3 1994 01589 6191

D0449563

Kiss Collector

SANTA ANA PUBLIC LIBRARY

WENDY HIGGINS

Kiss Collector

HARPER TEEN
An Imprint of HarperCollinsPublishers

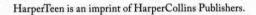

HarperTeen is an imprint of HarperCollins Publishers.

Kiss Collector
Copyright © 2018 by Wendy Higgins
Emoji icons provided by EmojiOne
All rights reserved. Printed in the United States of America.
No part of this book may be used or reproduced in any manner whatsoever without
written permission except in the case of brief quotations embodied in critical
articles and reviews. For information address HarperCollins Children's Books, a
division of HarperCollins Publishers, 195 Broadway, New York, NY 10007.
www.epicreads.com

Library of Congress Control Number: 2018938737
ISBN 978-0-06-279521-2

Typography by Michelle Gengaro-Kokmen
19 20 21 22 PC/LSCH 10 9 8 7 6 5 4 3 2
❖
First Edition

To the students of Potomac Senior High School
in Dumfries, Virginia,
past, present, and future.
Dream big. This world is yours.

Junior Year

One Week before Spring Break

CHAPTER ONE

After eight months of gentle begging, I finally gave in to Wylie. Not as fully as he would have liked, but I did something for him I'd never done before. I can't say I enjoyed it, necessarily, but he did. And Wylie had gotten plenty more than that from girls before me—girls who weren't his girlfriends. Wylie is wild like that. The life of the party. The guy who steals beer from peoples' garages and runs away laughing when an adult yells at him. But he's good when we're together. I get to see the sweet, tame side of him that others don't.

I love him, and I wanted to show him.

That was a week ago, and this party will be the first time I've seen him since. We go to rival high schools. He lives in the richest part of our northern Virginia county. Every day is a fashion show at Hillside High where Wylie goes. I live in the least wealthy and most multicultural corner of the county, where Peakton students wear sweats to school and have rap wars in the locker bay between classes. Just how I like it.

For all its flaws, I love Peakton. Wylie, on the other hand, has no school pride. He's awesome at soccer, but got kicked off the varsity team last year in tenth grade because of bad grades. He just skates by like it's all a big joke, waiting for it to be over.

I park our family's ancient minivan down the street in front of one of the neighbors' brick houses and walk past the manicured lawn. March weather can be iffy, but it's nice tonight. Not too cold. I just wish my girls were with me—I hate rolling up at Hillside parties alone—but they all had family stuff, and this was a last-minute decision.

Wylie's not expecting me. I'd been itching to text him and let him know I was coming now that I have my phone back, but I wanted to surprise him. I'm supposed to be grounded with no phone for skipping class—Dad's punishment—but my mom is a huge pushover these days. Too many early morning shifts at the bakery. But whatever, I'm not going to think about family crap. Tonight I'm here to relax and surprise my man.

I've met a lot of Hillside kids through Wylie, but none of them are friends. I always feel the girls looking down on me with my natural brown curls pulled back in a ponytail, and knockoff jeans, which, by the way, flatter my ass just as well as their designer ones. I don't need their approval because I know practically everyone at my own school, and when I walk down the halls of Peakton, I feel the love.

I'm only here for Wylie. His giant smile and infectious laughter make all the other stuff go away. After all this time together, I still crave his attention.

Rube is the first friend of Wylie's I see when I push my way into the hot, crowded house. Ugh. It smells like pot, sweat, and potpourri, a sickly sweet-and-sour combo. Rube is hard to miss, towering over everyone like a scowling giant. He's my least favorite of Wylie's friends. He made it clear months ago that I was cramping his style by "not letting" Wylie go out and party as much as he used to. But I don't control Wylie. He does what he wants, and chooses to hang out with me. Not that he'd admit that to the guys.

I don't bother with niceties when I get to him. "Where's Wylie?"

Rube's grin turns my stomach. "Well, hey there, little Miss Not So Prude after all."

"What?" I ask, and then it hits me like a wrecking ball and my cheeks flame.

Wylie told him?! Oh my God. I didn't think to tell him *not* to tell his friends because I assumed he would know better. These idiots have no boundaries!

"I mean, it took you long enough." Rube tilts his head back to finish his beer.

I flip him off, something that's uncommon for me, and he lets out a malicious dry laugh. I turn and switch directions, getting as far from that jerk as possible.

I'm going to kill Wylie for telling him. I can already imagine Wy laughing it off and saying, "Girl, don't listen to that mess. You know he likes to tease." *Blah, blah.*

Wylie is so dead.

I spot Jade, his other friend. Wylie and his gang are an

3

eclectic group. Wy is Dominican and Haitian, with precious freckles across his nose and cheeks that make him appear innocent. Rube is a hulking guy who fools adults into thinking he's a big, polite teddy bear. Jade is a heavy-metal rocker with a shaved head. They grew up on the same street, and the three of them have more money among them than I can fathom. Their parents never tell them no. It's kind of sickening.

"Jade!" I call. He stumbles toward my voice, drunk already.

"Zae! What's up, girl?" His voice is raspy from too many cigarettes, and he slings a skinny arm around my neck, giving me a wet kiss on the cheek. "I didn't know you were coming."

I discreetly wipe my cheek. "Neither did I. Have you seen Wylie?"

"Uh . . ." His eyes jerk toward the hallway and back to me. "Nope. Hang with me and have a beer. I'm sure he'll find his way in here soon. Did you call him?"

"No, I wanted to surprise him."

Jade runs a hand over his smooth head and laughs, sounding strange. A nasty feeling settles into my gut.

"Is something going on?" I ask.

"Huh? Nah. Have a drink." He tries to hand me a can, but I shake my head.

See . . . the thing is, Wylie and I have been fighting a lot lately about his . . . recreational entertainment. He's been sampling different drugs when we're not together, so I don't trust him. The boy has no self-control and he's a thrill seeker. Now I'm nervous. He's probably smoking pot or sniffing something somewhere in the house after swearing to me he wouldn't do it anymore. My gut churns at the thought.

When Jade's eyes nervously flick to the hallway again, I turn and head that way, ignoring when he calls out.

"Aw, c'mon, Zae, be cool. Have one drink with me!"

I stop at a door in the hall where light shines from the crack at the bottom, probably a bathroom. I put my ear to the door and hear shuffling noises, so I knock.

"Occupied." The sound of Wylie's voice sends an excited and nervous jolt through me. If he's high, we are going to throw down.

I knock again, harder.

"Dude, fuck off!" he says now, a hint of amusement framing his words.

"Wy, it's me." I try not to sound annoyed.

I hear him whisper "Oh, shit!" and my heart drops. "Hold on! I'm just . . . talkin' to someone."

More whispers and shuffling. My heart is pounding too hard. I cross my arms and wait as the door opens a couple of inches. My stomach spins like it always does when I see his creamy brown skin and wavy black hair.

"Hey, baby, what are you doing here?" He smiles. His eyes aren't red, and there's no smoke. I suddenly feel sick, knowing he's doing something more hard-core than weed.

"Surprise," I say, holding up my palms innocently. He still only peeks at me through the crack of the doorway.

"I'm almost finished talking to someone about this thing I need to take care of—"

Okay, enough BS. "What are you doing in there, Wylie?"

"Nothin'. For real." That big smile again. "Just dealing with some drama from school, but we're getting it figured out.

Can you get me a drink real quick?" he asks, giving me his cute, pouty look. "Pretty please? I'll be done by the time you get back, and we can hang."

I hold back a sarcastic snort. "Sure. Be right back." I move to the side and he closes the door. I'm sweating now as I wait in the darkened hall, not moving.

After ten seconds the door cracks open and a girl slips out backward, giggling and whispering. She looks maybe fourteen or fifteen. Wavy hair and big cocoa eyes.

What the hell? He's getting high with some freshman?

Time slows as the girl smiles at Wylie, reaching for his hands. He steps out with a finger to his lips, and with his other hand gives her a gentle push away. Then they both catch sight of my steely face in the dim hall and freeze.

Not drugs. Another girl.

Inside my chest, my heart begins to rattle, quaking, then it explodes, landing in my stomach with a flame that claws up my throat. Acid. Realization. Jealousy.

Wylie is a bad boy as far as following the law's concerned, but cheating has never been an issue. Has it?

The girl stumbles back like she's scared, and her eyes dart between us. She's at the end of a dead-end hall, trapped. I glare at Wylie, who wears the crap-eating grin he always does when he's in trouble. This cannot be happening.

"Did you . . . ? What's going on, Wy?"

He reaches for my hand, and I let him, because I'm his girl. I'm the one he *should* be touching. "I told you, we were talking." His words are quick and jittery.

I want to believe him. It's possible they were just talking, right? But the look of horror and guilt on the girl's face is too much to ignore. I wrench my hand from his and push away, moving into the girl's face. I don't usually resort to intimidation tactics, but she is obviously scared, and I need answers.

"Zae . . ." Wylie warns.

"Did you kiss my boyfriend?" I ask her. I might puke.

If possible, her face becomes more terrified. Ashen. Instead of answering, she whimpers and looks past my shoulder at Wylie. My stomach is wrung tight. The hall behind us is starting to fill with people.

"What did y'all do?"

"I—I d-didn't know he had a girlfriend." She glances past me again to Wylie.

"Zae, come on." Wylie tries to pull my waist from behind, but I slap his hand without looking away from the girl.

"What's your name?" I lower my voice at the girl, trying to sound kind and soothing, like a friend.

"Vonia," she says, breathless.

"Vonia, okay." I'm shaking so hard. I clench my hands into tight fists. "I need you to be honest—"

"Zae," Wylie says louder. "Let's go. Come on. You and me can talk."

I ignore him, focused on the girl. I'll narrow down the worst possible scenario first. "Did you have sex?"

Deny it.

She swallows hard and covers her mouth, cowering back from me.

Please just say no. Why isn't she saying no?

I speak gently, though inside I'm raging. "Just answer the question."

"Zae, baby, come on. You're scaring her. I already told you—"

"Shut up!" I snarl at him, snapping my head to look at his shocked face for one second before turning back to the girl. She's crying now.

"I'm sorry!" she blurts. "I didn't know! I thought . . ." She looks at Wylie again, betrayal in her eyes. "He said—"

"You should go." Wylie cuts her off. "Vonia, go!"

"No," I say, looking at the girl again, trapping her between the wall and me. "He said *what*?"

She sniffs, still cowering, having no idea I'd never hit her. "He said you broke up."

Bile rises in my throat. My breaths become shallow. Even *I* haven't had sex with him.

Wylie throws his head back, pressing the heels of his hands into his eyes. "Oh my God," he groans.

I can't form a coherent thought. A long moment passes where we all stand there expectantly in shock, like it's a nightmare. And then all my thoughts rush at me at once. Last weekend meant *nothing* to him. Here I was, thinking we were closer than ever, that something bigger was building between us. But apparently it wasn't enough. *I'm* not enough.

Why couldn't he have been getting high? Why this? I can handle anything but this! The thought of them touching, of them . . . I almost throw up right there. The room spins. I need air.

I shove past Wylie, pushing my way through the gawking people, ignoring the sound of my name being called.

The air outside has cooled when I slam the front door behind me. Hot tears roll down my cheeks as I run through the thick grass. I hate its plushiness. Its *fakeness*.

I can't believe he would do this. He loves me—I know he does. My first love. I thought he was my forever love. I would never cheat on him.

Sounds of the party filter through the air as the door to the house opens and shuts.

"Zae! Baby, wait!"

I don't stop, even when I hear his footsteps slamming up behind me. He jumps in front of me and grabs my shoulders, looking frantic. This is a first. Nothing dishevels Wy. My stupid, weak heart thrums with pain.

"I'm sorry." He pants, and I can smell alcohol on his breath. "I'm so sorry. I drank too much. And then she started talking to me. She's been trying to get with me all year, Zae. Tonight . . . I don't know. She reminded me of you. I missed you. I swear, I was thinking of you the whole time."

"Oh my God, Wylie!" I'm full-out crying now. "That is not okay! First of all, that poor girl likes you, and you lied to her so she'd sleep with you! How would you feel if I did that with some other guy?"

He winces. "You wouldn't. You're so good. I— You know I'm not strong like you. I can't stop messing up." His voice cracks as he grabs his hair in anguish, and I want to kill him for having the nerve to be serious and emotional for the first time ever. Because truly all I want to do is slip my arms around his waist and comfort him, which is so backward. I want to tell him he can be good, too. Tell him we can work it out and actually believe it.

But I don't believe it. The innocence of our relationship has been polluted.

"It's called self-control, Wy! You could be strong if you wanted to, but all you care about is yourself. All you want to do is have fun, no matter who you hurt, and I'm sick of it. Sick of making excuses for you. I'm not going to share you. Drunk or not, what you did was wrong. And, oh! You told Rube what we did!" I shove his chest in anger.

His eyes get big, and a nervous smile flits across his face. "I didn't mean to. I just . . . you were fucking amazing, and—"

"Shut up!" My hands clench into little fists. "Just shut up! I hate you for this, Wylie. Get out of my way."

I run past him down the sidewalk.

"Zae!"

"Leave me alone!" I scream the words, not caring when a neighbor's porch light flicks on, probably wondering what on earth is disturbing their perfect peace.

Wylie doesn't try to stop me again. He stares at me with a pitifully lost expression as I start the minivan and speed past him, past the perfect lawns, sprawling houses, and overpriced cars the other kids drive.

Damn it. I've never felt so cheap. Used. Stupid. Disgusting. But the worst part is, I feel like I've lost something vital, and my heart is stretching, reaching, trying to get it back.

I miss Wylie already.

CHAPTER TWO

I hate stereotypes. Especially the one about cheerleaders being stuck-up mean girls or annoying airheads or sluts. Me and my friends cheer, and I wish they'd put our squad in one of those movies. Crazy, fun, diverse girls. Most important, we're nice—at least the four of us are. And smart . . . *ish*. And virgins, though not completely innocent. My night with Wy, for example. Stupid Wylie. My heart and stomach ache with pitiful pain as I stare unfocused at the whiteboard. Stupid Monday. Stupid math class.

My girls were there for me after the breakup. They showed up at my house on Sunday with essentials. Homemade churros from Monica—her mom knows they're my fave. Countless Boys Suck memes on Lin's phone. And Kenzie's '80s hip-hop playlist. We listened to it on my bed while Lin played with my unruly curls, giving me fishtail braids, the four of us getting cinnamon and sugar everywhere as we rated the images on my walls. I have posters of all the places I want to go: Paris, Buenos Aires, Berlin, Edinburgh, Dublin, Prague, Tuscany, the Swiss Alps, to name a few. My walls are covered.

"Zae?" My math teacher's voice comes to me from far away as Kenzie elbows me in the ribs, and I realize I was daydreaming again. My face heats with embarrassment as everyone stares.

"Yeah, uh yes, Ms. Lane?"

"What do you have for number seven?"

"Um . . ." I look down at my trigonometry worksheet. Oh, thank God, it's one of the triangle ones. I understand those. "Side *AC* equals ten?"

She nods and turns back to the board. I exhale while my heart rate slows. Kenzie discreetly holds out her fist between us, her tawny brown fingers bumping mine. We hate trig, but we get by.

I've been a mess all day. Sadness makes my stomach feel off. Everything feels off. I woke up super early this morning and couldn't go back to sleep. Then I went to get a drink and found Dad sleeping on the couch. He tried to jump up and throw the blanket down to play it off like he just came in and sat, but I knew. He slept there, which means he and Mom were probably fighting. Again.

He rubbed his face and said, "Hey, Zae-bae. I got in late last night and didn't want to disturb Mama."

I hardly think having your husband crawl into bed with you after a long shift is an unwanted disturbance, but I've never been married, so what do I know?

Dad lost his job as a retail manager at a department store in the mall last year, so he's the manager at a barbecue restaurant now. The problem is that the pay is less, and he has to work night shifts. I know it's hard, and it sucks, but my parents need to get their acts together and adjust. My eighth-grade brother, Zebediah, and I are ready for some stability again.

Thank God it's the last week before spring break. And thank God there's no cheer practice now that basketball season has ended. Tryouts for senior year are in a couple of months, but for now I'm a free woman.

I meet Lin, Monica, and Kenzie at our usual corner at the end of the junior class locker bay. Their hushed conversation stops when I walk up, and the three of them take in the sight of my downcast face. All at once they converge on me with hugs.

"Wylie deserves to lose his balls. Painfully." Ah, lovely Lin.

"He doesn't deserve you." Girl power Monica. "You're better off without him."

Kenzie nods in agreement, her tender heart making her eyes well with tears on my behalf.

"Thanks," I whisper.

A mob of fellow eleventh graders begins to surround us, some with genuine concern and some just nosy for drama.

"You guys broke up?"

"Ah, that sucks."

"Sorry, Zae."

I hug people back, trying to pull myself together, but it's hard when I hear people whispering " . . . cheated on her with a freshman!" Then looks of pity. I clear my throat.

"I'm okay," I say. Don't think I don't notice the way guys are suddenly looking at me like fresh meat back on the market. Thankfully the warning bell rings, and the throng scatters, except my three girls. My squad.

"So this means you're single again," Lin says carefully.

"Yeah," I tell her. "And it's going to stay that way."

They give one another skeptical looks.

"I mean it," I tell them. "I never want a boyfriend again." *Ever.*

"Okay." Kenzie pats my arm with gentle care and I feel myself scowling a little.

The second warning bell rings, so we dash off our separate ways.

One more week before break. I can do this.

I plop down at my desk in English class.

"Open your books to page three seventy," Mrs. Warfield says in a chipper voice. "We'll be doing a short modern poetry unit this week."

The whole class groans, me included.

"It's almost spring break!" whines one of the football players in the back. Jack Rinehart, a jock. Let's just say this is one of those times when the stereotype is dead-on.

Mrs. Warfield seems amused by our complaints. She smiles as she passes out the assignment sheet. Then she gets all mushy-gushy, talking about letting our bottled feelings explode onto the page with a handful of carefully chosen words. Behind me, I hear Jack's forehead hit the desk.

Our first assignment is to capture one of our emotions in

14

a poem. I stare at the page, annoyed. I'm not feeling creative. The emotions I'm dealing with are not appropriate for Mrs. Warfield's eyes.

"It can rhyme, but it certainly doesn't have to," she says. "Let yourselves reminisce on good times, like holidays, et cetera. And bad times, like experiencing a loss, et cetera."

Against my will, an image comes to mind. A vivid snapshot of my parents on Christmas morning when Zebediah and I were younger. Mom was sitting on Dad's lap while Zebby and I opened our presents. I remember thinking how comfortable they looked. And in love. The way his fingers twined with hers, and how he kept absently kissing her hand over and over, like he didn't even realize he was doing it.

I'd give anything to have that moment back. My parents haven't shown affection in a long time. They're both focused on work and trying to make enough money to pay the bills. I just want them to be happy again.

All at once my hand is flying across the page, scratching out words as they flood my mind. It's weirdly freeing. I'm not artsy by nature. Foreign languages are my thing. So the flow of words feels both strange and exhilarating.

I barely hear Mrs. Warfield talking. "It doesn't have to be long. I simply want to feel what you're feeling in several lines. I'll give you fifteen minutes."

I'm done in ten. And it's more than four lines. I read it over and over, feeling the punch of emotion each time. I erase words and change them, wanting each line to be perfect as it summarizes the nostalgia and longing I feel.

"Okay, class," Mrs. Warfield sings. "I want you to pair off, but I've learned my mistake from the last time I let you pick your own partners."

More groaning from the class as she pairs us off into couples of her own choosing.

"Zae Monroe and Dean Prescott."

My heart flutters. It actually does, I swear, which feels bizarre because I've been wholly devoted to Wylie for so long that other guys don't affect me. But Dean had been one of my many crushes in ninth and tenth grades.

The girl next to Dean moves, so I stand and go to her seat.

"Hi," I say.

"Hey."

I take the opportunity to stealthily look him over. Dean is a large guy. A football player of the anti-stereotype variety— quiet, kind, and smart. And did I mention big? He's over six feet and as broad as the doorway. Okay, maybe not that broad, but for real. His chest and shoulders are massive. He's got a linebacker body with an adorable smile and wavy brown hair.

He stares at me as if he can read my thoughts, and I look away.

A wave of guilt crashes over me for thinking Dean is sexy, but that guilt is chased away by an indignant voice screaming *You have every right to check out guys! You're single now!* My stomach tightens at the reminder.

"You okay?" he asks.

"Yeah." I clear my throat.

The room gets loud and Mrs. Warfield has to shout instructions over us. She wants everyone to share their poems and "gently critique" one another. Everything she says after that is drowned out by the panic of blood pumping into my eardrums.

I can't share this poem. Not with Dean or anyone. It's way too sappy and personal. I haven't even shared these feelings with Lin, Monica, and Kenz. Everyone's parents fight sometimes. I don't even know why I'm writing stupid poems about it.

The poem sits facedown on my desk, and when Dean reaches for it, I snatch it to my chest. I feel my eyes go unnaturally large.

"Whoa," he says. "Sorry."

Embarrassment stings my cheeks. "No, it's okay. I just . . . it's bad. Like, really, *really* bad. I didn't know we'd be sharing."

He watches me in a way that feels like he can see under the surface of my lie.

"It's all right," he says. "Mine sucks, too."

Man, his voice is deep. I chew my lip as he hunkers over his paper with his arms crossed in front of him, biceps bulging. I stare for too long and when I finally look at his face again, he gives me a slow grin, two adorable indentations dimpling his cheeks.

When he first moved to the area in eighth grade, we were science partners and I talked his ear off, forcing him to converse with me. It'd always been my personal objective to draw out the quiet ones.

"So, do you want me to critique you?" I nod to his poem.

"Only if I can do you, too," he says. Then he blinks. "Wow, that sounded bad."

I burst into laughter and watch as his ears redden. He shakes his head, grinning.

"What I *meant* is, I'll let you read mine if you let me read yours."

I clam up. "No deal."

"Man, you're really embarrassed about it, huh? Don't worry. Dean don't judge."

I laugh again but shake my head. "I'm not a poet."

"Nobody here is. At least tell me what it's about," he urges. "Is it your boyfriend?"

"No . . ." Damn that stupid wave of sadness and loss that keeps crashing over me when I'm not expecting it. "We broke up."

"Oh." He gets quiet, studying my face. "My bad."

I shake my head. "Um . . . okay, my poem. It's about Christmas when I was little. And my family. Dumb stuff."

He stares at me like he doesn't believe the downplay.

"Okay," he says. "Well, mine's about a girl I used to see."

If I were a dog, my ears would have gone straight up, all pointy-like.

"Who?"

He gives a nonchalant shrug. Okay, now I *have* to read his poem.

"Was it that girl from last year? The one from Brooklyn?" I ask.

His face goes a little slack. "The Bronx, yeah."

I'm rapt. "Let me read it. Please?" I may or may not tilt my head cutely and pout with duck lips.

His eyes go straight to my mouth and he pauses, wavering. Yes! Dean is not immune to my charms! His hand wavers over his paper before he suddenly puffs out his chest in defiance.

"Not unless I can read yours."

Dang it! I really wanted to find out about that girl. I think her name was Jenna. The name was far too sweet for her, though. Rumor was, she'd been sent to live with her aunt and uncle here in Virginia to avoid being put in the New York foster-care system. She'd had a wicked accent and a permanent badass scowl. I never officially met her since we didn't have any classes together, and before I knew it she'd been sent back to New York. She got in two fights during the four months she was here, and the only person she ever talked to was Dean. Rumor also had it that they "did it." A lot.

"Okay, class!" Mrs. Warfield called. "Let's wrap it up. The bell's about to ring. Place your poems on my desk as you leave."

I give Dean a fake angry glare, letting him know he wins the battle this time but I'm not done with him. He chuckles.

"Whatever, girl. You're too cute to scare me."

I stop glaring. Dean Prescott just called me cute. He's always been friendly, but never flirtatious. Before I can think of any joking comeback, the bell rings and Dean is out of his seat, moving toward the door.

I notice with some satisfaction that his ears are, once again, tinged red.

CHAPTER THREE

I drive Lin, Monica, and Kenzie home from school. Lin doesn't have a license yet. Monica's mom only has one car. And Kenzie ran over her family's mailbox the first week she got her license, so she's scared to drive now. That was three months ago. As long as they're not too embarrassed to be seen in the fourteen-year-old minivan that sometimes sputters when it starts, I'm happy to keep giving them rides.

I drop them at their houses and drive to my neighborhood of crammed-together brick-and-siding town houses just as my brother, Zebby, is getting off the middle school bus. I wave when I see his curly brown hair, and he trots over. Each day I give him a ride to our home around the corner, at the end of the street. We live in an old neighborhood bordering some of the only forests in the county that haven't been torn down for more houses and stores.

Zeb slumps in the passenger seat and crosses his arms, staring out the window.

"What's wrong with you?" I ask. "Hey, put your seat belt on."

"Seriously? We're only driving for a minute."

"Have you seen how some of the crazies drive around here? Why are you so grumpy?"

His response is an incoherent grumble.

I pull into a visitor's spot down the street, since our parents use our two assigned numbered spots. I wish we had a garage. Sometimes I have to park two streets away and run through the rain. Zeb reaches for his door handle, but I grab his arm.

"Tell me what happened," I say gently.

He huffs out a loud breath. "This kid on my bus is a dick-wad!"

Whoa. "Don't say *dickwad*. What'd he do?"

"Every day on the bus he's like, 'Dude, your sister's so hot. When you gonna hook me up?' And when I tell him to shut up, he laughs and keeps going. Talking about all the stuff he wants to . . . you know . . . do to you."

Ah, one of *those* boys. I want to laugh at the thought of this middle schooler who thinks he's got game, but I hold back because Zeb is too out of sorts. His cheeks are splotchy with anger. Aw, my cute, protective little bro.

"Who is it?" I ask.

"Rob."

"Weren't you on the track team with that kid? I thought you guys were solid."

"Yeah, we were. Kinda. He's always had a big mouth, though."

"Zebby, you need to ignore that idiot. He's just trying to piss you off. He knows exactly how to get to you and he thinks it's funny. Some people are like that."

Zeb grinds his teeth together. "I'm gonna kick his ass someday. I swear."

I rumple his hair and open the door. "Don't say *ass*. And you better not get in a fight. That sh— stuff will follow you." I climb out, silently vowing that if I ever see that little Rob creep I'll kick his ass myself.

We trudge to our home at the end of the row and I let us in. During cheer season I have practice most days, so I've been enjoying this after-school time with Zeb. Cheer tryouts are in two months, and then our crazy summer practice schedule begins. All this free time feels weird. My brother throws his bag in the middle of the floor and I kick it aside. He goes straight to the couch and turns on the television while I make a snack—celery and peanut butter, raisins for me but not him.

"Thanks," he says before he shoves one in his mouth.

I munch one as I watch him zone out, staring at animated warriors, and I feel a surge of protective love. As kids, Zebby and I fought like crazy. He drove me nuts with all his annoying and gross habits. But in the past year since our parents' schedules got crazy, we've had to rely on each other, and we fight less. I kind of like my brother now. As a person. It's weird.

I pull out my phone and check all my social pages while I eat.

An hour later we're still lounging in those same spots on the couch when Mom comes home carrying bags of groceries. Her bun hangs loose.

"Hi," she says, sounding weary.

"Hey," I reply. Zeb grunts, half-comatose. "Any more groceries to carry?"

"Nope, that's it."

Mom dumps her large purse and the bags on the counter with a sigh. "I feel like ordering Chinese tonight." This makes Zeb perk up.

"Really?" he asks.

"I think so."

She gives a small smile when we both cheer. Our parents rarely order out. Mom's a baker at a tiny shop, which is getting less and less business because people get their baked goods at the grocery store for convenience—even though Mom's bakery items are way better. Between the DC area's cost of living and our family's bills, it's no secret in our house that we're broke. But if Mom wants to splurge, I'm not complaining.

I help set the table, noticing the bags under her eyes seem heavier than normal. Plus, up close I see she still hasn't colored her hair, which she normally does every month, so the gray at her roots is showing. I don't say anything, but it makes me sad.

Dad gets home just after the food arrives. For a second I wonder if he'll gripe at Mom for spending money on Chinese, but he doesn't seem surprised, so they must have planned it. Dad kisses my temple and squeezes Zeb's shoulder before he sits.

"How was school Xanderia? Zebediah?"

I cringe inwardly at his use of my full name. Nobody calls me that except him, probably because he's Xander, and I was named after him. When he was a toddler, Zeb called me Zae, because *Xanderia* was too hard to say, and thankfully the nick-name stuck.

"Fine," we both answer.

Zeb looks at me as we all sit. Mom and Dad haven't even acknowledged each other. I shake my head, telling him not to worry, though I wish I could take my own advice. We fill our plates in silence, and I don't mean silence of the comfortable variety. I can hardly even enjoy my amazing spring roll and sesame chicken with the blanket of awkwardness stifling the room.

"So," I say. "I think I'm going to get a job this summer. Try to help out."

"Oh, Zae." Mom smiles softly. "That's so sweet of you, but you'll be busy with cheer, won't you?"

"Well, yeah," I say. "But maybe I can find somewhere that will work around my practice schedule. I can pay for my own camp this year." Just the thought of taking that burden off my parents' shoulders fills me with pride.

Mom and Dad share a quick glance, and Mom grabs her napkin to wipe her eyes.

"Allergies have been killing me," she says. "Cherry trees are blooming."

Dad spears a piece of broccoli.

My brother must be sick of the weirdness because he shovels down his food at hyperspeed and pushes back his chair to stand.

"May I be excused?" he mumbles.

"Actually," Mom says, "Dad and I want to talk to you guys."

24

Talk to us? I set my forkful of food back down on the plate, appetite lost. The half meal I'd eaten churns inside me with apprehension.

"Finish eating, sweetie," Mom whispers to me.

"I'm done," I whisper back.

I don't like family talks. They only happen when something bad is going on. Last year it was Dad losing his job.

The room is so quiet I can hear the clock ticking, filling the room with an echoing dread.

Mom and Dad both set down their utensils and look at each other. He gives her a nod and I want to scream *No! Don't say it!* Whatever it is, I don't want to hear it. I grip the edges of my seat and hold my breath.

"Your dad and I love you both so much." She looks back and forth between Zebby and me, her eyes misting. "And I promise you it's not your fault—"

"That's right," Dad says. "It's about your mom and me."

No. No. No. I'm going to be sick.

Mom pauses, then opens her mouth in what seems like slow motion. "We're separating."

The world tilts as I stare at my food, which now looks revolting.

"We can't afford to keep this house when your dad moves out, so the three of us will be getting an apartment." My head snaps up, my heart racing, frantic.

"What?" Zeb asks. "We're moving?"

Zeb and I have lived in this town house our whole lives!

Mom swallows and nods. "I got us a two-bedroom apartment in Southern Ridge, and Dad will be living outside of

25

town with a roommate. You two will have to share a room, but it's only temporary until—"

Oh my God! She's serious! I stand so fast my chair makes a horrible screech on the linoleum. *"Why?!"*

Mom drops her head, but her shoulders are tense.

"We'll still get to see each other," Dad promises. He reaches for my hand and I yank my arm away, making him frown.

"Things change, honey." Mom's voice cracks. She sounds so defeated.

"No crap. Really? Things change? Uh, yeah! That's life! And people *adjust*."

"It's not that simple." Dad is using his hard, paternal voice now, and it only makes me angrier.

"I can't believe you guys are just giving up!" I yell. "After, like, nineteen years? Just because we're going through one rough time?"

Mom closes her eyes and presses her fingertips to her lips. Dad stares off, his face plastered with something like regret or guilt.

When I look down at Zebby, his face is streaked with tears. I cover my mouth against a giant sob. Our family is splitting. Cracking. Breaking. Is nothing in this world sacred?

I have to talk through tears now. "You took vows. You're supposed to be together forever, for better or worse."

Visions of our summer road trips to the beach flash through my mind. So much laughter. So much love. How does that change? How did this happen? Then my mind turns to Wylie in that room with another girl. Oh, God, what if . . . ?

"Is one of you cheating?" My voice is filled with ugly

26

accusation. I know I shouldn't ask. I'm crossing a major line, but I don't care.

Mom's wet eyes bug. "Honey! We . . ."

She looks at Dad, desperate, until he finally speaks, his face rigid. "The details are nobody's business but ours. All you need to know is that we fell out of love, Xanderia. And we couldn't find our way back."

How convenient. No map for that.

"We need to start packing," Mom whispers. "We move out on Saturday."

"*Saturday?*" My voice breaks as the room feels off kilter. Four days from now? I heave for air as their words sink in. This is happening, and I can't stop it. "This is wrong! You guys suck!"

Mom is crying now and Dad puts his elbows on the table, rubbing his face. I run from the dining room, down the stairs to my room in the basement, and slam my bedroom door as hard as I can. Then I curl into a ball on my bed.

First Wylie and now my parents. Love is a sham. Marriage is a mockery. Everything I believe in is tarnishing and crumbling.

I feel a touch on my shoulder and look up to see Zebby. The same overwhelming loss is in his brown eyes and furrowed forehead. I tug him down, and we hold each other tight, crying.

Mourning.

CHAPTER FOUR

The next morning in the minivan, Monica is rubbing her long legs with plum lotion and telling us about the party happening at Jack Rinehart's house this Saturday. Her long brown hair is braided in a fishtail over one shoulder. I feel so empty, I hardly hear her words.

I should have texted them last night. I tell my girls everything. But this . . . it's so big. And last night I kept thinking any second my parents would say they'd changed their minds. That they were going to work things out. That we didn't have to move.

When I woke up this morning after tossing and turning and crying all night, nothing had changed. Except that Dad wasn't on the couch. He was gone.

My chest tightens and I rub it with one hand as I drive.

"You okay?" Kenzie asks from the front passenger seat.

I just keep rubbing. I'm afraid if I open my mouth I'll start crying and I won't be able to see the road. Just one more mile till we're at school. So I nod. I can feel Kenz watching me as Monica and Lin talk about who all's going to be at Jack's party.

I pull into a parking spot and let out a ragged breath.

"Do you think you can drive us Saturday?" Monica asks.

I blink and slowly turn my head to her. Monica's forehead scrunches.

"Zae?" she whispers.

"I can't," I say. "I—I'm moving that day."

A long, silent pause passes before Lin shouts, "*What*?!" She unbuckles and flies forward between the seats to look at me. I turn so I can see all their confused faces.

"You've been crying," Kenzie says. "What's going on?"

My voice is deadpan as I try to protect myself from the ugly words that spill from my mouth: "separation," "apartment," "roommate."

My friends' faces reflect the direness of the situation.

Lin, who was adopted from China as a toddler, is the only girl in the car whose parents are still together. "Oh, Zae, I'm so sorry. And I'm so glad you're not moving far away. You freaked me out when you said that."

Kenzie wipes her eyes. Her mom, a white Texan, fell in love with a black classmate in college, which apparently was a big deal in the town she'd lived in, so they moved to the DC area. Her parents split when Kenz was in elementary school, and her dad moved back to Texas, but she's still close with him, and her stepfather, too. She calls them both Dad and sees her real father for two weeks every summer.

"It'll be okay," she whispers. "Maybe they just need some time apart. Maybe they'll get back together."

I catch Lin shooting Kenz a warning look, and I know she's telling her not to get my hopes up, but it's too late. I don't want stepparents someday. I want my family. Just the four of us. It's all I thought about all night. Deep down, I know this separation will make them miss our family. It has to. I didn't even want anyone else to know they're separated, because when they get back together we can get a new, better house and pretend like this never happened.

"Don't tell anyone, 'kay?" I say.

They're quiet as they nod, looking around at each other.

Monica reaches over and links her pinkie finger with mine. "No matter what happens, we're here, and you're gonna be okay. All right?"

I tighten my pinkie around hers. Monica's mom never married. Her dad was a marine from Quantico base, and now he sends child support, but otherwise he's not part of her life. She lives with her mom, little sister from another father, her aunt, two female cousins, and her grandmother—a household of loud, bold Latina women.

My friends surround me with love as we walk up to the school. The dreary, cold day matches how I feel, especially as I sit through math class. By the time I trudge into English, I'm heavy, and my stomach churns every time I think about my parents or Wylie. I slump in my seat, zoning out as Mrs. Warfield drones on and on about the power of words.

Our assignment is to write another poem, this one about how we perceive someone else to be feeling, and it has to include a metaphor or simile. Something empathetic. But

30

mine is just pathetic. I write two lines about Lin's smile being like sunshine. Lame.

It's not until near the end of class that Mrs. Warfield sparks my attention.

"I have a special treat. Someone, who shall remain anonymous unless they so choose to reveal themselves, wrote a gorgeous piece of poetry yesterday. I wasn't expecting anything of this magnitude in the short span of time I'd given, so I feel I *must* share it with the class."

Discomfort prickles the back of my neck.

It can't be mine. I mean, yeah, the poem was emotional for me, but writing's not my thing, so it can't be any good. And then it dawns on me that maybe it's Dean's poem. I shoot a quick glance over my shoulder. His eyes meet mine immediately, and his brows go up with interest.

For the moment I'm not thinking about my family tragedy. I'm thinking how I'd love a glimpse into Dean's mind and his relationship with that Jenna chick.

She clears her throat. I feel unreasonably nervous, shaking on the inside as she begins in a low, somber tone.

"I woke my little brother and we crept to the den
To see presents where empty space had once been.
A blue bike and a dollhouse with red velvet bows
Stood near our stockings laid out in neat rows."

Great God above. She is reading my freaking poem. Scalding heat takes over my face and I slink down in my seat. The teacher never looks my way, never gives away my secret as she continues, but I want to scream *Shut up! Stop!*

31

*"Mom was there in her nightgown, her head on Dad's
shoulder,
Smiling so broadly at something he'd told her.
That's when they still laughed and kissed and held hands,
Long before they happened to stop being friends."*

Mrs. Warfield enunciates each word with ripe emotion, and my heart squeezes like a fist inside my chest. Yesterday when I wrote the poem, I was sad, but I still had hope. Today I'm a different person, and the words hold even more power over me. Each line nearly strangles me as it slides from her lips. The way her face contorts with feeling. Each stanza coaxes my tear ducts, urging them to spill. I fight it with every ounce of energy and self-preservation I have. I refuse to melt down in front of my peers.

*"Colors on the tree blinked bright and shimmered,
As nutmeg and clove in the oven did simmer.
Then Dad sang out in his tenor soft and low,
'Let it snow, let it snow, let it snow.'"*

She puts a hand over her heart and closes her eyes dramatically. The class is quiet for a moment, and then everyone applauds. As an afterthought, I clap, too, so as not to give myself away. I hear classmates murmuring and whispering about whose it could be. From the corner of my eye I feel the stare of Dean, causing me to remember how I'd told him my poem was about Christmas and my family. Damn it.

I struggle for breath. He has to know it's mine. I feel

exposed and raw and edgy as hell.

When the bell rings, I spring from my seat. I see Mrs. Warfield trying to catch my eye, but I refuse to look at her. I know she had good intentions, but I wish she'd have asked me first.

Behind me I hear Dean's deep rumble of a voice as I hit the hallway. "Hey, Zae. Wait up!"

Nope. I hitch my book bag higher on my shoulder and ghost into the crowd.

I manage to avoid Dean for the next two hours, which is good because I cannot fake the funk. If he confronts me, I will cry. I can't force a smile for any amount of money. All day people ask me what's wrong. I reply with "family stuff" or "not feeling good," but I go from being numb to feeling cynical and angry.

At lunch, Kenzie and Monica try to make light conversation, but I can't concentrate. I find myself glaring at happy couples, thinking about how it's only a matter of time before their feelings change and they end up hurt. Why does anyone even bother?

I half-heartedly sip the Capri Sun Mom packed with my elementary school–worthy lunch. Every day I drink the kiddie drinks and eat string cheese with crackers, or PB and Js with potato chips. She says it's cheaper than the school meal plan, so I eat without complaint. But today I have zero appetite.

Monica eats the school's mac and cheese with Lit'l Smokies, the teeny weenies, which I usually make jokes about, but can't bring myself to today. Kenzie is sipping a can of something inside a Koozie, but it doesn't look like a regular soda can.

33

When she turns to talk to someone, I pull down the top to look.

What the hell? A weight-loss drink? Monica and I both look at each other with dread. Kenzie is naturally tiny, but she has this weird, warped image of herself. She doesn't see what we see. She sees fat where there is only skin and lean muscle.

Kenz turns around and snatches the can from me, saying, "Hey!" Her light-brown cheeks turn a mottled red.

"Kenz—" I start, but she cuts me off with a groan.

"Oh, my gosh, please don't start with me. My mom made me eat a huge breakfast, so I knew I wouldn't be hungry at lunch. Okay?"

She doesn't wait for a response, though. She packs her bag and gets up, leaving us.

"We'll keep an eye on her," Monica says, and I nod. It's been over a year since we had to show Kenz some tough love. We even got her mom and older sister involved, which Kenzie probably still holds against us. Her mom is a workaholic Energizer Bunny who is as naturally thin as Kenzie, but where Kenz is super sweet, her mom can be super severe. Her sister is awesome, though, and was a huge help.

"Did you hear that Lin and John had a fight?"

"Oh, no." Lin isn't in this lunch period with the rest of us. "That sucks."

"Yeah, she was hoping they could hang out more now that cheer is out, but he keeps going to his friend's house to play basketball after baseball practice instead of coming to see her."

All I can do is roll my eyes. Relationship drama. They've been together two months. It's doomed.

I take one last sip of my pouched drink and toss my lunch in the trash, then wave bye to Monica.

My next class is Spanish III, my favorite. The second I walk in, Mrs. Hernandez smiles at me, cocks her head, and says, *"¿Qué está mal?"* *What is wrong?* Of course she can tell. She's the best teacher ever.

"Mis padres," I answer. She gives me a sad nod, and pats my shoulder, not prying further.

When I take my seat, for the first time that day I feel a sense of comfort. Everything outside this room has completely gone to crap, but in here I can get lost in the beauty of the language, knowing there is something I'm good at. Something I can't screw up beyond repair. Something that won't hurt me.

Everyone is quiet in the van on the way home, careful, like we're walking on eggshells. Lin tries to keep the conversation light, attempting to make us laugh. She tells a story about how she got embarrassed at a Chinese restaurant when the hostess spoke to her in Chinese and she had to admit she didn't understand.

"I feel kind of guilty, you know?" she says.

"We could learn, if you want," I tell her absently. Seems like a reasonable solution to me. I catch Lin's look of surprise in the rearview mirror, as if I'm speaking Mandarin right now.

"You know it has different symbols for the alphabet, right? That would be *so* hard. I can barely keep my grade up in Latin!"

I shrug, and the car goes quiet again.

It's so tense that I'm relieved when I drop them all at their homes and get to drive five minutes by myself.

When I turn into my neighborhood, a crowd of kids stands in a circle at Zebby's bus stop. Foreboding settles in my stomach, and I swerve toward the curb, throwing the van into park and jumping out. Sure enough, I hear Zeb's raised voice. As I run closer, he pushes a boy in the chest and the kid shoves him back. Nope. Not happening. I run. The mob of middle schoolers shouts and shuffles closer for better views.

I push my way through them, yelling, "Hey!" and put a hand on each kid's chest. "I don't think so, guys." I look at Zebediah. He's panting. Red-faced. Enraged.

The other kid is smirking.

Let me guess. "Are you Rob?"

His smirk disappears, replaced by surprise, and he runs a hand through his long, shaggy hair. I swear, the kid bounces his eyebrows, proud that I know his name. "That's me."

"Was he talking crap to you again?" I ask Zeb, who says nothing, just continues to glare at the other kid. I take that as a yes.

Rob puts his palms up. "You snitched to your sister, man? I was only messing around."

Yeah, well, he messed with the wrong kid.

I smile at Rob, Mr. Wannabe Bad Boy, and turn to face him fully with my back to Zeb. The kid tries to mirror my confident smile, but I can see his chest rising and falling quickly with either nervousness or excitement. His gaze tumbles downward to my long legs in tight jeans and back up in awe.

"Tell me, Rob." I touch the curve at the bottom of his neck with my pointer finger, and let it trail down his T-shirt. His breath hitches and all the kids watch with open amazement. "What exactly would you like to do to me?"

He makes a funny sound in the back of his throat, and I hear kids snickering with shock. I move closer to the boy, talking as sweetly as I can muster. He's nearly as tall as me.

"Not gonna tell me? Well, let me be clear with you, *Rob*. You will never touch this." I motion up and down my body with my hands. "And if I hear that you've said another word about me to my brother, or messed with him in any way, I will find you and kick your tiny balls so hard they'll be in your throat. Choking you."

Mortified is how I'd describe his expression now.

"Got it?" I ask with a small smile.

"Y-yeah," he croaks.

"Come on, Zeb." The crowd parts and we walk to the minivan. The bus-stop jerks gawk at us until we drive around the corner to our street, and Zebby lets out a giant *whoop*.

"That was the most awesome thing ever! Did you see his face! That was priceless!"

He laughs and slaps his thighs. I laugh for the first time today, so glad to see his glee. To be sure, it felt good to release some of the wickedness inside me on that poor kid.

"Damn, Zae. You are the coolest sister ever."

"Thanks. But don't say *damn*."

"I've heard *you* say *damn*."

I sigh. Hypocrisy is not cool. "Okay, fine."

He smiles at me and I smile back, glad to have a comrade.

Chapter Five

Not another poetry day. I lay my head on the desk. Last night Mom made me start packing my room and taking down my posters. Now it doesn't feel like home. I don't want to be there, and I don't want to be here. I don't want to be anywhere. I hate everything. So when we have to take out paper to write today's poem—ode to an object—I choose an ugly, square, dry, boring cardboard box. It will make no sense to Mrs. Warfield why I have destroyed boxkind with words. And I don't care. As soon as I finish, I put my head back down on my desk.

"It's time for our daily dose of mystery reading!" Mrs. Warfield says in an overly cheerful, warbling voice.

I keep my head down, confident that my piece of crap poem from yesterday will not be the chosen one today. But still I listen, wondering whose soul will be displayed.

"Sadness," she begins in an ominously low voice that sends a chill across my skin.

"Bowed spine. Downcast face.
I see you, a dark thundercloud amidst cumulous puffs,
their smiles fake, your frown real.
Sadness.
Even a sip of Capri Sun cannot cast the shadows away."

I lift my face, and look at Mrs. Warfield as if I'd heard her wrong. But she only continues, oblivious to the cyclone that is suddenly circling inside me.

"What steals your color, lovely bloom?
What seeps the water from your petals?
The softness from your lips?
Sadness."

My heart is thundering, like the cloud mentioned in the poem. I sit up, clapping along with my classmates. It hits way too close to home to be a coincidence. Or am I being an ego-maniac, and it's not about me at all? There could be tons of people drinking Capri Suns at Peakton that I haven't noticed. But what if? I pretend to fiddle with my backpack on the floor while I stealthily glance around the room. The bell is about to ring, and everyone else is starting to shuffle, too. I've known most of the kids in this class since middle school, and some even from elementary school.

Who in the world wrote it? I look at the back row. Emberly

Bray, track star, hard asleep on his desk. Joel Ruddick with his sweatshirt hood up and arms crossed, also sleeping, but with his head leaned back against the wall. He's new to Peakton. I heard he might be a drug dealer. He transferred here from Hillside, and he never says much. Did he know Wylie? Stupid Wylie.

Next to him is John, Lin's boyfriend. Definitely not him. I keep glancing around. Raul is on the cheer squad, but he's not into girls, plus he can't keep a secret to save his life. Could it be Mike, my lab partner from last year? He's nice, but he's a scab picker, definitely not a poet. Angelo Garcia? We kissed in eighth grade. He's a loudmouth, so I can't imagine him not taking credit for the poem, but maybe? Super shy and quiet Flynn Rogers, who I think is in a band? Elliott Fields, the dirty-blond redneck break-dancer? No, seriously, he wears camo and talks nonstop about fishing, but he can break-dance like nothing I've ever seen. It's hard to picture him writing that, but maybe?

I continue browsing. Brent Dodge, the baby-faced varsity baseball player, who's currently flirting with Jana from the step team? Not likely. Then there's skater boy Taro Hattori, who's currently doodling a Japanese anime sketch. He's definitely creative. And cute in his skinny pants, with black hair that hangs across half his face. I eye him, but he doesn't look up. Quiet and mysterious. Hm. A definite possibility.

As I'm gazing, Dean catches my eye. It's as if he's been waiting for me to get to him. Our eyes hook and snag, and I feel a shy, miniature smile slip onto my face. His grin is bigger. Dimplier. I abruptly look away, heart thrumming.

When the bell rings, I rush out. I don't know what to do with this feeling. It's . . . nice, I admit, but I don't want it.

I'm paranoid as I drink my Capri Sun at lunch. My eyes dart all around the cafeteria, trying to spot people from English class watching me or other people drinking Capri Suns. I keep looking over at Dean and his group of athletes, but I swear he doesn't look at me once. Also, there's not another Capri Sun in sight.

"You okay?" Monica asks.

"Yeah." I decide to tell them. "You know how I drink one of these every day?" I hold up the pouch and the girls nod. I tell them about the poem. Monica is grinning like the Cheshire cat, and Kenzie leans across the table, a serious twinkle in her brown eyes.

"Name every single guy in your English class," Kenz says.

I tell them every one. "But after the poem was read, Dean was the only one who looked at me."

Both girls stare over at his group, and I hiss at them, "Don't look at him!"

They snatch their gazes back, giggling.

"Dean is a sexy beast, damn." Monica's face is vibrant. I can't help but steal another look at Dean and nod.

"I love a good mystery," Kenzie says. "Let's figure out which ones from your class are in this lunch." We stare around the crowded, loud room, and I count. Nine of the twelve straight guys in my English class are in here. And none of them are making suspicious eyes at us. This is going to be hard.

"Maybe it's a girl." Monica waggles her eyebrows, and I shrug.

"Wouldn't that be a twist!" Kenzie laughs.

I bite off a hunk of my cheese stick. Whoever wrote the poem, I'm grateful because it's the only thing that's been able to numb the sting of this horrible week. Guy or girl, I want to hug them.

Across from me, Kenzie stiffens and looks pointedly down at her tray of half-nibbled taco salad. Monica and I turn to see Sierra, Meeka, and Raul from the squad coming at us. My stomach clenches. Sierra and Meeka are as high end as students get at Peakton. Sierra's dad owns the huge car lot on Route 1, and Meeka's parents work at the Pentagon. They both live in the same neighborhood as Kenzie.

I suddenly remember Raul is in my English class, so I shove the Capri Sun into my lap under the table. I don't want him to think the poem might be about me.

Sierra sits right down next to me and says, "Hey, Zae. What's up?"

"Hey," I say. She glances over at Monica with a nod, but completely ignores Kenzie, as always. They have bad blood that dates back to seventh grade.

Meeka stands there smiling down at us, her long, muscular legs on display in a skirt. Raul looks down at his filed nails, as if bored.

"So . . ." Sierra's eyes are smiling as she faces me, sitting super close. I stare at her sculpted eyebrows and eyelash extensions. She could totally be a Hillside girl.

"What's up?" I ask.

For a moment I feel a sense of shame because there is something satisfying and exciting about having the full attention of the two most popular girls in school. Funny thing about popularity, though. There's the kind that stems from being well liked, and the kind that happens because you're feared. These girls could ruin your whole reputation with just one offhand comment.

"You and that Hillside guy broke up? Wylie Janac?"

My stomach drops at the sound of his name. "Yeah."

She gives me a sad look, a press of her red lips. "Is it true he cheated on you right after you guys had sex?"

"What?" Here we go. "No. We didn't have sex." I'm not going to mention what we *did* do. They'll tell the whole school.

"Oh." She looks disappointed.

"Really, Zae?" Meeka says. "Y'all were together a long time." She gives me a look like she knows I'm lying.

"They didn't," Monica says. Kenzie crosses her arms, her mouth pursed.

"But you were up in the girl's face, right?" Meeka says. "About ready to fight her?"

I clench my jaw. They're wanting details they can tell everyone. If I don't play along, they'll make up whatever story they want. But I hate this. I hate having my personal business on display. Yet here I am giving them info.

"I got in her face so she'd tell me what happened, but—"

"He fucked her?" Raul asks, and I cringe, my heart deflating.

"I guess." I shove my trash into the paper bag. "He's not my problem anymore, so whatever, you know? I'm done with that."

My end-of-discussion stance leaves the three of them looking annoyed. I'm sure they're not used to being dismissed.

"All right, then." Sierra stands, and without a goodbye, they walk away from us, whispering, and then Meeka throws her head back in laughter. The three of us watch them in silence.

Meeka and Kenzie are next-door neighbors. They were best friends all through elementary school and middle school. Sierra moved to their neighborhood in seventh grade, and she slowly stole Meeka, making sure Kenz was left out little by little, and then completely. But it wasn't enough to have Meeka all to herself. She had to make sure they displayed their new friendship all over social media, having parties where everyone was invited but Kenz.

By the time I met Kenzie in ninth grade, she was lonely and brokenhearted. I can see why Sierra would feel threatened and jealous. Kenz is her opposite: petite, bubbly, cute, naturally kind. Sierra has a more severe, womanly beauty, tall and big-boned. Controlling and conquering. Meeka and Sierra don't acknowledge Kenzie unless they're lifting her in a cheer stunt. I used to fear they'd drop her, but thankfully they keep it professional when it comes to the squad. Still, I prefer it when Lin and I are her bases, with Monica as the back spot, just to be on the safe side.

"Basic bitches," Kenzie whispers, and then she crosses her arms and looks kind of guilty for saying it.

"You okay?" Monica asks me.

I nod, though I'm shaken.

"Why does Raul hang out with them?" Monica asks. "He's like a different person when he's in their claws."

"He plays with my hair when they're not around." Kenzie sighs, running her fingers down the strands to her shoulders, dark-brown to light-brown ombre at the tips, sleek from great products and hours of straightening.

I ball up my paper bag and toss it like a basketball toward the trash can. When it makes it, the table of athletes cheers, making me and the girls laugh. I stand and give a curtsy just as the bell rings.

I decide right then that I'm going to focus on the positive. On the people who lift each other up. Not the ones who try to tear us down.

Chapter Six

Mrs. Warfield is smiling way too big when the rest of us roll into English on Thursday. I'm so tired and grumpy, I can hardly stand it. Mom and Zeb got in a fight last night because she got a call at work that he'd been involved in a spitball war at lunch and accidentally hit a girl in the eye. And then they fought harder when, instead of packing up his bookshelf, Zeb threw every item across the room. They both ended up in tears, which meant that I did, too.

Fun times.

"I think we should begin class with another mystery poem, this one being a sort of continuation of yesterday's." She actually giggles, and I sit straight up in my seat, my heart sprinting. I want to look around, to see whose face looks like the guilty culprit, but I'm too nervous.

Mrs. Warfield raises an eyebrow and scans the room to be sure we're all paying attention before she begins.

"Ode to the straw that fits in the pouch that rests in your hand.
The straw that meets your lips, pink as blossoms.
The proud, cylindrical piece of plastic that stands up to greet you with its chest out, ready to be used by you, to quench you.
Oh, to be that straw, partially submerged in 66 percent fruit juice,
And partially submerged in your mouth. Enjoy, little straw, enjoy."

Flames engulf me. Mrs. Warfield fans herself and winks as the class erupts into riotous cheering and laughter. My eyes are bulging out. I openly stare around the class, just as others do, trying to figure out who wrote it. Everyone but the sleeping Joel and Emberly in the back row is smiling and talking.

Then Dean says in a loud voice above the din, "All right, fess up! Who's the smooth Shakespearean up in here?"

"Me!" Angelo Garcia stands, putting his forearm across his abdomen, and bowing regally. "Ladies, you can reach me at seven-oh-three—"

"I'm sorry, Romeo, but I cannot allow you to take credit," Mrs. Warfield tells Angelo with a wink.

"Aw, man!" He sits, and everyone is laughing.

Now I'm totally confused. Dean smiles at me when we make eye contact, but I can't figure out if he said that to play it off and take suspicion off himself or what.

"Oh my God, this is so cute, I can't handle it," Raul says.

"It was you, huh, Raul?" Dean asks him with a smile.

"You know it, babe." Raul gives him a sexy look and everyone laughs.

"Okay, class, settle down," Mrs. Warfield says. "And for the record, that's as risqué as I will allow the poetry to be in my class. Keep it clean." She winks again, the dirty birdie, and then tells us to open our books.

Needless to say I'm completely distracted the rest of class, which leads into glorious distraction for the rest of the day.

"Dad's here!" Zeb opens his door while the van is still moving into the spot, and I holler at him, but it's no use. He jumps out and runs. We haven't seen Dad in days, but it feels like so much longer.

Uninvited hope rises in my chest as I get out and go inside. I find Dad in the kitchen, putting some of the large travel mugs and his coffee cups into a box. I drop my book bag, my heart dropping with it.

"Hey!" He gives a half smile as Zeb runs into his arms. "How's my main man?"

"Good." Zeb looks up at him, eyes full of love.

Dad turns to me, not letting go of Zeb. "Xanderia."

"Hey," I say quietly. I glance around at how many more boxes are piled up in the room. Pictures have been taken down and boxed up, the bigger ones leaning in a pile against the wall. Photographs of the four of us together. Will we even be allowed to display those anymore? My chin trembles, and there's a sudden burning at the back of my eyes. I swallow and turn away from them.

Mom comes down the stairs and hefts a heavy box onto the kitchen counter. "Here's your movies and CDs from the bedroom and the last of your dress shoes."

"Thanks," he says.

As Mom wipes her hands down her thighs, they look at each other, and the sorrow that looms between them sends a shock wave through the room that makes me choke. I know I'm being dramatic, making things worse, but I can't help it. I slide down the wall and bury my face in my hands. The sobs that come rack my body. I can't control the grief that takes over.

This house feels like a tomb. A place where something joyful has died and left behind a gaping chasm of distress and regret. Through my sobs I hear Zeb begin to cry, and Dad consoling him. Then I feel Mom's arms go around me. She whispers over and over into my hair, "I'm sorry . . ."

And I believe her, but it doesn't take away the pain. It doesn't make things better. It doesn't give us back our family.

"Why don't you stay home from school tomorrow?" Mom says to both of us. "Sleep in and get some rest. It's almost spring break anyway."

"Yeah," Zeb quickly agrees.

I look up to see Dad give Mom a disapproving glance for letting us miss school, but he blows out a breath and lets it go.

"I can't miss school," I say stubbornly.

"Okay, then." Mom sounds disappointed that I've denied her consolation prize. "Just leave your phone for Zeb if he stays."

"Fine." I push to my feet and get away from them.

A ding wakes me in the middle of the night. It took me forever to get to sleep. I immediately smell the must of boxes and dust, and my heart fills with the wretched feelings that kept me awake to begin with.

I look at my phone and nearly scream. It's two in the morning.

Wylie: **I'm sorry about your parents.**

Wy heard the news. I'm not surprised with how fast the gossip mill works between our schools.

Oh my God, my heart. I could so easily go to him for comfort. He was always good at making me feel better, making me laugh, cuddling me; and he was there for me the past year while my parents fought. Then I remember what's-her-face, and how he told her we broke up so he could get with her, and those comforting vibes are chased away.

I text him back: **Thx.**

His response is immediate. **I miss u.**

I miss him, too, but I'll never tell him that.

I made a mistake, he says. **I will never ever do that again, Zae. I swear.**

It's too late. My chest shudders in memory of today's crying spree.

Wy: **I want to see u. Plz. I'm coming over.**

Me: **You don't have a car or license.**

Wy: **I'll take my mom's car.**

Me: **No!! Don't. I just want to sleep. I'm turning off my phone.**

I do exactly as I say, switching the sound off, and I fling an arm over my eyes. Now I'm wide awake and pissed off. Leave it to Wylie to use my parents as a way to try to get what he wants. He probably doesn't even care. I swear, if he comes knocking at my window in twenty minutes, I will go out there and punch him.

And now I can't get back to sleep. I hate everyone.

CHAPTER SEVEN

I know I told Mom I was going to school, just to spite her offer, but when my alarm goes off, not even the possibility of a Capri Sun poem can pull me out of bed. Once when I was little, my parents took us to the Renaissance Fair in Maryland. I remember trying to pick up a knight's chain-mail vest, and struggling. I couldn't imagine someone walking around with that heavy thing on his body, much less battling.

That's how this feels.

I text the girls to let them know I'm not coming, and I roll back over. An hour later I hear Zeb moving around on the floor above me, probably trying to find something to eat since Mom's at work, and I'm so heavy. A ton of chain mail is on my chest, and I'm on the constant verge of weeping. My plan is to lie here for hours, worthless, ignoring my basic needs, but I suddenly remember. I have a Spanish presentation today! With all the moving crap going on, I completely forgot.

I drag myself out of bed. When I go upstairs, I see the countertops covered in boxes, and the chain mail weighs heavier on my shoulders.

I'm in the middle of maneuvering my way around boxes to make a cup of ramen when Zeb comes out of the bathroom. He takes one look at me and says, "Whoa."

I'm rocking the cave-woman look in my baggy sweats and oversize T-shirt, hunched over, ponytail askew with half my hair falling out of it.

"I don't feel good," I say defensively, not bothering to point out his own bedheaded bouffant.

He puts his hands up. "Sorry."

I pour boiling water into my Styrofoam cup of noodles and weigh down the paper lid with a fork. "Want one?" I ask.

"For breakfast? Nah. I had toast." Despite his jab against my breakfast-food choice, he grabs a bag of off-brand barbecue chips.

The glasses are packed, so I pour us both paper cups of orange juice and we sit at the table. I have to push back two boxes so I can actually see my brother's face.

I peel back the paper lid on my noodles as Zeb talks.

"Mom says the neighbors are helping us move tomorrow since Dad has to work a double shift."

I don't respond because I know a tirade against our parents will ensue, especially my dad. He can't take a couple of hours off?

"It might be kind of fun living in an apartment, right?" Zeb asks. "It has a pool."

I nearly choke as I force myself to say, "Right."

I proceed to stuff my face so I don't have to lie to Zeb anymore. Likewise, he shoves in handfuls of chips as his eyes glaze over in thought. I wonder what he's thinking, but I don't have the energy to ask.

Instead, I open the family laptop so I can work on my presentation. I have to pretend I'm a news reporter, using a real news article from a Central American country of my choice, and talk for three minutes. I chose one about the Panama Canal, and I already did my research and written portion at school. Now I search for images of the canal to go along with my visual presentation. Then I type up my verbal part and go over it several times. I'm allowed to use notes, but I want to memorize as much as I can.

I barely finish in time, and there's not even a minute to spare for a shower. I change real quick, yank a brush through my hair, yell "Bye!" to Zebby, and race to school.

Chapter Eight

A buzz of excitement fills the air at Peakton, knowing we have the next week off from school, but I can't bring myself to fully share the enthusiasm. Tomorrow I'm moving from the house I love. The only house I've ever known. And why? Because my parents, who I *know* love each other, cannot get their shiz together and make up.

I check in at the office and race to Spanish, skidding in right before the bell. I'm actually kind of excited for my presentation. Nerd alert.

As I begin presenting my project, Mrs. Hernandez watches me with her head cocked, a look of proud wonder on her face that she often reserves for me. Over the years, she's given me more compliments and one-on-one time than any other teacher.

I'm so tuned in to my project that my three minutes fly by. The smile on my face feels foreign when everyone claps.

Mrs. Hernandez waves me over, and I notice for the first time there's someone standing at her desk. It's that Joel guy from English, the possible drug dealer who sleeps through class. I vaguely remember him coming in during my presentation.

"Zae, ¡excelente!" Mrs. Hernandez says. "And now you are being called to the guidance department."

I look at Joel with the pass in his hand. Wow, he's actually awake, and his hood is back. He's got light-brown, almost blond, buzzed hair and small onyx earrings. He doesn't look at me, just turns to go, and I follow.

He doesn't talk as we walk, and normally I'd fill the silence, but when I left my Spanish room, the gloom descended on me again, so I stay quiet. He leads me to the guidance wing, to Mrs. Crowley's room, and leaves me.

The older woman smiles and pulls off her glasses. "Ah, Zae Monroe, come in."

She motions to the seat across from her desk, so I sit. A dramatic pause happens while she looks at me, and my eyes wander to the motivational posters on her walls.

Walk the Talk.
Dare to Soar.

"Your mom called and explained everything that's going on at home." Oh, great. Her voice is calm and soothing, but I am not soothed. I'm immediately uneasy. She pauses like she's expecting a reaction, so I give a stiff nod.

"No matter how common divorce is, it's never easy—"

"They're not divorcing," I quickly say. "Just, like, a temporary separation."

I know how naïve I sound. And I see the pity in her eyes, like I'm a being a fool, which makes me want to scream and bolt from her presence.

"Well, you never know," she says. "These things are delicate, and difficult on everyone involved. Is there anything you'd like to talk about, Zae?"

"No." I should have probably pretended to think about it instead of blurting out my response, because she gives me that pitying look again and I want to rail. Then I make things worse with the most famous lie in history: "Everything is fine."

She lets out a thoughtful hum. I wonder what her face would look like if I brought my fists down and pounded on her desk.

"Sometimes when things are hard, I find it's best to look ahead. To plan. To keep my mind busy. What are your plans after high school? Will you be applying to colleges this fall? If so, perhaps you can begin looking now. Researching. Filling out paperwork. It could be therapeutic."

Uuuugh. I have no idea what I want to do with my life. I know that's crazy since it's the end of my junior year, but it's one of those questions that makes me really anxious. Kenzie wants to go to James Madison, like her mom, to become a biology teacher. Lin already has a stack of applications for places she can study business and finance. Monica is big into marketing, publicity, and communications. They're all so sure of themselves. College bound.

The only things that interest me are languages, so when people ask what I want to be, I say a Spanish teacher so they'll leave me alone about it. But I really don't love the idea of standing in front of a classroom every day. In fact, I want high school to be the end of my classroom days, even as a student. I've never told anyone that. Am I a total loser for not wanting to go to college?

I want to travel and learn even more languages. I've looked into being a professional translator, but most places are looking for advanced degrees for certification. I thought about being a travel YouTuber, showing people the world and other cultures through interaction, but that obviously takes money to start up. I keep telling myself I have time to figure it out, but it's moments like this that I feel the walls closing in.

"Okay, yeah. Thanks. I'll do that." I force a smile and her eyes narrow like she's consulting her inner lie detector.

I must pass because she says, "Please come to me any time if you need to talk."

"Yes, ma'am." Look at my manners.

I stand and head for the door before she can say anything else. When I get outside, Joel is sitting in a chair with his hood up, head leaning against the wall, eyes closed. I walk past and barely hear when he says, "Nice presentation."

I turn in surprise. He's not even looking at me—his eyes are still closed.

"Me?" I ask dumbly.

He grins and cracks one eye open. "*Sí.*" Ah, he's talking about my Spanish class.

I snort. So random. "Thanks."

He closes both eyes again, so I leave, shaking my head. I should've asked him if there were any Capri Sun poems today. Though he'd probably been sleeping.

When I get home, I find Zebby on the couch where I left him. I plop down beside him, and we zone out mindlessly in front of the television until Mom gets home. She sets down her huge purse.

"Zeb, you didn't answer any of my calls today. I've been worried sick!" She walks in and crosses her arms, her eyebrows scrunched up at my brother, and he looks at me.

Oh, yeah—crap. "I forgot to leave my phone with him," I admit.

We don't have a landline. For a second I feel bad, knowing she worried and he didn't have a way to call anyone, but in the end I only shrug at her gaping face, because he's fine. Everyone's fine. Her mouth gets tight.

"What?" I ask, annoyed that she's freaking out. "Nothing happened. Maybe it's time to get him a phone." I know I'm being disrespectful, and I brace myself against her verbal comeback, or even a slap, but she looks almost scared of me.

"Maybe you should watch your mouth before you lose your phone again." The threat is as weak as her voice, and for a second I feel power over her—a power I never wanted to have, and yet, all the anger living inside me is eating it up like candy.

Still, I don't want to lose my phone over spring break, even for a day, so I snarl "Sorry," in a way that shows I'm not sorry at all. She shakes her head and lets out a sigh as she turns away. God, I feel gross about what I can get away with lately, but another part of me screams that I deserve to have an attitude against the people who are turning my life upside down.

I feel dirty right then, inside and out. I stand up and stomp toward the bathroom to shower. As I pass the kitchen, I see Mom pulling out all the ingredients for taco soup, my favorite, and my stomach sours with guilt.

Our last night in the house is the saddest night of my life. All the beds have been taken apart, and they lean against the walls in the front hall. Zebby and I share an air mattress in my empty room with our sleeping bags on top. We eat popcorn and play with flashlights. He wants to hear a spooky story, so I look one up on my phone, and it's so cheesy that we end up laughing hysterically. It's the kind of laughter that stems from stress, when it's not really funny but you can't help yourself. You can't stop. It's either laugh or cry, and we're so tired of crying.

But after Zeb falls to sleep, in the quiet of my empty room with its barren walls, I do cry.

Spring Break

CHAPTER NINE

Brutal, seething anger. It's all I feel as I stand in the cramped apartment on my first day of spring break, wondering how it got to be this bad. We had a yard sale this morning and took the leftover stuff to Goodwill since we can't afford a storage unit. Now we're down to the bare minimum in every sense of the word.

I keep my earbuds in, music blaring, as I unpack stuff in my and Zebby's room, ripping open boxes with aggression. Mom said we could sell my full-size bed from the old house and get a bunk bed instead, but Zeb offered to sleep on the couch at night to let me have the bedroom to myself, which is really solid of him. The bedroom will be where his clothes and few belongings are stored. There isn't room for both our dressers, so we're using storage bins that slide under the bed.

This whole thing blows.

My heart leaps when my phone buzzes against my thigh.

Kenzie. **U sure u can't come 2nite?**

Jack Rinehart's party. I'm not in the mood to be sociable.

I text her back. **I'm sure. Sorry, sweets. Have fun.**

She sends a crying face.

When I take my earbuds out to go to the bathroom, I hear Mom and Zebby talking in her room.

"Why can't I help him move, too?" Zeb asks.

"He's got it under control, honey."

"Okay, fine. But when can I see him?"

"Maybe next weekend?"

"A whole week?"

"He needs to get settled in, baby." There's a plea in Mom's voice, like she wishes this whole thing would go away. She's always been a strong yet sensitive woman. I know she has to be hurting, but I still can't help but be angry with her. She let this happen.

Zeb stomps out of the room with a scowl and I duck in to the bathroom doorway before he has a chance to bowl me over.

At ten thirty that night I get another text while I'm mindlessly scrolling videos. This time from Monica.

OMG. Major drama. John broke up w Lin. Now she's wasted & making a scene.

Oh, crap. Poor Lin. Granted, we've all been waiting for this to happen, but still.

I call Monica and it's loud when she answers.

"Seriously, Zae. I wish you were here." Her voice sounds thick.

"You need to drag her away," I tell Monica. "Get her out of there."

"I want to, but we've all been drinking. John was supposed to be our ride home!"

Double crap. My girls need me.

"I'll come get you guys."

"Oh, thank God!" Monica sighs into the phone. "I freaking love you."

I redo my curls into a ponytail, making it higher and cuter, switch out my oversize T-shirt for a fitted black one, and pull on my snuggest jeans. I slip my toes into sparkly flip-flops, despite the chill in the night air, wishing there was time to do my makeup, but there isn't.

I grab my tote purse and run to tell Mom where I'm going. She probably won't like it, but she's always given me a lot of freedom, and now I have her guilt on my side. I lift my hand to knock on her door and hear her voice on the other side—a low, emotional murmur. I press my ear to the door.

"—not going to lie for you anymore, Xander. Hurry up and tell them or I will!"

Tell us what? My chest tightens. I knock twice and open the door before she answers. She hangs up, and we stare at each other. Her eyes are bloodshot and she looks older, crumpled in the middle of the bed.

"Is everything okay?" she asks.

"What's going on with Dad?"

She blinks, an innocent look plastered on her face.

My voice softens. "Tell me the truth. Please, Mom."

A war of indecision battles in her eyes.

"I really want him to tell you himself," she says.

It feels like a stampede of horses is thundering through my chest.

"Just *tell* me."

She swallows hard. As each word is torn from her mouth, it seems to pain her. "Your dad . . . he's not moving in with a regular roommate."

Different scenarios tumble end over end through my imagination, landing on the most terrible option.

"He's moving in with a woman?"

I wait for her to scoff and tell me "Of course not!" but she doesn't. Instead her chin dips in a small nod.

"Oh my God," I whisper. "Like . . . a girlfriend?"

Again with a slow, small nod. My stomach is clenched by an evil fist.

Dad has been cheating. I lose respect for the man I've always admired in that moment and it's a horrible, disgusting feeling, as if something once precious has shown its true nature and turned to rust. Dad is no better than Wylie. Is no man capable of being loyal to the woman he supposedly loves?

"Honey, please," she says. "Don't be angry with him."

What? "How can you stick up for him?" I hiss, trying not to yell.

Mom shuts her eyes. "It's . . . complicated. But he loves you and Zeb."

Yeah. Sure feels like it. All the vivacious color in my life has turned gray and ugly in a matter of days. I feel dizzy as I stand there.

"Don't tell Zebby," Mom begs.

I can't think straight. I stumble a step backward into the door. "I have to go pick up my friends from a party and take them home. Their ride bailed."

This seems to surprise her. "You shouldn't drive right now. You're upset, and it's late. They can call their parents."

"I'm *fine*," I say. "If it wasn't for the move today, I would've been with them anyway."

She sets her jaw. "Be careful, Zae. Do you have your pepper spray?"

"Yes."

"Don't stay out late. Take them home and come right back."

I don't answer. Turning, I rush down the hall. Zeb is passed out on the couch in front of the flickering TV, fully clothed. That was fast. Then again, it has been a long day. I shut the television off and pull the blanket from his old bed up around him. He snuggles down.

Something changes inside me as I leave our apartment—the bland, tiny box that will never be home. I feel the protective coating of my childhood innocence shed away, leaving me painfully exposed. Agony flares from every nerve ending, burning my eyes.

This is not just a break for my parents. They won't be getting back together after some therapeutic time apart. Dad is with someone else—*living* with her. And nothing will ever be the same.

CHAPTER TEN

The drive to Jack's house takes only ten minutes. My body shakes the entire way. I park across the street and make sure my eyes are dry and lipstick applied before I climb out, on a mission to find Lin and rescue her from pain and humiliation. Caused by a boy, of course.

I walk with purpose up the long driveway toward the house that's thumping with life. I think about all the boys who've hurt me and my friends over the years. The boys who are looking for casual hookups with no plans of getting to know us. The boys who couldn't care less if they hurt us, as long as they get what they want, moving on the moment they get bored. The boys who will be just like my dad someday.

Stupid, selfish creatures. Each one of them needs to be taught a lesson. They deserve to be treated the way they treat us. Used.

I burst into Jack's house with vengeance in my heart. People yell my name and I raise my chin in mock nods, but my radar is poised to find my friends. Lo and behold, all three of them are shoved into the tiny hall bathroom where a line of grouchy girls waits. I knock and yell for them to open up. My heart clenches at the sight of Lin's puffy red eyes, reminiscent of my mother's. I hold out my hand and when she takes it, I pull her from the bathroom.

She digs her heels in. "I'm not leaving!"

Oh, boy. It's her drunk voice. "Okay, fine, but let's at least get some fresh air." I pull her to the back deck. The four of us huddle in a corner and I squeeze her tight while she cries, leaning into me drunkenly.

Over her shoulder Monica and Kenz shake their heads at me with big eyes, letting me know what a disaster the night's been.

"You know the best way to make him pay?" I ask.

Lin sniffles.

"Move on," I tell her. It's strange to be giving this advice, especially when I still feel so torn up about my own breakup.

"I don't want to move on," she sobs.

"I know, but he doesn't deserve you, just like Wylie didn't deserve me."

"How can you be so strong?" she asks.

"I'm not strong," I assure her. "I'm just really, really pissed off."

That makes her crack a smile. "Can I have another drinkie?"

"*No*," the three of us say in unison. She pouts.

A loud group of guys comes out, laughing and talking crudely. The stench of cigarette smoke wafts toward us.

"Oh, hey," Monica says in a hushed whisper. "It's Rex Morino, professional fukboi."

I glance over my shoulder at the group. Sure enough, Rex Morino is right in the middle, leaning back against the deck rail with one elbow while his other hand holds a cigarette between his thumb and finger. His four friends circle him, all in clunky boots and grungy T-shirts. I know for sure one's been in juvi and the other goes to an alternative school.

Last year Lin and Monica had simultaneous crushes on Rex, and it got ugly. He toyed with them both during the class they had together. For six months there'd been a rift in our friendship. All because of this stupid guy.

I don't look away fast enough, and Rex captures my eye. His are practically black, and partially hidden by his dyed bangs, also black. They all have overgrown hair. I try to be nice to everyone at school, but I don't bother with these guys. I avoid them like the scary dudes they are.

Rex Morino gives me a nod and blows smoke through his lips and nose. "See somethin' you want, rah-rah?"

His whole group turns to see who he's talking to, and they snigger. My friends freeze under their scrutiny.

"Let's go," Kenz whispers.

"No, hold on," I say to her, feeling emboldened.

How many girls has Rex Morino hurt? He was my crush in the eighth grade. I wonder if he remembers dancing with me at the Snow Ball, telling me he'd be right back with cups of punch for us, then slinking out the side door with some other girl. I'd obsessed over him for months. Clinging to every look he gave me. Every word he uttered near me. Looking for some sign that he wanted me and hoping his leaving was all a big misunderstanding.

I walk toward him now, feeling a strange pull. His friends part to let me in, malicious grins on their faces. A surge of confidence that stems from a lack of caring fills me.

"Zae, what are you doing?" Monica hisses behind me. But I only have eyes for Rex Morino. The heartbreaker.

He grins now, amused beyond belief that I have moved into his bubble—that I haven't blushed and run away.

"Careful, girl," he says, never taking those lazy, dark eyes off me, even as he crushes his cigarette in the raised flowerpot next to him. "Once you taste this, everything else is bland."

Oh, please.

His friends cackle at the purposefully stupid line, and he laughs, too.

I have no idea what's gotten into me, but it feels good to stand face-to-face with Rex Morino without fear. To surprise him. To be in his sights and have his complete attention. He's bad. An untouchable. Close up, I see the red in his eyes from when he smoked up tonight. He's high.

"Something you want?" he asks again, but this time his voice is low, careful.

"A kiss," I say. I can feel my heart pounding all the way up in my throat.

One of his friends whistles, but Rex and I never lose eye contact as his friends act like heathens around us. My pulse is still racing, but I embrace it. It's been almost a year since I've kissed anyone other than Wylie. I feel a jab in my gut, like I'm being unfaithful, but I swipe it aside. I belong to *me*.

Rex doesn't say a word. Nor does he smile again. Or hesitate.

His tattooed hand slips under my ponytail and to the back of my neck with complete ownership as he pulls my mouth to his.

In a distant land, I hear my friends screech my name in shock, but I'm focused on that smoky, masculine mouth. Those expert lips and tongue that possess mine. My hands slip into the thick, silky hair at the back of his head, as his hands slide down my waist to the belt loops of my jeans. There he hooks his fingers and yanks my hips closer to his.

This kiss is different for me from any others I've experienced. I'm lost in the physical sensations but emotionally detached from it.

Like a guy.

Rex's hands roam farther down, cupping my butt, which is my cue. I slowly pull away, taking a steady step back. When he stares at me like I'm some kind of glowing anomaly, it's my turn to grin.

"Thanks," I say.

His mouth is still open as I turn away. His friends gawk. My friends gawk.

"Come on," I say to the girls.

They follow me, our hands automatically linking. I pull us like a train through the party, refusing to stop for anything.

The moment we hit the driveway out front, my friends are shrieking questions at me, jumping up and down, flipping out.

"What the heck was that badassness?"

"Holy freaking shit, Zae!"

"Are you *crazy?*"

For the first time all week, I let out a real laugh. There's something freeing about not giving a crap.

"I think it's time we turned the tables, girls."

We stop at my car and I lean against it. They stand in front of me, a wall of shocked faces. "Boys use girls all the time. They want things from us, but they don't want to give anything in return. They hurt us and lie to us and make fools of us, and I don't know about you guys, but I'm over it."

"How are we supposed to turn the tables?" Lin asks.

I smile. "We use them for one of our favorite things."

They stare at me, baffled, as if I hadn't just demonstrated my intentions on the most infamous bad boy we know.

"Kissing!" I clarify. "This spring break, we kiss as many boys as we can. We don't fall for them. We don't care about them. We kiss them and we compare them and we bring them to their knees."

Kenzie giggles and covers her mouth.

"That is genius." Monica's eyes dance as she imagines it. Moonlight glints off her thick cocoa hair, courtesy of her mother's Salvadoran genes.

Only Lin frowns. "I don't think I can."

I move forward and take her hands. Tonight she's hurting and still in denial that it's over with John. But one thing I know about Lin is that she's competitive.

"You can, Lin. Let's make it a contest to see which one of us can kiss the most boys before the end of spring break." Nine days.

Kenz and Monica both let out little squees and clap their hands at the idea. Lin still frowns, but it's tinged with frustration now.

"I don't know if I can do this." Her voice is a little slurred.

"Take all the time you need," I tell her. "Meanwhile, we'll be racking up our numbers. If I can kiss Rex Morino, then you can kiss anyone you want."

Her eyes widen in indignation, knowing I'm cornering her.

"The contest began tonight," I say. "And I'm in the lead."

"Hey, no fair!" Kenzie says.

"Yeah," Lin cries. "You can't count Rex. We didn't even know it was a contest yet!" She nearly falls over putting her hands to her hips.

I smile to myself as I climb in the van, knowing I have her now. Monica gives me her fist and I touch it to mine. Our fingers explode.

I turn to Lin. "So, if I erase Rex's kiss and we're on even ground, you're in?"

She cuts her sexy gaze to me and crosses her arms. "Fine."

I smile and say, "Everyone buckle up." In the compacted space, I can smell the alcohol on them. The seat belts click and I put the minivan in drive.

"I'm not gonna lie, Zae," Monica says. "That was hot. You freaking owned him. You should have seen him staring at you when you walked away!"

Cruel pride parades through me.

"Is he a good kisser?" Kenzie leans toward me from the front passenger seat.

"Yeah," I admit. "Except for the weed taste. But his

74

technique was awesome. He's very . . . confident."

Kenzie sighs.

"I still can't believe you kissed him," Lin says. "So, *if* I decide to do this, what are the rules?"

I inwardly cheer.

"No kissing each other's exes," Kenzie immediately says.

That should go without saying.

"No going after guys who have girlfriends," Lin says. "We don't need any psychos hunting us down, and we're not home-wreckers."

"It has to be a real kiss. With tongue," Monica clarifies, waggling her eyebrows.

"Does it count if we end up kissing the same guys?" Lin asks.

"Ew!" Kenzie giggles.

"What? It's like sharing a drink." Lin grins. "I don't mean we're kissing him at the same time or anything."

"Sure," I said. "But we have to remember that we're using *them*. Not the other way around. So, no getting mad at each other. If y'all want sloppy seconds, go for it."

The four of us laugh, giddy.

"Be forceful," Monica says, punching the air with a strong arm.

"Be aggressive," Kenzie adds with a growl.

Like the huge cheer dorks we are, we automatically break into a catchy cheer from middle school, clapping and chanting at the top of our lungs:

"Be aggressive. Be, be aggressive, say B-E A-G-G-R-E-S-S-I-V-E!" And then we laugh hysterically at our own absurdity.

Yeah, we'd die if any living soul saw us do that.

"We take what we want!" I yell. "And we don't feel guilty for saying no to what *they* want. We're the bosses. And the biggest rule of all is *no falling for any of the boys we kiss*. This is our time to rule! No love. No emotion. Just kisses and fun. Got it?"

"Got it!" they respond together.

I turn up the radio as loud as it will go without blowing out the speakers and we car dance with hyper, reckless abandon. I'm taking back my life, one kiss at a time.

CHAPTER ELEVEN

Sunday

Three o'clock in the morning is not a good time to wake me.

OMG, Zae. Did you kiss some dude 2nite? Some asshole? Stay away from him, k? I'm goin crazy. I miss you.

Is he out of his mind? In what messed-up world does he think it's okay to cheat on me, and then give me a hard time when I kiss a guy after we've broken up?

I turn on all caps. **MIND YOUR OWN BUSINESS AND STOP WAKING ME UP IN THE MIDDLE OF THE NIGHT!!!** Then I turn off the sound.

I'm too pissed to go back to sleep. Over and over I formulate more scathing comebacks that will put him in his lowly place, but I know my silence will hurt him more than anything. He's a spoiled boy used to getting attention whenever he wants it. Especially from me.

When I pull my butt out of bed at ten the next morning, Mom is still at work. She works the four to ten a.m. shift Sunday mornings. Zeb is sitting up on the couch, hair askew, playing a video game. I make us both bowls of cereal and he pauses the game to eat with me. For some reason, his slurping bites don't irritate me like they used to.

"You doin' okay?" I ask when he's finished. He looks so young in his Pokémon pajama bottoms with his bird chest and milk mustache.

"Yeah," he says quietly, wiping his mouth on his bare forearm. He grinds his teeth as he looks down at his lap, a sure sign he's upset. Not being one to talk, he loses himself in the game again. I make a mental note to do something fun with him this week.

When I get out of the shower, Mom is home with two-day-old pastries they can't sell anymore. My mouth waters as I put an almond croissant in the microwave and then eat it while it's hot enough to burn my fingers and mouth.

"Careful, Zae!" Mom scolds.

"I smell bread." Zebby comes into the cramped kitchen like a zombie.

My phone dings, so I sit at the table to read my text while I eat.

Kenzie: **Are u going 2 the baseball fund-raiser at the mall?**

Oh, crap, I'd forgotten about that. The pizza parlor and arcade are donating a certain percentage of their proceeds to our baseball team from noon to two this afternoon. I still don't feel like being social, though. Plus, I'm not asking for money from Mom for overpriced mall pizza.

No $. I tell her. **LMK if you do something tonight.**

OMG just let me pay for your pizza. Plz come?

I glance over at Zeb, who is inhaling a cold cheese Danish in one hand and a smashed bear claw in the other. **Do you care if I bring Zeb? He'll just play at the arcade the whole time.**

Aw, my lil' boyfriend! Of course I don't care!

I laugh. "Hey, Zebby. Wanna come to the arcade at the mall?"

"Yeah!" He spews crumbs, and Mom gives his arm a small whap.

"Okay, I've got some quarters in my piggy bank," I tell him. "We'll leave at eleven thirty."

"That will be nice," Mom says, and I realize I didn't ask for her permission, and she's trying to make me acknowledge her.

"There's a fund-raiser for the baseball team," I force myself to explain.

I brush my hands over a napkin, then hole myself in my room until it's time to go.

The girls flirt mercilessly with Zebby in the van, hugging him and ruffling his curls. He gobbles up their attention like candy, and I think his face might break from smiling. It makes me glad I brought him.

My plan is to let Zeb have my piece of pizza, but it turns out Mom slipped him a fiver, which he uses to get his own slice with sausage, then I fill his pockets with quarters and send him on his way.

"Don't leave the arcade," I call after him. "And if anyone tries to steal you, dig your fingers into their eyeballs and

79

scream!" He rolls his eyes and heads to the blinking, bleeping room, looking taller and skinnier than ever.

"I can't get over how cute he is," Kenzie says.

I'm glad we got here right on time so we could get a booth, because now the place is getting packed. Two guys from the baseball team, Kyle and Callum, wearing their blue Panther hats, squeeze onto the edges of our booth seats, squashing us in.

"Thanks for the support, ladies," Kyle says with a cocky smile.

"Oh, is there something going on here for the baseball team?" Monica asks. "We were just craving pizza."

The guys laugh at her sarcasm.

"Hey, my parents are leaving tomorrow for a cruise," Callum says. "You guys wanna come over tomorrow night?"

Kenzie opens her happy-looking mouth, and I grab her leg under the table.

"We'll think about it," I say.

"Cool." Callum stands, and Kyle follows. "Y'all know where I live, right? Around the corner from Monica? We'll have beer." He knocks twice on the table and turns to bother another table of girls.

"Will John be there?" I ask Lin since John's on the team.

She shakes her head. "His family's out of town for spring break."

The three of them look at me, and I say, "Good. Then we're going."

They cheer.

"I call dibs on Kyle!" Kenzie whispers.

"Not if I get him first," Lin responds with an evil laugh.

"You're feeling better, then?" I ask Lin.

She gives a shrug and her face falls. "Not really, but I think I knew it was coming."

"You seemed pretty crushed last night," I say.

"That was partly the beer." She gives an embarrassed eye roll. "I mean, I'm still upset, but I thought about it all night, and . . . I'm not sure I loved him, you know? Not like you loved Wylie. So, I guess if you can move on, I can, too."

I put my fingertips together and hold them out. She does the same and we touch them together, like our fingers are smooching.

Kenzie's phone starts blaring Harry Potter music, her ringtone, and she sighs. "It's my mom. Be right back."

The rest of us eat until she comes bouncing back in with a huge grin. "Someone at work gave my mom four tickets to the country jamboree tonight, but they already have plans. She said we could have them . . . ." She bites her lip and watches us expectantly while Monica, Lin, and I share *What the what?* looks.

"Is that a jug band?" Monica asks, making me snort.

Kenzie sighs, exasperated. "It's a huge country concert. Come on, you guys, it'll be so much fun!" She starts to name off the bands and singers who will be there, and I recognize a few of the names from online and television.

"Is this an old people thing?" I ask.

Kenz gawks at me. "I only went to one in Texas, and there were tons of country boys."

The other three of us perk up now, and Kenzie goes for the kill.

"Cowboy hats. Cowboy boots. Super hot guys who call

you ma'am, and not in a you're-an-old-lady way but in a sexy I-respect-your-womanhood way. And the music is fun, I swear! It's outdoors. The weather is supposed to be beautiful."

"What would we wear?" Lin asks. "And do we have to square dance?"

Kenzie laughs. "No! It's all about cute comfort. Jeans. Boots. Maybe something flannel tied at the waist. Pigtail braids. I have some hats— Ooh, Monica, I have a leopard-print one that would be amazing on you. We can get ready at my house!"

We're all smiling now, because her excitement is contagious.

"I'm in," I say. The others agree, and Kenzie claps her hands. If nothing else, it'll be an experience.

When we finish eating, we start to get dirty looks from the people who are standing with trays, so we get up to let others sit. I lead us into the arcade where I find Zeb immersed in a race-car simulator. I crouch next to where he's sitting.

"We're going to walk around the mall. Call me if you need me."

"Okay," he says without looking away from the screen.

After the phone incident the other day, Mom bought Zeb one of those pay-as-you-go ones from a gas station.

We go out and walk the mall, rating outfits in the windows and commenting on prices. When we get near the food court, Lin stops and pokes me in the ribs.

"Ow!" Lin is buff from throwing flyers on the cheer squad, so when she pokes it hurts.

"Is that Rex Morino?" she whispers.

Oh, no. I look over to see Rex with a handful of goons and some tough girls by the wall near the cookie stand. He's looking right at us. My first instinct is to tuck and run, but I look straight forward and whisper, "Ignore him." We start to walk, but Kenzie hisses, "He's coming over!"

Sure enough, Rex is swaggering in our direction. I swallow hard and meet his eyes as he makes his way into our circle.

"'Sup, girls?" One of his dark eyes is hidden behind his black hair. He smirks, all sexy like. I look at his yummy lips for a second and then his eyes again.

"Nothin'." I cross my arms.

"Zae, right?" he asks.

I want to choke him. We've only been going to school together for five freaking years. Does he even remember dancing with me in middle school?

"What was up with you last night?" He runs a hand through his hair.

I shrug. "Just having fun. Nothing I want to repeat."

"Burn," Monica says under her breath.

Rex laughs and puts a hand to his heart like I've hurt him. It's true, though. I have no plans or desire to kiss him again, no matter how good it'd been. I'd gotten what I wanted, and now I'm ready to get it from someone else.

"Pretty sure you enjoyed it," he says.

"Yep. I did." It's my turn to smile. "See you later, Rex." I turn and catch the mirth and disbelief in my friends' eyes.

We walk away and don't give him a second glance. The girls can barely hold it together, tittering under their breath until we get around the corner and they let it all out. I can only laugh. I have no idea what's come over me.

My eye catches a Help Wanted sign in the window of Clara's Bowtique, a cute jewelry and accessory shop. "Hold on a sec," I tell them.

We go in together, and while they browse, I approach the ancient-looking lady at the register.

"Hi," I say. "I saw your sign. I'm still in school, though, so I can't work during the day."

"I need someone to work weekends and summer," she says. She leans down and gets out an application, sliding it to me with a pen on top. "Do you have transportation?"

"Yeah," I say.

"I prefer 'Yes, ma'am.'"

My eyes go wide. "Oh, sorry. Yes, ma'am." I almost laugh because I get awkward when I'm embarrassed.

She looks down at the application with her hands behind her back, and I realize she wants me to fill it out now. My friends are giving me funny looks, but I ignore them and fill out the application as quickly as I can. I've never had a job, so there's a lot I have to leave blank.

"Zae?" the woman asks.

I nod, then quickly say, "Yes, ma'am."

"Interesting name. I'm Mrs. McOllie, the owner. I will call you to set up an interview."

"Yes, ma'am. It's my spring break, so you can call any time." I hope she doesn't call too early.

She gives a curt nod of dismissal, so I leave with my girls trailing behind me.

"Did you just apply for a job?" Kenzie asks.

"Yeah."

"Cool," Monica says. "I love that store. Do you think you'll get a friends' discount?"

I think about the strict old lady. "Doubtful."

When we get back to the pizza place, the crowd has cleared out. I peek in the arcade to make sure Zeb is okay, and then we find a table with four plastic chairs. The baseball guys are still there, being loud and obnoxious as their family members buy out all the tiramisu to get the team every penny possible.

While Kenzie and Lin jump up to talk to Kyle, and Monica runs to the restroom, the chair next to me pulls out and my heart leaps as Dean Prescott slides into it. Dean! He rests his big linebacker forearms on the table, turning his gaze to me.

"Big weekend, huh?"

My mind immediately goes to the new apartment. "Yeah. Sucks."

His eyebrows pinch with confusion and I want to kick myself. He has no idea about my moving. That means he'd heard about the stupid kiss with Rex. Crap.

"Oh," I say. "No. That was . . ."

Man, it's hot all of a sudden. His eyebrows lift, as if he's waiting.

I let out a nervous laugh. "Nothing."

"Yeah." He sits back in the chair now and the plastic groans. "Probably not best to rebound with that dude."

"I'm not. I'm really not. I don't even like him."

Once again his eyebrows go up, and his lips purse like he doesn't believe me.

"I don't! I swear."

He laughs and reaches out to tug a curl of my brown hair. "Just be careful."

85

I open my mouth to argue as Monica returns and sits down, facing him. "Dean! Hey, boy."

"Hey, girl." He's grinning at her the way boys can't help but grin at Monica. A twinge of jealousy jabs my gut at how easily Monica was able to shift his attention. She's the total package with her high cheekbones, curvy body, and commercial-worthy hair. All my friends have appeal. Lin's got an hourglass shape with a tiny waist, plus a soft, triangular face. Kenzie's super cute with nice, full lips and even has a dimple. My friends claim to envy my long legs and brown eyes with flecks of light gold. I feel pretty when my natural curls are on point, but I guess everyone's their worst critic.

"What are y'all up to for spring break?" he asks.

"If there's a party, we're there," I tell him. "Know of any?"

He pushes his phone toward me. "Gimme your number and I'll hit you up if I hear anything."

A thrill shoots through me as I pick up his big phone in its rugged case, so much heavier than mine. I smile at his Washington Redskins wallpaper. My family are huge fans. We watch all their games together. Or . . . we used to. My smile falls.

"Go, 'Skins," I say as I program my number in and slide the phone back.

"That's right." He grins and stands, giving Monica a nod, then leaves us to join two other guys from the football team at the counter.

"God, I haven't talked to him in forever," Monica says.

"I really hope he texts me," I whisper.

Her eyes light up. "Ooh, he's totally kissable."

"He's mine." I'm trying to joke, but it feels like it comes

across territorial, especially when she gives me that teasing look.

"I thought you said we could share?"

I shrug, looking over at him, laughing with his friends in line.

"Oh," she says. "You *like* him?"

"No." I'm never going to like a boy again. But then a lingering thought slips out . . . "I mean, if he's the one writing the poetry, then . . . I don't know." Ugh, I shouldn't have said that. Yes, Dean seems like a nice guy, but he's got the Y chromosome, so he would eventually hurt me like any other boy. God, that is so depressing.

Monica's eyebrows shoot up. "I forgot about that! Do you think it's him?"

"I have no idea," I say honestly. "Maybe?"

My eyes move back toward the ordering counter where they roam over Dean's form. Over his defensive linebacker body that makes my average height feel petite. Over his square jaw, which is a manly contrast to his dimpled cheeks. Over his light-brown eyes and wavy brown hair. And those lips. Perfectly formed. Nice teeth, too. I even thought he was cute back in the day when he had braces.

I'm going to kiss him. That will prove to him just how much I'm not falling for Rex Morino. At some point soon, Dean Prescott's lips will be mine.

CHAPTER TWELVE

In the mall parking lot, I pull out right behind Kyle, who has the top off his Jeep, even though it's not quite warm enough for that yet. His vehicle is full of guys who need to put their seat belts on. Kenzie opens my sunroof, and she and Lin stick their torsos through, calling out to them.

"Hiiiii, Kyyyyyle!" they sing simultaneously. Kyle holds up a fist and the other guys stand, turning around to face the van. They're all banging their chests like Tarzan, and my friends are laughing uproariously.

Zebby hollers from the back, "What is wrong with you people?"

Monica is falling over in the middle seat, and I can't help but join the laughter. Then Kyle tries to show off by gunning his engine and flying up on a grassy median. I gasp as the guys barely grab hold to keep from falling out.

"Y'all sit down!" I grab Lin and pull. "They almost died!"

"They did not!" Kenzie says with laughter, but she gets back in. Her cheeks are tinted from the wind.

As Kyle continues his off-roading adventure through the mall parking lot, I see lights flashing behind us, and I yank the van to the side. A mall cop zooms past me and gets near the curb, yelling on his speaker for Kyle to stop and pull over. We drive past them, and the five of us cannot stop laughing at the look of dread on Kyle's face, and how the other three guys are scrambling to get their seat belts on. I can't wait to make fun of them at the baseball party tomorrow. We're dying the whole way home as I drop the girls off.

It's weird how Zeb's mirth and mine completely dissolve when we enter the apartment. The place is soul sucking, with its lack of space and character. Not to mention the random boxes still sitting around.

Zeb immediately goes to the couch, and my shoulders slump. This will never be home.

Monica's staring at her phone as we get ready in Kenzie's frilly room. It's been decorated in mauve and eyelet lace since forever. "Holy crap, Rex Morino just started following me, so I followed him back, and he freaking immediately messaged me to ask for your number!"

"Don't give it to him!" I say, swiping blush over my cheek as Monica works on French braiding my hair down both sides.

"I won't. Jeez, you're really doing a number on his ego. It's like he can't believe any girl wouldn't want to be with him."

Kenzie claps her hands in glee. "This is so awesome!"

"It's just the thrill of the chase," I say, not sharing her amusement. "Boys want what they can't have, and what they *do* have is never good enough." My sad attitude puts a damper on our pregame excitement, and I feel bad. I used to be all positive, all the time. But that was the me who let herself get hurt.

"Alright, then," Kenzie says. She turns on the radio to a country station and pulls a pair of bona fide cowgirl boots out of her closet. Pointy toes, one-inch heels, brown leather with embellishment designs around the edges. She pulls a matching cowgirl hat from an upper shelf and puts it on. With her hair jutting out, snug jeans, and a pink-and-white checkered shirt, this girl needs to be in a music video.

Lin lets out a "Yee-haw!" and I say, "Well, howdy, little lady."

Monica makes her spin for us. "Where have you been hiding this stuff?"

"My grandma got it for me when I went to San Antonio at Christmas." Kenz admires the boots on her feet. "It's only the second time I've worn them."

I put a hand on my hip. "Exactly how long have you been a closet country girl?"

She rolls her eyes. "It's all my mom listens to, and it sort of grows on you. I know y'all aren't into it, but I'm hoping we can have fun anyway."

Honestly, I don't care where we're going or what kind of music will be playing. I'm just glad to be with my girls, hunting guys, collecting kisses.

My French braids are complete, and my red, glossy lips

match the red-and-black-plaid shirt I'm wearing with leggings.

"I feel like a lumberjack," I say, looking down.

"You're a hot lumber Jill," Kenzie assures me. "Just own it."

Monica sticks the leopard-print cowgirl hat on her head, and it complements her dark eye makeup perfectly. Lin's shiny black pigtails hang over her shoulders, her jean skirt hugs her hips, and her ankle boots are rocking. Kenzie smiles at what she's created. We're ready to go.

CHAPTER THIRTEEN

Sunday Night

The pavilion is a forty-five-minute drive in a town that's on the cusp between northern Virginia's built-up suburbia and mid-Virginia's sprawling countryside. We listen to Kenz's music the whole way. Some of the songs are catchy and sexy and sassy. We end up singing along before we know it. By the time we roll up, I feel like we've been country girls for ages, and I'm ready to do this.

Kenz was not lying. The first thing we notice in the parking lot are the hordes of young people everywhere. We smile at the big groups who are tailgating as we pass, and everyone returns the smiles. Some linger on us longer than others, and we soak up the looks.

Lin says, "There are, for real, hot guys in hats everywhere!"

"Right?" Kenzie laughs. "I told you! And legit Wrangler jeans!" I catch sight of the *W*s on the pockets of the guys moseying in front of us.

A natural buzz builds among the four of us, and we're giddy as we walk up hundreds of steps and enter the lawn of the pavilion. Kenzie buys us all sodas and we find a spot to sit on the grassy hill looking down at the stage. The way we're laughing and carrying on, people around us probably think we slipped a little something in our drinks.

The music starts with a kick-ass female artist singing about throwing her man's no-good, cheating tail out the door. I'm immediately on my feet, arm raised, learning every word of the song. Kenzie shouts the lyrics and we dance, shaking our hips and punching the sky as the singer's ex-boyfriend undergoes a series of mishaps: being fed to the crocs in the lake, getting tossed onto the old railroad tracks, losing all his hair to a newbie barber. I'm ridiculously entertained.

As the next song comes on, one we recognize from the car ride, we move into a circle to dance and sing the words at the top of our lungs. I spot a group of guys a little way behind us, sitting in a row on the ground. It's almost comical how they're each on their bottoms, legs bent, boots down, arms draped over their knees or leaning back, each of them totally at ease. But what I notice first is that every pair of their eyes is watching us. I freeze, which makes Monica start to turn, but I grab her hand to stop her.

"We're being watched. Don't all look at once . . . but definitely look."

Kenzie is first to sneak a peek. "Oh my gosh," she says,

turning back to us. "The one in the brown hat is mine because we're matchy."

I dart my gaze stealthily. Brown Hat Boy is kind of small and wiry muscled, a good fit for her petite form. Before I can look away, my eyes are drawn to the guy next to him.

Black Hat Boy. Yes, that's his name.

He's got a Styrofoam cup dangling from his hand, which is lazily draped on his knee, and he totally watches me as he brings the drink to his mouth and sips. His eyes look dark from here, and his jaw is a rugged, sexy line. I give him a wry grin and slowly turn away, feeling the heat of his attention.

"Black hat," I say under my breath.

"I knew you would go for him," Kenzie tells me with a giggle. "He looks bad. You should just wreck every bad boy, Zae."

"With pleasure."

We pucker our fingers and touch them for a kiss.

"They don't have girls with them," Lin says. "That's good."

"Okay, they *are* kind of hot," Monica admits reluctantly. "But I don't want a hat boy. I like the guy on the end with the black ponytail. He looks Native American or something." She stares hard until Lin elbows her. "Sorry, but look at him! He's got that lost-in-thought look, like he's . . . deep."

Lin bursts out laughing, clutching her stomach like Monica said something dirty. It makes me laugh, too.

"Shut up," Monica says. "Which one do you want?"

Lin shrugs, and I can tell she's still kind of nervous after her breakup with John.

"Wait and see once we meet them," I tell her.

"Should we go now?" Kenzie asks.

I look at her like she's lost her mind. "We definitely do not go now. We have their attention. If we move too fast, they'll think we're desperate."

"But you moved fast with Rex," she points out.

"That was different. I know him. He would have never come to me, and I didn't want to play games. We don't know these guys. Let's flirt from a distance, act like we don't care too much, and make them come to us. Tonight, a little gaming is in order."

Kenzie sips her soda daintily and peers over at Brown Hat Boy. She gives him a naughty sort of smile with the straw between her lips, and I'm hit with a burst of pride as she looks back at the stage and says, "Oh, we are so winning this game."

For the next half hour we dance to the sounds of guitars and fast fiddling. We're careful to keep the boys in our sights and to cast glances and smiles in their direction. The pavilion fills up even more as the sun begins to drop and the lights illuminate the sky. The guys are forced to stand.

"Oh, they've got a stash," Monica says. "I just saw Black Hat Boy pull something out of his pocket and pour it in his drink. The others moved around him to block him."

Nice.

"I knew he was the bad one," Kenzie says, giving me a grin.

I peek over now and see that the guys are passing the drink around. Ponytail Boy shakes his head.

"Aw, my deep thinker is a good boy." Monica sighs. "That's sweet. I hope he's not too good to kiss a stranger, though."

"Well, there's six of them," Lin points out. "Two extra dudes, just in case."

"Okay, now we really sound like guys." I laugh.

A new band comes onstage, and they start with one of the songs we learned and loved in the car. We all holler and raise our hands, dancing and belting out the words again. Everyone on the stage looks like mini action figures from here, but that's okay. The music is amplified and shakes the earth beneath our feet.

"I need to pee!" Kenz says. "I drank my Coke too fast."

"I'll go with you," I tell her. Girl code. Nobody goes alone. It's not the bathroom we worry about—it's the trip to and from.

We leave Monica and Lin, and as we pass the six sexy country boys, I swear they all nod in unison, and it's so adorably polite we can't help but laugh a little as we nod in return.

The bathroom line is long and takes forever. I start to get antsy. Kenzie and other women sing in their stalls when a new song comes on that raises a huge cheer from the crowd. I haven't heard it before. It's a slow ballad.

When Kenz is finally done, we rush back through the crowd. It's even darker now, and I'm lost for a second. I'm looking for our line of guys, but I can't see them. My heart sinks. Did they leave already? All that flirting for nothing?

"There's Monica!" Kenzie says, and when she points she gasps and I see why. Our friends are surrounded by the six guys, and they are chatting away.

They struck when our group was halved. Very smart. Less intimidating and easier than approaching all of us at once. Kenzie gives my hand a squeeze and we move forward.

"Be cool," I whisper. Kenz nods and tries not to smile.

As we join them, I can't help but see villainous possibilities in each of these guys—the way they size up my friends, just as we sized them up—probably thinking of how they can use us and be done with us. Think again, boys.

Black Hat Boy turns his head and lifts his chin when he sees us coming, making my stomach flip. Up close, he's shorter than I expected, but his face is even hotter. One of those guys with dark-brown eyes and flawless skin that you can't help but stare at.

I look away and focus on Monica and Lin instead.

"Y'all made some friends?"

"Yeah," Lin says. "This is . . ." She starts naming names and I nod at each guy, but the names fall straight through my memory. Until she gets to Black Hat Boy. Mike. I'd been expecting him to be an Austin, Tucker, or Hunter, but nope. Just Mike. I give him a nod like the others and look away, pretending to be interested in the flashing, colorful lights from the show down below.

The main act is starting onstage, so the lights around us dim, and the volume gets even louder as the crowd cheers. Kenzie cups her hands around her mouth and lets out a *wooo!* as Brown Hat Boy next to her claps his hands. Above us, the stars are twinkling in a cloudless sky, and it couldn't get more perfect.

Mike sidles up next to me, and I continue watching the show. Everyone around us is on their feet, dancing, swaying, singing. I sway, too, then flash him a smile and focus on the band again.

"Enjoying the concert?" Oh, my. He's got a country lilt.

"Yeah," I say. "It's my first one."

"Ever?"

"My first *country* concert," I clarify.

He nods. His eyes are hooded under the black brim of his cowboy hat.

"Where you from?" I ask.

"Culpeper." Ah, lots of farmland. "You?"

"Dumfries."

I wait for him to give me an *ew* look or reaction, but he just nods. We do some basic chatting while keeping our eyes on the band, and I find out he's a senior headed to Longwood University this summer. All these guys are graduating in less than two months, and they've got the carefree attitudes to show it.

Another song comes on that we learned in the car, and the four of us girls gather together in a huddle to sing. The boys surround us, watching us with confidence, giving off clear vibes to everyone else that they've claimed us. But really, us girls are the ones who own them. The four of us share knowing smiles as we shake our booties.

We dance through one more song, paying little attention to the guys. When the third set comes on, something slower, I turn to Mike in his black cowboy hat, and put my arms on his shoulders. A small grin graces his face as he takes my hips and we begin to dance. He's waited patiently for this. I freeze for a second as he starts to sing along, his voice sounding smooth and perfectly in tune. I can't help but melt as he croons the romantic lyrics to me.

But I will not fall.

I tilt my head up and take his lips with mine. Without

hesitation, he kisses me back, his mouth firm and assertive with a hint of rum. I feel almost secluded and protected under the darkness of that wide-brimmed hat.

"You taste good," he murmurs against my lips, making me blush a little in the darkness. I wind my arms tighter around his neck and press my body to his. He moans into my mouth, burning me up.

When the song ends, I turn around and lean my back against his chest. He puts his arms around me, and we spend the rest of the concert like that. My friends do the same. I see them dancing with their guys, laughing, and, yes, kissing. The two straggler boys end up wandering off, I assume to meet other girls.

Mike sings in my ear with his lovely low voice, and we rock back and forth to the beat. He knows every word to every song. Several times he rests his chin on my shoulder, placing kisses on my cheeks, even nibbling my earlobe. I can't believe I'm snuggling with a cowboy. I take what I want from him: his affection, his kisses, his full attention. It's everything I need right now without the heartache that goes along with commitment.

At the end of the show, Mike whispers in my ear, "You gotta phone number I can have?"

I turn to him, looking up with a small smile. "You're going off to college. You'll meet lots of girls."

He looks at me funny, as if surprised. "You don't wanna hang out before I go?"

I shake my head. "I'm not trying to get my heart broken by a boy who's on his way out." I go up on my tiptoes and press my lips to his one last time. His eyes are still sort of bulging with shock, and I'm guessing no girl has ever denied him her digits.

"I had fun tonight," I tell him. He's gawking, staring at me as I back away, the crowd surging around us with people trying to leave. I find Kenzie and take her hand.

"Bye!" she's telling Brown Hat Boy.

"Wait," he says, but she's already turning away, giggling as I pull her. Lin and Monica are ahead of us, getting pushed along by the surge of concertgoers. I take one last peek over my shoulder and see the four guys standing in a line, just like they were when we first saw them, watching us. But their expressions this time are baffled. Not a single one of the poor guys knows what hit him.

CHAPTER FOURTEEN

Monday Night

It's time for night two of kiss collecting. Right now, the four of us are tied. I pull up in front of Monica's old brick rambler and climb out, grabbing my things. We're all staying at Monica's tonight since she lives so close to the party.

Thank God for friends. Mine are crazy and silly, and I love them so hard. They have been just what I need.

As always, dressing for the party is a free-for-all. We throw our clothes on the bed and start digging through, since we wear similar sizes, though nothing fits us exactly the same. Monica ends up with my lime-green V-neck tank pulled low over her chest.

"Dang, *chica*, this shirt's too small." She peers down at the inches of cleavage on display.

"Um . . . it doesn't look like that on me," I tell her.

Kenzie giggles. "That tank can't handle D-dub's cargo."

Now we all laugh. It's been a while since we used our nicknames. In the beginning of sophomore year we realized the four of us had different cup sizes. Monica was a D cup, Lin was a C, I was a B, and Kenzie was an A. We started calling each other D-dub, C-kat, B-diddy, and A-dawg.

Stupid, I know, but we thought we were so witty to be able to talk about our bra sizes in public with nobody catching on.

"Yeah, this isn't gonna work," Monica says. "My girls are getting squished too hard."

She peels the tank over her head and tosses it back on the pile. We aren't comfortable enough to go naked around one another, contrary to the fantasies of our guy friends, but we're okay with being in our undies.

Monica leans over me to grab another shirt off her bed, and her boob side smacks me softly but firmly in the forehead.

"Arg!" I laugh, hunkering down. "You just boob punched me in the head!"

"Sorry!" Monica laughs. And then Kenzie lets out adorable giggles that shake her whole body.

"Boob punch!" Kenz grabs her stomach and rolls around. It's near impossible not to laugh when Kenzie gets like this. "I wish I could boob punch someone! No fair."

"Don't worry, I can't either," I say.

I grab a pink scoop-neck shirt of silky material. I think it's Kenz's.

"Can I wear this?" I ask her.

She finally catches her breath and says, "Of course!"

A good song comes on the playlist and Lin dives toward

the music dock, turning it up so we can sing along. Kenzie is as off-key as always, but still sings at the top of her lungs. Monica's two little cousins try to come in and dance with us, but she wrangles them out and locks the door.

When we're finally dressed, and every strand of hair has been either straightened or curled, we apply lipstick and gloss for the maximum kissable look. Then we join arms and set off into Monica's neighborhood for Callum's house.

Watch out, baseball boys. Here we come.

It's more of a get-together than a party. Most of the varsity baseball team is here, along with a few of the more popular boys from JV. Their girlfriends are here and a smattering of other girls who crush on them.

I'd been hoping for loud music and bad behavior, but everyone is crammed into the living room watching a game on television.

I'm so not feelin' it.

Kyle is in a recliner, and I hold back an eye roll when Kenzie and Lin both rush over and sit on the arms of the chair on either side of him. He smiles like he won the lottery, which he did in my opinion. A tenth-grade girl who's on the floor by his feet frowns.

This better not end badly.

Monica and I stand against the back wall and wave to the girls we know, trying to catch the eyes of the ones we don't and smile at them. Girl camaraderie is a must. After a few minutes of boredom I cross my eyes at Monica, and she pretends to nod off, eyelids fluttering as her eyes roll back. Her head bangs against the wall and I snort as she rubs the spot, saying, "Ow!"

My spirits lift when an older boy comes in carrying two cases of beer. All the guys jump up and run into the adjacent kitchen, talking animatedly now.

"Callum's brother," Monica informs me. He drops the beer off, accepts money from Callum and his friends, then leaves us.

The energy in the house goes up as beers are passed around. All four of us girls take one. We're not huge drinkers—let's be honest, we'll all be buzzed and acting crazy after one or two— but we let loose now and then. Kenzie threw up all over the inside of my van once, so I've tried to keep her from getting that drunk again. Cleaning puke is not my idea of fun.

Soon the group breaks off—guys with girlfriends going into the formal dining room to hang out and play cards as couples—the other half standing around in the kitchen, laughing and talking. It begins to feel more like a party. I lean against the counter and take sips of my nasty, lukewarm beer. Eyeing the crowd, I narrow down the selection to Brent Dodge from English class. He's a bit on the short side, an inch or two taller than me, with a baby face. He wears his baseball hat low on his forehead. When he catches me looking, he pauses in his conversation with one of the guys. I smile and look away, angling toward Monica.

"Brent is staring at you," Monica says through her teeth.

"Good. Who do you have your eye on?" I hold my breath and take three big glugs of the beer. *Blech.*

"Mateo," she says, then chugs and shivers. "He's cool."

I look over at Mateo, the lanky pitcher. Monica has a thing for tall guys.

"Incoming," she whispers.

Seconds later I feel body warmth from behind, followed by a voice.

"What's up, girls?"

I turn to Brent Dodge's smiling face. His cheeks are a little ruddy. Cute.

"Not much," I say. The familiar light sensation of a buzz is beginning to lift me.

"I'm trying to find some cards for a drinking game. You in?"

Ugh. Drinking games always get me wasted. I grin and lift my can. "How 'bout I just cheer you on?"

"Sweet. My own personal cheerleader." He beams at me once more before bounding off to find some cards.

"Too easy," Monica said with a sigh. "Not even a fair win."

"Go talk to Mateo." I bump her hip with mine and she sidles away without hesitation.

My slight smile disappears when I look over and see Kyle cornered by both Kenzie and Lin. He looks to be enjoying their attention, but I can tell they're trying to one-up each other. Lin bats her almond eyes and cocks her hip. Kenzie lets out a loud burst of laughter at something Kyle said.

Oh, brother. I hope they're at least giving him crap about the mall cop thing.

I scan the room, eyes landing on the incredibly handsome but often overlooked Vincent Romas, third basemen for the team. His painfully quiet personality makes him disappear into the crowd, which is a shame. He has the face and body and baseball talent to make any girl swoon. But it's a bit of a problem when he won't converse . . .

I march right up to where he's sitting in a recliner, my friendly smile in place.

"Hey, Vincent!"

He jolts and looks up at me. "Oh, h-hey."

I put a hand under his beer to feel the weight of it. He simply watches me.

"Drink up," I say, giving it a lift. He lets out an amused huff and shakes his head but complies, drinking the whole thing. Pretty sure he's blushing under all that tan skin.

"So . . ." I begin. Yes, I'm totally scheming. You see, Kenzie had it bad for Vincent this time last year. She tried and tried to get him out of his shell, and ended up feeling stupid when he wouldn't make a move. I'd always believed Vincent was the kind of guy who needed the girl to make the first move, but Kenz had been too nervous—too afraid of rejection. "Kenzie looks good tonight, huh?"

He glances over at her before dropping his gaze to the floor.

"Don't worry about Kyle," I tell him. "They're just friends."

He grabs another beer from the coffee table and pops it open. I continue talking, unperturbed by his lack of response. I know I have his attention.

"She was *so* into you," I said. Yeah, she'll murder me if she knows I'm saying this. "She's still sad that y'all didn't even kiss."

Vincent drinks half his beer in one go and gives a nervous laugh. "I don't think so."

"It's true." I lean closer to him and whisper, "I dare you to kiss her."

Again with the nervous laugh and a shake of his head.

"Why not? Are you seeing anyone?"

He shakes his head again.

I have to cover all my bases. "Do you like boys? It's okay if you do—"

"No," he says.

"All right, well. If you won't kiss her, let me ask you this. Would you stop her if she tried to kiss you?"

His tan gets darker and I realize he's definitely blushing. Vincent drinks more beer, tipping the can up high. I have to smile when he grins and wipes his mouth with the back of his hand.

"Yes or no?" I probe. "Would you stop her?"

Staring at the can in his hand, he quietly says, "No."

I grab his arm, jumping up and down two times before getting control of myself. He smiles and shakes his head yet again.

"You're crazy, Zae," he says in his quiet, deep voice.

I can't stop smiling. "I know. Nice talkin' to you, Vincent."

A flutter of anticipation hits my belly when Brent Dodge comes back in the room with cards. Several people cheer and pull out chairs at the kitchen table. Brent finds me in the crowd and his lips tip up, seeming relieved to find me still there. Another flutter ripples, and I realize this little game is all a prelude to a kiss—the exchanged glances and flirtations—the lead-up is sometimes the best part.

I move to the corner and grab ahold of Kenzie's elbow. "Excuse us," I say, pulling her away from Kyle. Her brow crinkles at the disruption, and Lin moves to fill the spot.

"I just talked to Vincent," I whisper.

"Vincent?!" Her brow wrinkles tighter. "You're gonna try to kiss him?"

"What? No! You are."

She thrusts a finger at her chest. *"Me?"*

We peek over at Vincent, who is pointedly staring straight ahead, as if he has no idea I'm talking to Kenzie about him at this very moment. He totally knows.

"Of course *you*."

"What did he say?"

"That he wants you to kiss him."

Her mouth and eyes fly open. "He did not!"

"Did so."

Her eyes go back to him, and she softens a little. "You're serious, Zae?"

"I promise," I say. "He really, really said it. He's shy, but he's still a guy. You have to take charge. Come on!" I waggle my eyebrows, and she chews her lip. A smile begins to form.

"Fine, I'll talk to him and see how it feels. Let me finish my beer first." She drinks all of it and makes a terrible face.

As she walks away I grab her arm again. "Remember, it's just a kiss. No big deal."

"'Kay."

I let her go and breathe a sigh of relief. All three of my friends are talking to guys, boys they are going to use and not be hurt by, and I have one waiting in the wings. Just having fun. No big deal. This is how it should be.

I pull up a chair at the table and watch. It's a good time— lots of laughing and making fun of each other. The guys get along like brothers.

When I see Kenzie and Vincent slip out the back door I almost whoop out loud.

"Vin and Kenzie?" Callum asks. "Hopefully he's gettin' some so he won't be so damn uptight."

I punch Callum in the arm. "He'll be lucky to get a kiss."

"True," Callum concedes.

Once all the beer has been consumed, and couples are drifting away from the group to find privacy around the house, Brent Dodge bumps my shoulder with his. We are the only people at the table now. Only one other couple is still in the kitchen and—oh, whoa. Lin is up on her tiptoes and she and Kyle are going at it against the counter. Just guessing, but I think she might be over John.

"Dude," Brent says with a laugh.

"Let's go out front," I tell him.

We end up on Callum's porch swing. It's dark out, and crickets are chirping in the bushes.

"So, Lin and Kyle?" he asks.

I wave off the comment. "Just having fun."

He raises an eyebrow. "Like you and Rex Morino?"

Oh, for crap's sake.

"All we did was kiss. Everyone is making a huge deal of it."

"Just a kiss?" He sounds skeptical.

"Yes, just one single meaningless kiss. Girls *can* kiss for fun and not want anything else."

He laughs. "No offense, but chicks always want something else. Tell the truth. Were you trying to get back at your ex?"

"No." I clench my teeth, annoyed, even though I know he's not trying to offend me. "I just felt like kissing someone."

"Okay." His voice lowers. "Well, what if I just felt like

kissing someone right now?"

"I'd say do it."

His eyes get wider as I remain right where I am, relaxed in the swing, a smile creeping onto my face as a sense of power fills me and my blood pounds.

"For real?" he breathes.

"You're taking too long."

When he leans toward me, I meet him halfway. Our lips sort of collide, and he kisses me so hard I have to grab his shoulders to keep from being pushed backward. To say his tongue is dominating my mouth is an understatement. I feel the nervous eagerness rolling off him, and I need to rein him in.

I pull my head back and look at him, giving us both a second. His eye search mine, questioning. So, I give him a soft peck. Then a longer one. I slowly slip my tongue back in his mouth and stroke his, showing him a better pace. He learns quickly and takes my lead, moaning into my mouth as we find a good rhythm.

Ah, kissing. It's truly a weakness for me. Everything else goes bye-bye when I let myself get wrapped up in the scent and feel of a guy. Letting go feels amazing.

Until the front door opens and we yank apart. I wipe the corner of my mouth inconspicuously as one of the guys and his girlfriend walk out. Brent lifts his chin and says, "Later, bro."

The guy nods, then both he and the girl look back and forth between us. I swing my legs innocently and smile until they get to their car.

When Brent turns back to me, I stand before he can try to

kiss me again. Maybe it's mean of me, but I'd gotten what I came for and now I'm done.

"I gotta go round up the girls."

"You're leaving already?" Aw, he sounds disappointed. Sweet guy.

"Yep."

"Can I, like, call you or something?"

I bite my lip. "Remember, Brent, this was just for fun. No expectations?"

"Yeah, I know. I just meant . . . yeah."

Again, I should feel bad, but I don't. I squeeze his arm and pass him.

"See you around," I say.

"Okay. See ya."

I leave him sitting there in a near trance and go straight to the kitchen, where Lin is still lip-locked with Kyle, only now she's sitting on the countertop with her legs around him.

"All right, Lin-lin," I say. "Time to go."

She groans. I walk up and Kyle moves aside for her to hop down. He catches her by the waist.

"Bye, Kyle," she says, smiling shyly.

"Bye." He runs a hand through his hair and walks off. Lin and I make evil genius faces, like coconspirators.

We go to the back door and I holler out into the darkness. "Hey, Kenz! Time to go!" A shuffle sound comes from around the corner and I hope she's used her time wisely. One look at her tinged cheeks as she comes into view tells me she has. Vincent is nowhere to be seen. Kenzie is in a daze when she takes my hand.

I lead Kenz and Lin to the door of the basement and yell, "Monica!"

"What?" comes her voice from the den below.

"Let's go!"

Seconds later she bounds up the stairs, grinning, her voluminous hair and chest bouncing. Mateo stands at the bottom of the stairs.

I give him a wave. "Later." He raises his chin in response, looking baffled by our sudden departure.

Monica smiles down at him, and then the four of us are out the door, arm in arm down the middle of the dark street like Dorothy and her gang headed to the Emerald City. It's just after midnight.

"Please tell me you girls got some kisses. I *know* Lin did," I said. "She nearly set the kitchen on fire."

"Yeah, baby," Monica says. "That skinny boy can kiss, too. How 'bout you and Brent?"

"Yep. It was a little rough at first, but we worked it out."

They laugh, and we all look at Kenz. Hello, Stargazer. Monica elbows her.

"Hm? Oh, yeah . . . we kissed." She sounds bashful.

"Two for each of us! Still tied!" I hoot, punching the starry sky and doing a cartwheel. Lin runs into the nearest yard and does a roundoff back handspring. Then we dance our way down the street, laughing as we pirouette and high kick like dance team girls. But we really aren't fancy dancers. To prove it, Monica stops next to a fire hydrant, eyes us with mischief, and breaks into a twerk, bouncing her booty in front of the hydrant. We crack up as we join in, gyrating like true Peakton girls until an old lady turns on her porch light and glares at us through her window.

Kenzie squeals, "Ahh! A witch!" and takes off running down the street at a sprint. The rest of us try to catch up, grabbing our stomachs with laughter.

When we turn the corner we hear the rhythmic beat of drums, and we gravitate to the front yard of the house where it's coming from, but it looks dark.

"I think it's coming from the basement," Kenzie says.

We tiptoe in the dark to the side of the house and peer into a small rectangular window at ground level to see a band. It looks like they're warming up. I recognize the main guitarist at once.

"That guy's a senior at our school."

"And I know *him*." Monica points to the bassist, the quiet redheaded guy from my English class.

"Flynn Rogers!" I say. We watch as they pluck strings to tune instruments, and the drummer runs through a few rounds of beats.

Flynn parts his reddish curls down the middle and tucks them behind his ears. It's weird to see him out of school, being all serious. As his fingers move fluidly over the strings, a rich, low current of music flows up to us. I'm impressed.

"Can I help y'all?" The voice comes from behind us, and we all jump, squealing.

A guy carrying a huge keyboard under his arm laughs at our startled faces.

"Sorry," Lin says, standing and adjusting her skirt. "We just heard the drums, and . . ."

"It's cool," says the guy. He looks older, maybe in his twenties. "We're practicing to audition for the battle of the bands thing in DC next week."

"That's awesome," I say. "Good luck. Sorry for spying."

He lifts a shoulder and grins, leaving us. We giggle as we sprint away.

We're panting when we crash in Monica's room, trying to be quiet. Kenzie flops onto the bed next to Monica, staring up at the ceiling.

"You guys," Kenzie whispers, "I think I'm in love with Vincent."

I stiffen and let out a bleating sound of shocked disapproval, then I leap up and jump over Monica to pounce on top of Kenzie, straddling her thin waist and grabbing her shoulders.

"No, no, no!" I say, playfully pushing her into the bed over and over, making us bounce. "You're not allowed to fall for him!"

"I'm sorry!" She lets out a swoony sigh. "He's just so . . . I can't believe . . . he actually started talking to me. It was like once we kissed, it broke some sort of silence spell and . . ." She sighs.

Kenz is a goner too early in the game.

I shoot from the bed and swing my gaze accusingly between Lin and Monica.

"Please tell me neither of you are in love already."

Monica rolls her eyes and waves a hand. "Girl, please."

Lin chews her lip. "Well, Kyle *is* really hot. . . ."

"Lin!" Monica and I bellow.

She giggles and falls over. "Hurry up and find me another boy to kiss!"

I sigh with relief. That's the spirit.

One friend down. I crawl to my spot on the air mattress and turn my back to the others as Monica switches off the light. Kenzie climbs down next to me and snuggles into my back.

Yes, Vincent is a nice guy, but how long until he breaks Kenzie's heart? Anger swirls inside me, courtesy of Wylie and my dad. No guy can be trusted. I can't stop my friends from falling; all I can do is be here for them when it ends.

As for me, I can never go back.

CHAPTER FIFTEEN

Tuesday Morning

H*aremos el chorizo y los huevos.*"

"*¿Compraste tortillas?*"

"*Sí, están allí. Mira.*"

Loud voices permeate the stillness of the room, joined by blaring bachata music.

Kenzie rolls over next to me and slings an arm over her eyes. "Oh, my gosh, is there a fire?"

"They're talking about breakfast," I whisper. She smacks her lips and snuggles closer to me, probably still dreaming about Vincent. Ugh.

Up in the bed, Monica groans and Lin shoves her head under the pillow. It's six thirty in the morning. This is the only downfall of staying at Monica's. Her mom and aunt don't even try to be quiet. And music at full volume, really? I sit up, blinking, fully awake. I pull on my jeans and leave my grumbling, half-asleep friends.

"Ah!" Miss Sanchez says when she sees me. We kiss cheeks, and I do the same with her older sister and mother.

"*Buenos días*," I say over the music, and they both beam at me. Monica prefers to speak English, so the Sanchez women love that I'll converse in Spanish. Miss Sanchez has been in the United States since she was eighteen, but her older sister and mother only came five years ago, so some of their English is still broken.

We talk for a few minutes in Spanish before Monica trudges in, glaring, bedhead in full effect. Her mother and aunt scoff at her. Monica tries to turn down the radio, but her grandmother smacks her fingers.

"You no brush you hair!" her aunt scolds.

"It's too early," Monica grumbles. "Can't we make an eight a.m. rule for the weekend?"

"*No es* the weekend," her grandmother says. "*Es* Tuesday."

"But it's spring break!" Monica puts her head on the table as Lin and Kenzie come in.

"You went to sleep too late," her mom says. "It's not our fault."

Kenzie puts a hand in the air and one on her stomach, and twists her hips back and forth to the beat, making Monica groan.

Miss Sanchez dances at the stove. She's short. Monica must get her long legs from her dad.

We're just sitting down to eat when my cell rings with an unknown local number. I almost don't answer, but then I wonder if it's my dad at his new house. So I get up and move to the hall.

"Hello?"

"Yes, hello. This is Mrs. McOllie from Clara's Bowtique. May I speak with Zae Monroe?"

The lady from the mall! "This is her . . . er . . . she."

"I'm calling to see if you're able to start this morning?"

My heart splutters. "This morning?" I look at the clock on the wall. It's seven now. "What time?"

"Nine o'clock. We'll first discuss your pay and hours. If you accept the offer, we'll have an hour before opening to show you the register and have you fill out the financial forms."

Wow! Excitement swirls in my head. "So . . . I'm hired?"

"On a trial basis, yes."

"Thank you! Yes, I can be there at nine." She can probably hear me smiling through the phone.

"Very well. Please be prompt. I will see you soon."

She hangs up and I squeal when I get back in the kitchen. I'm bombarded with questions and commands to finish my breakfast before I leave, so I do, then I rush off, smiling when I get back to the apartment to shower and get ready. Zeb is still sleeping when I leave, so I write a note to him and Mom and close the door quietly.

The register is easy to work, and I love the bleep of the little scanner. Actually, I love everything about the job. I help Mrs. McOllie open shipments of boxes and put the new items on shelves and hooks.

"I keep a very close inventory and itemization of my stock," she says sternly. "If something is stolen I will know."

I pause and look at her, offended. "I wouldn't steal."

She looks right back at me, chin lifted. "The employee you're replacing allowed their *friends* to shoplift." Mrs. McOllie glances up at the video camera in the corner, and I nod in understanding.

"That won't happen," I say, trying to shake off the feeling of hurt. This lady's been burned before, so I know I shouldn't take it personally.

"Good. Because there will be shifts when you are alone, and you will be trusted with closing the store and counting the money. It requires maturity, honesty, and responsibility."

"Yes, ma'am," I say, imagining being here all by myself and feeling a swell of pride.

She goes back to stocking, so I do the same. When a customer comes in, she shoos me toward the register, and I jump to my feet, smiling brightly at the woman with a toddler.

"Welcome to Clara's," I say too loudly. "Let me know if you need any help." The woman nods and starts to browse. I keep a stealthy eye on her, without being a creeper. When she's ready to check out, my hands are shaking, and I nearly forget every single thing I just learned, but I work it out.

Mrs. McOllie tries to force me out for lunch, but I tell her I'm not hungry. Truth be told, I don't have any cash to buy food. My stomach keeps clenching around its emptiness, but I'll survive until I get home.

A group of guys meanders by the store, and I make eye contact with one—Flynn Rogers. I wave, and he points to his chest in question, looking behind him. I laugh and nod. He says something to the guys and comes in. I notice his lightly freckled cheeks get a little color as he approaches. He's pretty tall. I guess I've never taken full notice of him before.

"Hey!" I say. "I heard you practicing last night."

"Oh." He scratches the back of his neck, smiling nervously. "That was you at the window?"

"Me and my nosy friends, yeah. Good luck at the auditions."

"Thanks."

Mrs. McOllie clears her throat and approaches. Oh, crap.

"See you around," I say quickly. He takes my hint and leaves. Mrs. McOllie gives his retreating back a disapproving glance before going back to whatever she was doing. Man, she's tough.

She lets me go at two, with instructions to be back the next morning. There's a bounce in my step when I leave, and I feel more grown-up and independent than ever before.

I text my friends before I leave the mall parking lot: **I love my job!**

Kenzie: **Yay!!**

Me: **Where's the party tonight?**

Monica: **IDK but we'll find one.**

Lin: 😒

Kenz: **Hey, guys?**

I wait for her to say something else, and when she doesn't, I get a bad feeling.

Me: **Plz say you're going.** I pause and grit my teeth, then type, **Vin can come, too, if you want.**

Kenz immediately responds: **Yay! He's out of town part of break, but on days he's here I'll bring him. Thanks!**

Oy. Just what we need. A guy in tow. A shy, seemingly nice guy, but a guy nonetheless, cramping our style, infringing on girl time.

I'm bitter and grumpy as I start the car, and before I can make it out of the lot, the minivan starts doing this weird bump, bump, bump thing on one side. My heart accelerates as I pull into a space and get out.

Oh, my freaking gosh. One of the tires is half-flat! What do I even do?

I text Mom and she calls right away from work, panicking. "We can't afford a new tire, Zae!"

My eyes well with tears. "Well, I'm sorry! It's not like I did it on purpose!"

"I know." She sighs and then uses her matter-of-fact tone. "Look, I can't leave work. I'm the only one here and there's sourdough in the oven. I'll give you the number of the insurance company. You have to call and tell them where you are. They'll take you to Ruddick's Auto, and you'll need to tell them I'll come in after work to pay."

"I don't know how to deal with insurance stuff and auto shops!" Now I'm panicking. "What about Dad?"

"He's at work, too. I need you to be a big girl, Xanderia." *Ugh!* "I will text you the information now. Take care of it." She hangs up.

I stare down at my phone, shaking. This is grown-up crap. I am way out of my comfort zone. She texts me the insurance phone number, our policy number, and the phone number of the auto place.

My hands are trembling as I call the insurance company. The lady who answers puts me at ease right away and takes care of everything for me. She says she'll have a tow truck to me in twenty minutes.

I sit in the van, feeling annoyed by the unexpected waste of time, until the tow truck guy comes and hooks it up. He's an older man, small and skinny. He seems nice enough, but I'm still weirded out when he points to the old tow truck and tells me, "Hop in the cab."

Yikes. It smells like dirt and something sour. I spend the entire drive to the shop going over ways to defend myself if Old Dude tries to make a move. But he's quiet and polite.

When we pull up in front of Ruddick's Auto, my heart speeds up again.

"Um, do I need to pay you?" I totally don't have any money.

"Nope," he says. "Your car insurance covers the tow."

"Okay, thank you."

I breathe a sigh of relief before walking into the shop. The first thing I see is a familiar face wearing a stiff, blue Ruddick's Auto cap and matching blue button-up shirt with the logo on the pocket. It's that Joel guy from school, the possible drug dealer slash guidance aide. The uniform makes his eyes look really blue. But I have to laugh at how his shirt is untucked and his pants hang a little low.

When he sees me walk in, he freezes for a second, then turns to look at the window to the shop where two men work on a truck on a lift. Before he turns back, he takes his hat off and turns it backward. Then he looks at me.

"Zae Monroe." He glances out at the tow truck driving away. "What kind of trouble'd you get into?"

"Flat tire." I walk up to the counter, still shaking a little. "I don't have any money, though. Can my mom come by on her way home from work?" I don't tell him that she doesn't have any money either. Parents always seem to find some way to make it work, but the guilt I feel is massive.

"Yeah. Carrie Monroe, right?"

"You know my mom?"

He shrugs. "She's been coming for years. And Xander." Wow, he knows my parents? He comes out from behind the counter. "Let's take a look."

I follow him out the door, watching as he hikes up his baggy blue work pants and continues to swagger, in no hurry.

He squats by the nearly flat tire and runs a hand over it, looking closely. When he gets down near the back, he goes, "Ah. There it is." He glances up at me. "A screw. Let me get it out and see if I can plug it. You can have a seat while I get the stuff."

I nod and sit on the sidewalk, which makes him chuckle.

"I meant a seat inside, but if you wanna hang with me, that's cool."

I feel my face flush warm as I nod. I am an idiot today. I sit there, feeling stupid, while he goes and comes back with a bunch of stuff. Then I watch him work, and I can't help but be impressed at how his biceps and triceps bulge while he handles the tire—pumping the jack to lift the car, yanking out the screw and getting the plug in, then filling the tire with air. It looks solid. His hands are dirty now, and there's sweat along his blond hairline. It's kind of hot.

I'd kiss him.

I'm so into my moment of lustful staring that I jump when he pats the tire and says, "That should hold it."

I stand and brush my butt off. "So, we don't need a new tire?"

"Nope."

Thank God! "How much will it cost?"

He shrugs again, pulling out a rag from his back pocket and wiping his hands absentmindedly. "Don't worry about it. Friend discount."

Gratitude rushes through me, making my stupid eyes water again. Judging by the concerned look that crosses his face, he notices. "You okay?"

I want to hug him, but I hold back since he's at work.

"Yeah." I clear my throat and swallow. "It's just been a long week. Thank you so much. Really."

"Just don't tell my dad."

"Your dad?"

He hitches a thumb to the sign. "The owner. He's a cheap ass."

"Oh." Ruddick's Auto. Joel Ruddick. I smile. "It'll be our secret."

"Take care, then." He shoots me a quick, cute grin and turns his hat forward as he goes into the shop, leaving me exhausted and thankful as I call my mom to tell her all is well.

CHAPTER SIXTEEN

When I get home, Zebby is sitting on the couch like a lump. He'll stay in that exact spot all spring break if I let him.

"Wanna walk with me to Seven-Eleven?" I ask.

"Eh . . ."

"I'll buy you a Slurpee." My piggy bank still has a few dollars in change.

This gets him to sit up. "Okay."

I make us both pepperoni, cheese, and spinach wraps to eat while we're walking. My brother is a bottomless pit. He gets a giant Slurpee of mixed flavors and finishes it as we get back to the apartment. Mom's not home yet, but she will be soon. We both stop and stare up at our building. Dread fills me at the thought of leaving the sunshine to go back into that dreary place.

"You know what? Let's go to the skate park until dinner," I tell him.

"Really? Yes!" He runs up the stairs and puts on his flat, wide skater shoes, grabbing his skateboard that he hasn't used since fall. It was a brutally cold winter plagued with too much sleet and slush for skateboarding.

Though the sun is shining, it's cool in the shade, so I pull on a hoodie with my jeans, but opt for flip-flops to show my purple-and-teal toenails.

The skate park is packed, and thankfully Zeb finds a couple of nice kids he knows from school who are happy to let him join them. I sit on a bench soaking up vitamin D. It's the most contentment I've felt in a while.

A few guys and a girl are doing amazing tricks and jumps over at the tallest ramp. Zeb and his friends stop to watch. I can't take my eyes off one of the guys with sleek black hair that shrouds his face under a backward hat. He's got total control of the board in a way that's super hot. He's effortless in his jumps, making the board spin under his feet, then landing gracefully back in place.

When he lands a 360 ollie, everyone cheers, including me. I stand and move closer to watch. What I see makes my jaw hang loose. I *know* that guy! Taro Hattori, from my English class, whose hair is always blocking the beautiful angles of his face as he's hunched over a drawing. I didn't know he had these kinds of skills. I take a short video to show my friends.

When they stop to take a break, and the crowd disperses, Taro catches my eye and his widen in surprise. He quickly looks down, taking off his hat and turning it frontward, low, hiding much of his face beneath the bill and his hair. That's the kid I know. But we've already made eye contact. I can't just walk away without it being awkward, so I approach.

"Hey, Taro," I say. "I didn't know you could skate like that. You're awesome."

He reluctantly takes the compliment, looking down. "Thanks."

We're both quiet. It feels like I'm making him uncomfortable, and I don't want that. I'm about to turn and go back to the bench when he asks, "You skate?"

I let out a laugh. "No." I point over to Zeb. "My brother does. Or tries to."

"Ever tried?" He lifts his head enough for me to see his shaded eyes, and my heart jumps as if we've touched.

"Not unless you count sitting on the board and rolling down a driveway."

He laughs, and I can't help but smile as his burst of personality shows. We look over at Zeb, who's trying and failing to do a trick he's been working on for a year now.

"I would, like, pay you to teach him how to do that . . . whatever it's called."

"Fakie frontside one eighty. Okay, yeah."

"Seriously?" I can't stop smiling.

"I mean, I can try," he says.

I take Taro over to Zeb and introduce them. He and his friends have stars in their eyes for the older guy and his skills. Taro works with them, and I watch with rapt attention. For the first time ever, Zebby gets the trick and we all cheer. He and Taro bump knuckles, and Taro joins me on the bench as we watch the younger boys trying to perfect the move.

Mom texts me to find out where we are, and I write back. I know we should head home for dinner, but I'm not ready to leave just yet.

"Thank you so much," I tell Taro.

He gives that nonchalant shrug again, as if embarrassed by the praise. Zeb and his friends take off down the smooth sidewalks, racing, leaving Taro and me virtually alone.

I stare out at the fluid bodies around the skate park, dipping low into the U-bends, then swooping back up. I glance over at Taro's lips, which are truly shaped like a soft, round heart. I would happily kiss him if he made a move, but I doubt that would happen. It has to be me. I try to picture Taro as the poetry writer. Could it be him?

My phone dings and I look down at a message from an unknown local number.

Yo, Z. It's Dean. Party tmrw nite at Devonshire Farm.

Everything inside me does a 360 trick, and I silently cheer. I can't believe he texted me! The first real party I went to in ninth grade was at Devonshire Farm. It's the last true farm on our side of the county, and it's owned by the grandparents of Bodhi Stein, one of the football players. When his grandparents go out of town, he offers up the back field for a party. Since it's private property and nowhere near neighbors, it's safe from cops.

Thnx, I text back. **See you there!** I probably shouldn't have put the exclamation point. It looks like I'm overly excited. Oh, well. I shove my phone in my back pocket. I need to get home and tell the girls.

I stand, giving Taro a wave. "Thanks again."

"No problem. Your brother's rad."

I have to agree. I call Zeb and he skates my way, stopping when he gets to me. "Hop on, Zae. I'll pull you."

I climb on his board and hold his shoulders as he walks down the sidewalk pulling me. Taro watches us go, shaking his head in amusement. We laugh the whole time as I try not to fall off. It's crazy how much coordination and balance I have when it comes to cheer, but put me on moving wheels and it all disappears.

When we get down the street I realize I didn't get to ask Taro if he was the poet, but I can't go back without looking stupid. Besides, I'm pretty sure I know who the probable culprit is, and now I have his number.

Zeb is sweating by the time we get back to the apartment. Mom points him directly to the bathroom since he stinks like only a boy can.

After dinner, before Zebby can get lazy again, I say, "Let's play," and toss him a controller. We play boxing, and I kick his butt two out of three times. He's a good sport, though, and we even manage to laugh a few times.

As he's switching games he asks nonchalantly, "Heard from Dad?"

My heart tightens with sadness, then burns with wrath.

"No," I say. "But I'm sure he'll call soon."

Whenever he can spare a moment away from *her*. Whoever she is. The woman he's playing house with. No kids to worry about. No wife to nag him. Just fun and freedom while we sit here hurting and waiting.

I wonder what she looks like. How old she is. If he'll get

bored with her eventually and miss Mom. Miss us. Would Mom accept him back? Would I want that? Right now, the answer is a definite no. I don't know when, if ever, I'll be able to forgive him. I don't care if I ever see him again, but Zeb does. Dad can ignore me all he wants—whatever—but it's unacceptable for him to ignore his son.

After we play a round of a game of Zeb's choice, in which he slaughters me without mercy, I go to the bedroom and text Dad.

Zeb misses u. Make time for him.

I don't care if I sound bossy, rude, or disrespectful. I hope it annoys him.

He doesn't respond. Jerk.

But then I hear a chirp from the living room followed by Zebby's voice. I open the door to listen.

"Hey! . . . Yeah, I'm good. When can I see you and your new place? . . . Okay, I understand." His voice falls, and I lock my jaw. "Okay . . . Love you, too. Bye."

I walk out just as he's hanging up, his shoulders slumped in despondence.

"He's working double shifts to pay his new security deposit," Zeb mumbles. The burn of anger is back in my chest, seeping up my throat until I swallow it down.

"I'm sure you'll get to see him soon."

I ruffle his hair.

Mom comes through the front door and smiles at me inquisitively. "So, how did you manage to get no charge for the tire?"

"I know the owner's son from school," I tell her. "Just don't

130

tell his dad that he did it for free."

Mom wears the same look of tearful gratitude that I had earlier today as she nods.

"How was your first day at the job?"

"Good," I say. "I'm tired though."

Her mouth opens like she wants to chat, but I turn and head for my room. I try not to feel guilty when I think about the look on her face, so hopeful, only to be denied again. We used to talk a lot. I enjoyed time with Mom. I loved confiding in her, but it's too hard now. Everything's changed. She and Dad upended our lives. If they can be selfish, so can I.

I put my headphones on tight and blast the music, staring up at my international dream-destination posters.

Let the forgetting commence.

CHAPTER SEVENTEEN

Wednesday Night

I can't believe spring break is nearly halfway over already, but I'm looking forward to tonight. Vincent is gone to Williamsburg with his family until tomorrow, so Kenzie is all ours. When she starts gushing about how amazing he is, I shut her up by passing around the video of Taro from yesterday afternoon and telling them all about it.

"Okay, that's hot." Monica.

"Damn, he's good!" Lin.

"Aww! He's so sweet!" Kenz. "Did you kiss him?"

"No. I was too distracted by the text from Dean."

"Mmm . . . Dean." Monica gives me a sly look from the front passenger seat, and I cut her some side eye.

"I will fight you, D-dub."

"You can try, B-diddy." She laughs and I shake my head,

watching the road. I sincerely hope she's joking.

It's dark when we arrive at nine, and a huge bonfire lights the way as we park in the dirt field and make our way through long grasses. The place is lit. Bodhi Stein's pickup truck is pulled close, filled with firewood. His doors are open and his speakers are blaring a mixed playlist of country, hip-hop, and rock. There's a keg of beer with a stack of plastic cups. I have no idea how they were able to get that, but people are crowded around it, screaming and laughing. I'm happy to see that I recognize almost everyone here from school. Athletes and pot-heads, dancers and hoodlums. All so different, yet so much the same. It feels comfortable, like we can all let loose without fear.

My friends get in line for a beer, while I sip a bottle of Coke, peering around for Dean. He must not be here yet. After the girls get their drinks, we move aside. A group of baseball play-ers spots us and they holler out, having apparently been here drinking a lot longer than us. Kyle is already stumbling.

"Oh, no," I whisper when I make eye contact with Brent Dodge. His poor face lights up when he sees me, and he jogs over.

"What's up, Zae?"

"Hey, Brent. Having fun?"

"Yeah." He adjusts his Peakton baseball hat, looking at me with that cute baby face. "Hey, can we go talk?"

"Brent . . ." I let out a quiet sigh, and he gives me a bashful smile.

"What?"

"No talking."

"More kissing?" His voice is hopeful.

"No. I'm single, and that's how I like it." I give him a friendly punch in the arm, and he throws his head back, staring up at the sky.

"Fiiiine."

Kenzie bounds over with half her beer gone already. "Hi, Brent!"

"Hey, you coming to all the games this season?"

"You know it." She wouldn't miss watching her third baseman for the world. Our team is supposed to be amazing this year. She takes another long swig.

"Are you getting drunkies?" I ask.

"Maybe." Her huge smile shows she's already headed in that direction. Then she frowns. "I wish Vinny was here."

"*Vinny.*" Brent chuckles. "That is awesome." He laughs heartily, and Kenz shoves him, laughing, too.

It doesn't take long for the party to get rowdy. The sweet, skunky scent of weed blows on the spring breeze, mixing with bonfire smoke and pine. Spilled beer soils the ground beneath our feet. Darkness. Music. Dancing. Drugs and alcohol. Guys and girls on the cusp of independence. Seclusion. It's a recipe for success. Or disaster. But I'm only feeling the success right now because Dean and a carful of football players just showed up to a chorus of low howls from their friends.

Kenzie with a buzz is like a butterfly, flittering around to chat with as many people as possible and to hand out her famous hugs. For a little thing, she has a strong embrace. Lin, Monica, and I laugh as we watch her go. Thankfully she keeps her distance from where Sierra and Meeka are standing with a few guys from the basketball team and some of their dancer friends. If Kenz has a run-in with those two tonight, she'll end up inconsolable, and drunk tears are the worst.

"Don't look," Monica whispers with her cup close to her mouth, "but Rex Morino is at three o'clock and he's staring hard."

"Crap," I whisper, not daring to look.

"Holy stalker," Lin says.

"Tell me if he comes this way so I can run," I beg.

They both nod, sipping their drinks and taking surreptitious glances in his direction.

"He's totally watching you, waiting for you to look his way," Lin says. "Man, he's super sexy when he's intense like that."

"Let's go to the other side of the bonfire," I suggest, not caring how sexy he looks.

I breathe easier when I'm out of his line of sight, and I realize we're standing right next to redheaded Flynn Rogers and two other guys from his band.

"Hey, Flynn!" I say.

He turns and blinks with surprise before smiling. "Oh, hey. Good to see you."

"Did you have the auditions yet?" I ask.

His face falls a little. "Yeah. There were hundreds of bands, and only ten made the cut. I don't think they were fans of Celtic folk rock." He gives a low chuckle.

"Aw, that sucks," Monica says.

Flynn shoves unruly red curls behind his ears. "There was a man there who runs a local pub, though, and he asked if we'd come perform some Irish music."

"That's awesome!" I tell him. "You'll have to tell us when so we can come."

"I think you have to be twenty-one," he says. "I don't guess you have fake IDs?"

"Nope." My mouth pulls to the side and I scrunch my nose to show I'm disappointed.

A girl from the marching band named Emi walks toward us and tilts her head at Flynn.

"Hey," she says to him. She flashes a look toward me and my girls, and just as I'm about to say hello, I spot Kenzie at the keg and I nearly scream.

"What is she doing?"

Two football players have lifted her tiny form in the air, upside down, her dainty toes pointed, and she's drinking straight from the tap as the guys cheer her on.

"A keg stand," Monica says. "This is going to be a long night."

"Or a really short one," Lin grumbles, moving straight toward Kenzie with Monica behind her.

"Bye, guys," I say to Flynn and Emi. He nods and she ignores me, keeping her eyes on him.

I don't have time to worry about the snub as I make our way over to the keg. When the guys put Kenzie down, we try to drag her away, but she clings to the stupid thing.

"Wait! I need to fill my cup!" She's not falling over yet or anything, so we let her have one more. "I have to pee." She bounces up and down on her toes.

"I'll go with you," I say. She takes my hand, and we march through the people and grass to the trees. I hold her drink while she disappears into the darkness. I hear her murmuring

"Drip dry, drip dry" in a singsong voice, and I stifle a giggle. Fifteen feet away, a plume of smoke drifts out of the woods. I walk down and see two dark figures, the tips of their cigarettes glowing.

"Wussup, Zae Monroe?" asks a smooth, somewhat familiar voice.

I move closer to see Joel. Kwami Russell, another guy from school, gives me a nod.

"Hey," I say.

"You brought me a beer?" Joel asks. His short blond hair is messy, like he wore a cap all day, then ran his hands through it a hundred times. His T-shirt is fitted, but his jeans hang baggy and low.

"It's my friend's, sorry."

"No worries. I don't drink anyhow."

Kenzie stumbles out of the trees, letting out a yelp when the brambles snag around her jeans. She comes over and takes my arm. I hand her the cup and she drinks before squinting into the trees.

"Hey, I know you guys!" And then, to my amusement, she goes straight toward them to hug them. Joel looks at me over her shoulder with amusement as he pats her back. And then Kwami opens his arms wide and Kenzie snuggles into his chest while he laughs. He takes a drag, turning his head to the side to blow out the smoke.

"We can stay like this all night if you want," he says.

"You're a good hugger," Kenzie slurs.

I cross my arms. "Yeah, she has a boyfriend now, but she'll always be the Hugging Bandit."

The guys both chuckle, and I look at Joel again, remembering how nice he was at the shop. Their cigarette smoke stinks, but I still feel more comfortable standing there with them than I do over at the main party. When Kenz finally pulls away, some of her beer sloshes onto Kwami's pant leg, and she gasps.

"Oh, my gosh, *Kwamiiii* . . . I'm so sorry!"

"It's all good." He grins and takes another drag.

I reach for Kenzie's hand and pull her closer to keep her steady. A lull passes.

"Well," I say, "I guess we'll see you guys later." They both nod, and we turn to leave them.

"I *looooove* sweet people," Kenzie says to me. "Like, legit sweet, you know?" I have to walk slower when she lays her head against my arm.

"Me, too, Kenz."

My heart gives a hard bang when I spot Lin and Monica standing with Dean. I pick up our pace, practically pulling Kenzie.

"Hiiiii, Dean!" Kenzie crashes into his wide chest and he gives an umph of laughter.

"Dang, girl, look at you," he says, holding her at arm's length now as she smiles goofily up at him.

"Dean is so nice," Kenzie says, swiveling her head to me. "You should put him on your kissing list!"

My face goes slack with horror. "Kenzie, shut up," I mutter.

Dean eyes me with a half grin. "Your *what*?"

"Nothing—"

Kenzie pushes out in front of me. "Zae's making a list of guys—"

"I am not!" I laugh it off as if she's crazy, though I want to die. "There's no list." I glare at Kenzie's pouting face. "I'm *not* making a list of anything, Kenz."

Her chin quivers. "Why are you yelling at me?"

"I'm not!"

"Come here, sweetie." Monica takes her by the arm. "I think there are people you haven't hugged yet." Lin shoots me an upset look before she takes Kenzie's other arm and they lead her away. I'm not sure if Lin's upset with me or about Kenz, but surely she has to understand how embarrassing this is for me. My face is hot with humiliation.

Dean crosses his strong arms over his wide expanse of chest as I peer up at him. It's like he's waiting for me to explain, and I feel compelled to do just that.

"Look . . . when Wylie and I broke up, I was really mad and bitter, and then crap happened at home." I swallow hard. "So, we all decided we were just going to be single and have fun and whatever. You know, just being crazy."

His arms tighten. "Like with Rex Morino? Be careful."

Now I cross my own arms. "I *am*."

Does anyone tell a guy to be careful when he's playing the field and having fun? Why should I have to be careful? Boys should take responsibility and have some freaking self-control whether a girl is being "careful" or not. I drop my arms and shake them out. I don't want to be mad at Dean.

"I was glad when you texted me. Thank you."

"Of course." He uncrosses his arms to tweak my chin. "Glad you guys could come."

My heart picks up speed as I look at him. "Dean?"

"Yeah?"

I have to go for it. I really wish there was a beer in my system, but I'm sober, and I have to push forward in a rush. "Did you write those poems? The ones Mrs. Warfield read out loud?"

He grins. "The ones about the girl making out with the straw?"

I roll my eyes with a smile. "Yeah, those."

He shakes his head slowly, and I narrow my gaze, trying to figure out if he's lying. He's still looking straight at me, like he's trying to figure me out, too.

"Why? Did you like them?" he asks.

"Yes," I say quietly as he continues to ponder me.

"I know you wrote that one about your parents." His face turns somber as my stomach wobbles. I look down at my feet. "It was good, Zae. But . . ." I look back up at him as he chooses his words. "Maybe when you're hurting it's best not to . . ."

"Best not to what?" I grit my teeth. "I haven't done anything wrong."

He looks away, running a hand through his hair. "I'm not saying that. It's just . . . not every guy's an asshole, okay?"

"I know that," I say, softer. But *do* I know that? Because lately all I can see is the negative. All I can see is that even guys like Dean and Vincent will hurt a girl at some point, like my dad did. And maybe I'm mad at myself because I still feel drawn to Dean—I still crave love—knowing it won't last. It *can't* last. I still desperately want the impossible, and I hate it.

"I need to go check on Kenzie," I say. He nods, and I turn away, swallowing back all the emotion he brought out in me. That did not go as planned. And I still don't know if I buy the fact that he's not the poet, though he has no reason not to admit it. Unless he's waiting until the perfect moment to tell me. Ugh. I want it to be him.

As I'm walking with my head down I see a pair of black boots and I stop, looking up into the gorgeous face of Rex Morino, all sharp edges and darkness. My insides seize as I jolt to a stop.

"Zae." His voice is nonchalant. Uncaring. But the interest in his eyes gives him away. I am not in the mood for this.

"Do you remember the eighth-grade dance?" I blurt.

His eyes scrunch. "What?"

"The eighth-grade dance. You danced with me. Do you remember that? And you said you'd be right back, that you were going to get us drinks, and then you left with another girl. Remember?"

He stares at me for a long time, and then his brow smooths. "Kind of."

"Well, I remember it clearly."

"Wait . . ." The corner of his mouth goes up in a smirk. "Is that what this is about? You're trying to get revenge for something that happened when we were kids? Something I barely remember?"

"I don't want revenge, Rex. I wanted a kiss. Just like you wanted a quick rub up against me at the dance and nothing more. No biggie. Let's both move on, okay?"

His eyes harden. "Damn, you're a bitch."

"And you're a dick. So we're even."

I push past him, feeling a heavy load fall off my back, making me walk taller. Hopefully I squashed his stupid, fake puppy love once and for all.

I find Lin and Kenzie dancing with a ton of other people by the truck, and I join them. Some of the kids from school are staring at me, and lean together to whisper. They must have seen me and Rex talking. When I get closer to my girls, Lin's eyes widen and she pulls me aside.

"Listen, don't freak out okay?"

My body tenses with an oncoming freak-out. "About what?"

"Kenz was really upset when we left you, and she was crying and people were, like, what's wrong? and she told them you were mad at her for talking about your kiss list."

Noooooo!

Lin bites her red lip, and my freak-out commences.

"Who did she say that to?"

Lin nods toward the crowd of dancers. "Just . . . them."

I close my eyes, forcing myself to breathe. There're at least twenty people from school in that group. Maybe they'll dismiss what she said since she's obviously drunk. Then I remember the stares and whispers, and I know it's not likely.

"I told them all there's no list," Lin says. "I'm sorry. Don't be mad. She doesn't know what she's saying. And who cares what they all think, right?"

"Yeah, whatever," I say, trying and failing to shake it off. "Who cares?" So they think I'm making a list of guys I've kissed. What's the big deal? I exhale loudly, trying to rid myself of the peevish feeling I have toward Kenz.

"Zae!" Angelo Garcia, crazy guy from my English class, rushes out from the crowd of dancers. I squeal as he swipes me off my feet, up into his arms, where he cradles me. I kick my feet, laughing.

"Put me down!"

"Nuh-uh, not until you put me on your list."

One arm is around his neck, and I use my free hand to smack his chest. "I don't have a list!"

"Aw, come on!" He tries to kiss me and I turn my face aside, making his lips hit my cheek. I can't help but laugh because he's such a clown. "Girl, don't be like that." He smiles down at me, looking so happy, and a black strand of hair falls over his brown forehead.

Oh, what the hell. I peck his lips with mine. It doesn't count, as far as the contest goes, but that's okay. He throws his head back and howls like a coyote.

I wiggle enough that he puts me down and dances his way back into the crowd.

"That doesn't count," Lin says, grinning with her arms crossed. "But I got one from Bodhi, so I'm in the lead."

"Yeah, yeah." I smile back, even though I'm still peeved. "I'm going to sit down." Lin reaches out and squeezes my hand before going back into the throng of dancers to stay with Kenzie.

I find a giant stump and sit. Where's Monica? My eyes scan until I find her.

Talking to Dean.

Their faces are close as they talk. Both smiling. She bats his big shoulder, and he throws his head back in laughter. I'm frozen like a statue as I watch, my heart hammering, my stomach twisting. They're touching a lot. He didn't touch me when we talked. My skin starts to crawl. My eyes burn.

I know this feeling, but I've never experienced it toward a friend. I'm seething with jealousy, and it's gross. I want it to go away. A plume of smoke from the trees catches my eye, and I get up to walk toward it.

Joel is alone, leaning against a tree. He lifts his chin in greeting.

"Kwami left?" I ask.

I follow his eyes and see Kwami flirting with Meeka. "Ah."

He takes another drag and I ask, "Why do you smoke?"

Joel gives a single-shouldered shrug. "It relaxes me. And maybe I have an oral fixation."

My eyebrows go up, and he takes another lazy drag. I move closer.

"Can I try?"

He lowers the cigarette to his side and eyes me. "No."

"Why not?" I'm weirdly offended. "Afraid of my germs?"

His lips quirk. "Definitely not. But I won't contribute to the delinquency of an innocent. Even if she does keep a naughty list."

His words punch me in the chest with surprise. Has the whole freaking party heard now? My hands clench into fists, and I stomp toward him. "I want to try. Please?"

His lips purse, and he holds it out. "Take it easy. Just a tiny breath."

I put my lips to the filter and suck air through it, hearing the tip sizzle.

"You got nice lips," he says softly.

His compliment hits my brain at the same time the smoke

hits my throat, choking me. I bend at the waist, coughing like crazy, desperate for fresh air. It burns and tastes nasty. Joel chuckles as he pats my back.

"Damn. Sorry 'bout that." He takes the cigarette from my fingers.

"How can you stand that?" I ask as I get my breath back. I lean my hands on my knees and look up at him through watery eyes. He drops the stub and crushes it beneath the toe of his shoe.

"You can get used to anything, Zae. Even things you don't like at first. One of the downfalls of human nature."

Deep thoughts. I stare at him, and a flutter sails through me. I brace myself and ask, "Did you write the poems in English?"

"English? Ah, you're referring to what I like to call nap time." Joel cocks his head, examining me. "Do I look like a poet to you?"

Damn. "Well, you don't have one of those beret things, but you're smart."

He laughs, and his teeth are bright white.

"You shouldn't smoke anymore," I say softly. "You'll ruin your nice teeth."

His smile falls, and he looks serious. "Thanks for caring. I'll keep that in mind."

A quiet moment follows, and we both stare at the party scene before us. I drag my eyes from Dean and Monica, who are still talking.

"How did you hear about the list? There's no list, by the way. I haven't written down a single name."

"Everyone keeps a list," Joel says, "even if it's up here." He taps his head, then inclines it toward his friend. "Meeka came over and told us. I told her I wasn't interested in her bullshit gossip, and she stomped away, pissed off. Then Kwami chased her like a damn tomcat." Joel shoves his hands in his deep pockets and runs his tongue over his bottom lip. I remember what he said about having an oral fixation, and it sends a zap of hyperawareness through me.

Joel looks out and curses under his breath. I turn to see Sierra walking toward us. What is she doing? Her curls are perfect in a way that I can never hope for. Maybe because hers are made by a curling iron and mine were made by Mother Nature. She stops in front of us and smiles brightly.

"This is an interesting sight."

"Sierra," Joel says in a tone that sounds like he knows her. "Can I help you?"

"Just saying hello." Her attention turns to me. "Zae, did you hear that you'll need a roundoff back handspring for try-outs this year? I know you couldn't do one last year." She gives me a look of pity. Joel chuckles darkly down at the ground, shaking his head.

"Yeah." I push my curls behind my ears. "I need to work on it."

She pulls a worried face. "You don't have much time. Good luck. Oh!" She gives my arm a playful touch. "I heard about your list, you bad girl."

I shake my head. "Kenzie is drunk. There's no list. Nothing like that."

"Mm-hm." Sierra gives me a huge wink with her long

146

lashes. "I don't recommend adding Joel to the list, though." She lifts a hand like she's telling me a secret, though he can clearly hear. "Smoker's breath."

Joel's expression never wavers from that of nonchalance. "Never stopped you."

Again, my eyebrows fly up as I look to Sierra in shock. She would never slum it with a guy like Joel, would she? The fire in her eyes as she glares at him makes me wonder.

"You wish," she says. Her hair swings as she turns and walks away.

I can't help but stare at him as the surprise still courses through me.

"You and her? You know each other?"

"Our dads were partners, back in the day."

I think about Sierra's family's car business "At the dealership?" I ask.

Joel nods. "My dad owned the mechanic side of things. They were best friends until they went into business together. My dad went bankrupt getting out of it. Never quite recovered." His jaw clenches like he's said too much, and he clears his throat.

Oh, wow. I can't wrap my mind around how bad it must have been for his dad to go to those lengths. "Did you and Sierra really kiss?"

He answers without hesitation. "Back in eighth grade, ninth grade, we did a lot of stuff. Till it became apparent she's as manipulative and greedy as her dad."

I gape at his complete transparency. In the firelight his eyes are light blue.

"Zae!" I turn to see Lin jogging toward us. "Kenz's getting sick."

I groan and give Joel a wave.

"Good luck," he says. He pulls out his pack of cigarettes and taps it against his palm.

I walk backward away from him. "You should think about quitting," I tell him.

Joel pops one between his lips and says, "I'll think about it." And he flicks his lighter to life as I shake my head and jog off.

Monica has walked Kenzie to my minivan, where she sits in the grass, leaning against the bumper. She's as pale as a vamp.

"I'll see if there's a bag in the van."

I rummage through until I find one. When I go to the back, a car is creeping past ours with its windows down.

"Party still going?" asks a guy. I recognize him as one of the skaters from the park.

"Yeah," I tell him. The back window rolls down, and my heart tumbles over my ribs to see Taro. His eyes go to Kenzie as Lin and Monica help her to her feet.

"I guess you're taking off," Taro says.

I walk to the window. "She drank too much. I need to get her to bed."

Taro nods, but when I see the hint of disappointment in his eyes I lean in the window and give his heart lips a peck. They're as soft and supple as I'd imagined. I hear his friends snigger with surprise. When I'm about to pull back, Taro cups my cheek with one hand and presses his mouth closer, opening his lips for our tongues to touch. Now his friends are clapping, and after a few seconds of melting into his warmth, I gently pull back.

"Thanks for yesterday" I say to him.

His eyes search mine, and he nods. I turn to the minivan, where Monica and Lin are jumping in, both giggling.

"Oh my God, Zae," Lin whispers. "We turn around for one second and you're kissing someone!" They both laugh as Kenzie moans.

I climb in and shut the door. "Well, you know I have to keep my *list* up to date."

"Aw, come on," Monica says in an annoyed tone.

I let go of my seat belt and turn to them. "Funny how it's just me who has a list. If she said it about all of us, making you guys look stupid, too, you would be upset."

"Zae," Lin says, "the whole kissing-contest thing was your idea. You can't be mad that it got out."

"It wasn't even supposed to be a contest. I only said that so you would join me and get over John because you're competitive."

Lin's face tightens in anger for a second, and then she calms. "I guess it worked."

Monica snorts, and I look at her, asking, "Did you and Dean kiss?" My heart goes erratic, and I wonder if I just sounded as mean as I felt.

"No." She's eyeing me strangely. "I thought you made it clear he was yours."

Um . . . "But you were flirting with him."

Now it's Monica's turn to get mad. "Excuse me, but I'm not even allowed to talk to him now? You didn't exactly go for it while you were with him. And then you kissed skater boy right after. You can't claim everyone." I love when she goes into diva mode against other people but not so much against me.

"Guys," Lin warns us.

I turn to face the wheel, tugging the seat belt strap harder than necessary. This is wrong. It's all wrong.

"No fighting," Kenzie whispers, followed by the crinkling of a bag and sounds of retching. I tense, feeling bad for her.

"We can't take her home like that," I say. "Her parents are going to kill her."

"Her parents are at a work party, remember?" Lin says. "Rae will be there." Kenzie's older sister from college. I'm ashamed that I only faintly remember the conversation.

The minivan is quiet after that except for occasional dry heaving from Kenz. We take her home first, then Lin. That leaves me and Monica in awkward silence the rest of the way to her house. We both whisper our goodbyes and she gets out quickly. I know I should have said sorry, but of all the guys at the party, of all the guys Monica could get with a simple flick of her finger, why flirt with Dean?

I don't want a guy to come between us. It's my number-one rule, and I'm breaking it. But so is she.

I'm sad when I get home and crawl into bed. Even the reminder of Taro's soft lips cannot soothe me. Everything feels like it's starting to spiral out of control, and an evil voice in my head keeps telling me it's only going to get worse.

CHAPTER EIGHTEEN

Thursday Morning

It's my first day working alone. I like the freedom Mrs. McOllie is giving me, but it's hard to enjoy it when I still feel icky from last night. Usually the girls and I will text with random stuff from the second we wake up, but it's been quiet today.

An hour into my shift I get a text from Kenzie. **I'm so, so sorry, Zae. I've been sick all morning. I can't stop crying. I've never been that drunk. I don't even remember everything I said, but Lin told me some of it. I KNOW there's no list. Monica said ur super pissed. What can I do to fix this?**

My heart pinches, and her apology washes away some of the grime from my dark aura. **I'm not mad at you. It'll blow over. Let's just forget about it. I was in a bad mood last night.**

Hopefully my words will get back to Lin and Monica as well.

ILY, she texts.

ILY2.

Loud voices come at me from the mall hallway. Some guys are yelling and laughing, being rowdy. One of the voices sends a chill down my back. I look up, filled with dread as three guys pass, roughhousing. The biggest guy punches another in the arm, and looks up into the store to catch me staring. My stomach drops like lead.

Rube. Wylie's friend who I'd hoped to never see again.

A disgusting cyclone builds inside me when he stops dead in his tracks. The two guys he's with stop as well. I don't know them, but they're just as smug looking as Rube when they come into the store, touching things, flicking at the scarves and feathery earrings. I want to tell them to get out, but I hold my tongue and try to appear unaffected.

Rube takes his time getting to the counter; I have no doubt he knows how uncomfortable his presence is making me, and he's savoring it. He smirks and leans down on the counter like he owns the place. His two friends walk up and flank him, still touching items on display. I hate how rigid I've gone. Behind them I hear another loud, rowdy group of guys passing.

"You really did a number on Wylie," Rube says. "Cold." His friends eye me with disdain.

"Oh, *I* did a number on *him*?" I ask. "Right."

"Yeah, you did," he says. "What chick is with a guy for almost a year and won't even bang him? Won't let him go out with his friends? Won't let him do *anything*? A control freak, that's who. But he's having fun now." His friends laugh.

My blood pressure is through the roof. I can't even swallow the lump in my throat.

"Y'all need to go."

His low laughter screams *Make me*.

"What's up, Rube?" comes a voice from behind them.

Rube and his two goons turn, and I'm startled by the sight of Joel Ruddick. He's with Kwami and an older kid I don't recognize. Immediate tension fills the store as the guys sort of face off, three on three. Joel and Kwami always seem so chill when I see them, but right now they look hard.

Oh, shit. I rush out from behind the counter, ready to yell for them all to get the hell out. I'm not getting fired over a stupid fight. But what I see is not what I expect. Rube suddenly sheds his bully persona, trading it for a teddy bear attitude.

"Hey, what's up, man?" Rube says with a smile. "Joel, right? Yeah, I remember you. I know your brother, Marcus, too."

Joel stares at him, unsmiling. He and his friends look like complete gangsters as they glare at the three Hillside guys, who seem to have lost all the bravado they walked in here with. Kwami and the other guy continue to pin them in place with stares while Joel looks at me.

"How you doin'? Everything okay?"

"Yeah," I say automatically. I don't want to be a punk and admit that Rube was bothering me, especially since it seems he already knows.

Joel looks at Rube and says, "See you 'round, man." But Joel doesn't move. Neither do his friends.

"Yeah, all right," says Rube, and he takes the cue, strutting away with pride, acting like he didn't just get kicked out. His friends follow, throwing shade over their shoulders but keeping their mouths shut. Kwami and the other guy walk to the entrance after them, almost as if they're keeping guard to make sure they actually leave.

I let out a sharp exhale and mutter a long curse about Rube that I'd been holding back.

Joel grins. "You could probably take that chump down if you wanted to. Quick hit to the throat. He's a big-ass baby."

I try to smile but still feel too gross. "He's friends with my ex—"

"I know." Joel's quick response sends a ripple through me. He knows?

"Oh." I swallow. "Well, thanks. That's twice this week you saved me."

He gives an easy shrug. "I'm just a model citizen."

This makes me laugh, and the other guys join in.

"Y'all are laughing a little too hard," Joel says with a grin. He gives me a nod as he backs away from the counter. "Take care."

He turns and leaves me to get back to work. I watch his slow strut out of the store. Backward ball cap, fitted white T-shirt, baggy jeans, and oversize tennis shoes. I take stock of what I know about Joel. Rube said he knew his brother, Marcus, who I'm pretty sure graduated already. Rube looked almost scared. Maybe Joel really is a dealer? Whatever he is, I'm grateful he stepped in. I hate to admit that Rube scares me, but he's never tried to hide his dislike of me, and he's unpredictable.

If I thought I was on edge before, it's nothing compared to how I feel after that scene.

Two hours before my shift ends I get a nice surprise when

Zeb walks in. At the sight of him, some of the slithering nastiness in my abdomen disappears. Then I see he's with two kids from our old neighborhood: that loudmouthed Rob kid and another rough-looking boy. Say what?

I pull Zebby over and whisper, "Who brought you here?"

"Rob's mom."

"You and Rob are friends again?"

"Yeah. He's been cool since you busted his balls."

Boys are so weird. I give Zeb a light smack on the back of his head and he goes off to hang with his friends. They go straight to the back corner, which has buttons and key chains with dirty phrases and cusswords. They're all three laughing and being obnoxious. I consider shooing them out of there but stop myself. It's harmless. I don't want to embarrass my brother.

As I'm opening a box of sale tags I notice it gets quiet. I look over, and to my utter horror, Zeb and Rob are both sliding something shiny into their pockets. All at once, the three boys glance toward me and freeze. The kid I don't know puts his hands up in the air, shaking his head.

I'm suddenly hot, my heart sinking in a torrent of lava. It takes every ounce of self-control for me not to hop over the counter and sprint toward them, screaming like a banshee. Instead, I don't dare move. They are behind the rack, hidden from the security camera, and I don't want to draw attention.

My voice is deadly. "Both of you take them out of your pockets and put them back."

The shakes that racked me last night are back. I'm barely holding it together.

Rob looks at me blankly, like he has no idea what I'm talking about, but Zeb's pained face holds back none of his guilt. His chin trembles as he pulls a button out of his pocket in a limp hand. Rob gives him a hard glare.

"Now you," I say to Rob.

He huffs through his nose and pulls out a button, smacking it back onto the magnetic strip. I slowly come around the counter to face them, pulling out my phone.

"What's your mom's number?" I ask Rob.

The small freckles across his face pale. "I— It was his idea!" He points to Zeb.

Oh, right. Nice try.

But when I look at Zeb, he swallows. His eyes are wide and watery. He's trying not to cry, and I realize in that moment Rob is not lying. Fear and panic rise inside me, and it's as if my baby brother slips into a dimension I can't quite reach.

I point to Rob and the other kid with a shaking finger. "Go. Tell your mom I'm bringing Zebediah home."

"Are you gonna tell her?" Rob croaks.

I waffle. The right thing to do would be to tell his mom, and my mom, too, but I can't bear to. Because it was Zebby's idea. My sweet, not-so-innocent-anymore Zeb.

"No," I say. "Just get out."

The boys rush from the store, and as soon as they're gone, Zeb's head falls and his body is racked with sobs. I point to a spot behind the counter.

"Sit there until I'm done working."

He pulls himself together enough to crumple into the spot I commanded. He wraps his arms around his bony knees and

156

keeps his head down, sniffling now and then. My heart feels more ragged than it's ever been. I can't help but blame my parents. It all goes back to them. Especially my stupid, selfish, cheating dad.

I pace the store, robotic as I deal with customers, and feeling eternally grateful that nobody else was here when the incident happened. I hope to God Mrs. McOllie or mall security don't look at the surveillance tape. I'm relieved when my replacement, a girl who commutes to George Mason University, shows up for the late shift, and Zeb and I can leave. I finger the coupon in my pocket that someone gave all the mall employees today: a free pretzel from Uncle Andrew's.

I stop in front of the shop and get an almond one, Zeb's favorite. I don't look directly at him, but I can see him wiping his nose and face on his sleeve. We walk silently from the mall to the minivan and both climb in. I set the pretzel in his lap. Zeb looks up at me in confusion.

"It's for you."

"What? Why? No, I can't."

I turn toward him, grabbing his hand. "I love you, Zebby." I swallow hard. "You're a good boy who made a bad decision. But if anyone else had been there, you would be in police custody right now. I want you to think about that really hard."

His entire face crumples, and I pull him toward me, wrapping him in a strong hug as he lets out a low, wounded wail. I know his pain, because his pain is mine, and mine is his.

"I'm not going to tell anyone," I say. "I just need you to learn from this. Can you do that? Can you never, *ever* do anything like that again?"

"Yes." He hiccups. "I'm sorry."

"I know you are." I pull away and wipe my face, then inhale deeply and put the car in drive. "Now eat your pretzel."

I want to put him in Bubble Wrap and make all his decisions for him—better decisions than my parents and I have made for ourselves. I don't want it to be like this for him, and it kills me that I can't keep him safe and innocent. Why is life so hard and complicated?

CHAPTER NINETEEN

Thursday Night

My phone buzzes as I sit on the couch with Zebby. He's still off after what happened at the Bowtique.

It's a text from Lin. **Porpoise Beach party. Wanna go?**

I'm relieved that she's texting me. She and Monica have been quiet today, barely responding to my texts about what happened with Rube and Joel. I know they're still annoyed, but maybe this night out will be what we need to get back on track.

Porpoise Beach isn't really a beach. It's a local lake with sand brought in for a makeshift beach. It's Garrison High territory, another rival, but not as vicious as Hillside. Lin has some friends at Garrison who she knows from gymnastics classes.

Before I can agree to go, I need to clear the air.

Is Monica still mad at me? I ask.

No. She's over it. Are you?

Yep.

Will you be mad if she talks to Dean again?

This gives me pause. **Does she like him?**

My heart beats too hard as I wait too long for her to respond.

IDK.

She's lying. She totally knows but doesn't want to get in the middle of it. Monica likes Dean. Whatever.

See u tonight, I write back.

At that exact moment, Zeb's phone rings. "It's Dad!" His face lights up in a way that breaks me, but the conversation ends with my brother ecstatic, punching the sky when he hangs up.

"Dad's getting us at six and taking us to dinner and laser tag!"

What the eff? Since when does Dad take us to restaurants and fun activities? Not for years, and in the past it was always Mom's idea. Where's he getting the money? Borrowing from his girlfriend? I try to envision myself having fun with Dad, but it sickens me.

"Sorry, Zeb. I already have plans. You guys will have fun though."

His face falls, but only for a fraction of a second. It will be good for them to have boy time. I don't want Zeb to hate Dad like I do. I don't want him to have to feel this way.

Mom must have heard Zeb's excited shout because she comes out of her room, eyes rimmed in red. I can't even look at her.

"How was work?" she asks.

"Work was fine," I lie. "I drove Zeb home since he was there with his friends and I was getting off soon."

160

"Good. I wondered if he'd make his way to see you while he was there."

I see Zeb watching me, unsure if I'm going to keep my promise not to tell.

"Zeb's going to dinner with Dad, and I'm going out with the girls."

"Oh?"

I turn from her to text Dad while Zeb tells her the details: **I can't go.**

Xanderia, he responds. **Please come. I want to see you.**

I turn from Zeb's watchful eyes as I feel my stupid emotions sprouting. I wish Dad would act like the villain he is and not bother with fake niceness. My fingers type as I walk into the living room.

I have plans. Thanks for taking Zeb.

I swallow hard to rid myself of the urge to cry.

I miss my family. I hate this irreparable, broken feeling.

"Okay," Mom says to both of us, sounding resolved but a little sad that she'll be alone. On my way to my room to get ready, I hear Mom get a text on her phone in her room. I grab it off her nightstand and see the text on the screen from Dad.

You need to talk to Zae. I can't take her attitude anymore.

My attitude? Forget that. I drop the phone back onto her nightstand and stalk to my room, slamming the door and turning on my music as loud as I can without disturbing the neighbors.

Ten minutes before Dad is supposed to show to pick up Zebby, I give my brother a quick squeeze.

"Have fun," I tell him.

"You're not going to stay and see Dad for a minute?" he asks.

I feel Mom's eyes on me, but I focus on Zeb, forcing a regretful expression onto my face. "No. I have to go now or I'll be late."

I grab my purse and dash out before anyone can make me feel worse.

Time to pick up my girls, meet some Garrison boys, and get my kiss on. Things have been strained between us since the Devonshire field party last night, but maybe it'll be better tonight since we'll be partying with people we don't know. People who aren't Dean. And maybe, if I'm lucky, Monica will fall for a Garrison guy and back off.

I'm happy the weather is nice enough to wear my tight capri jeans and a newish shirt that hangs low on my shoulders. But I'm not happy when I show up at Kenz's and Vincent is with her. I forgot he was back and that I told her she could bring him along. She gets teary eyed when she hugs me, acting like a puppy who's in trouble. I give her a smile so she'll relax. They sit together in the third row of the minivan, holding hands and whispering, in their own little world.

I grumble about the car going too slow in front of me, and the fact that we're hitting every single freaking red light. I smack the steering wheel with my palm.

"What's wrong?" Monica looks at me from the front passenger seat.

"Nothing," I lie. This is usually when we would blast the music and get silly, but I don't feel like we can do that with a guy around. Not that Vin would care, but just the presence of a penis in the car is making me grumpy.

Lin scoots forward from the middle seat. I glance at her perfectly applied "dramatic cat" eyeliner and red lips in the rearview mirror.

"Parker is going to be there," she says.

"Ooh!" Monica claps her hands. "The hot guy from your gym?" We've heard lots about the male gymnast but never met him before.

"Yes, and he's so good, you guys. He competes at the national level. Anyway, he flirted with me the whole time John and I were together. Let's see if he's still interested now that I'm single."

"He'd be stupid not to be," Monica says, and I agree, though that *is* how guys work. A girl out of reach is always more appealing.

I park in a tiny lot surrounded by trees, and we take a trail down to the sand. We kick off our shoes, and the sand is cool. It's dusk now, still light enough to see everyone's faces, but it'll be dark soon. The first thing I notice is that all the Garrison girls are in spring dresses, like they just came from church. And we . . . are not. The huge group turns to watch us all at once, and I feel completely conspicuous.

Then one of the girls shouts, "Lin!" and comes running. Another girl and a short, muscular guy follow. Lin introduces us, and I forget their names immediately, except for Parker, who is just as cute as Lin said. He's an inch taller than her, with broad shoulders and arms.

He hugs her with a big grin, and Monica gives me the look that says, "Yeah, he's into her." I bounce my brows in agreement. Winner.

Kenzie and Vincent bypass everyone and walk down to the

163

water together. I try not to be sad. I know I should be happy for her. The way he puts a hand protectively on her lower back is sweet, but all I can see is the potential heartache that's to come and how she's not really ours anymore, so I look away and follow Lin as she leads us down into the group.

It turns out the fancy girls are pretty nice. Definitely more welcoming than Hillside High girls. They offer us drinks, but I pass since I'm driving. My eyes scan the guys to see which ones are with girls, or have their eyes on girls already, and which are ripe for the picking. I see Monica eyeing a loud group at a picnic table, but they're a little preppy for my liking, all in polo shirts and whatnot. I should have expected this. Oh, well. No time to be picky. I'm not looking for a boyfriend, after all. Just a pair of nice lips.

Once the sun dips low enough to darken the sky, and enough beer has been consumed, things start to get lively. Someone turns on a portable speaker connected to a phone that blasts punk rock, and it all sort of clicks. Laughter. The glimmer of lake water. Two drunk guys banging their heads like a couple of crazies in the middle of it all.

Vincent goes to stand in the drink line while Kenzie stands with Monica and me. Lin and Parker are straddling a picnic-bench seat, facing each other in close conversation. Monica nudges me, and I look up to see three guys walking our way, beer cans in hand, confidence plastered on their well-groomed faces.

"Hello, hello," says a tall blond one. "I'm Ranger."

"Hey," Monica says. "I'm Monica. This is Zae and Kenzie."

Ranger points to a super tall and thin guy in a buzz cut.

"That's Arik." And then a polished, all-American boy with brown waves perfectly gelled. "And this is Bauer."

I give a wave and smile.

"What school do you go to?" Bauer asks.

"Peakton," I tell him.

Each one of them visibly reacts with surprise—raised eyebrows, pulled faces.

"What?" Monica asks.

Arik gives a short laugh. "I didn't know there were any hot girls at Peakton."

Now it's our turn to scoff.

"Surprise," Monica says in a deadpan voice. I hold back a guffaw.

Bauer gives Arik a small shove and says, "Idiot."

"What?" Arik laughs and drinks his beer. "I thought Peakton was all ghetto—"

"Stop." Monica holds a hand up, and I *wish* she'd go Latina on his ass.

"Seriously, dude." Ranger laughs. "Shut up."

"Sorry! I'm not trying to be an asshole." Arik crushes his can and throws it far into the trees. This Peakton girl does not approve of littering. Then he looks at Kenzie. "You're cute."

"Um, thanks." She glances toward the line where Vin is almost at the front.

The guy, Arik, keeps looking at her, and says, "So, like, what are you?"

I cringe hard enough to tweak a nerve in my back.

"What the fuck?" Monica says, putting a hand on her hip.

"What?" the guy asks, grinning stupidly. His friends smack

165

themselves in the heads, groaning, and Kenzie smiles tightly at Arik. He's asking for her heritage. It's not the first time I've heard someone ask her like this, and it pisses me off worse every time. I'm about to tell him where he can shove his question, when Kenzie raises her pixie-like chin.

"Female cisgender," she says. "All American. What are *you*?"

I hold back a cackle of pride as the other two guys laugh outright, and Arik crosses his arms.

"No, I mean, like—"

"I know what you meant." She loses the fake smile, done. I know she's not ashamed of being biracial, but she also isn't in the mood to explain anything to a dumbass. I want to hug her for how fierce she looks right now.

"O-*kay*," he says, clearly peeved that she's not going to answer.

"Go get another beer." Bauer nudges Arik, and he complies, seeming glad for an excuse to leave us, shaking his head. Ranger and Bauer sidle up closer.

"Sorry about that," Ranger says. "He's missing some sort of connection up here." He points to his head. Kenzie shrugs, but discomfort pollutes the air.

"You okay?" I whisper.

She glances behind us and nods tightly. "Here comes Vin. I'm gonna take a walk."

Monica and I watch her go, taking her beer from Vincent, then twining her hand with his as they disappear into the woods.

Monica sips her drink and eyes me sideways with meaning,

as if making sure I'm okay. If I wanted to leave now, she'd be cool with it. I give her a small shrug, then a roll of my eyes and a nod. She nods back, silently saying it's up to me.

I look at the two boys. "Yeah, I don't really want to hang around him. No offense to you guys."

"Yeah, he's a buzzkill," Ranger says. "I'll text him and tell him not to come back." He pulls out his phone and taps away, grinning when it's done.

"Hope you won't hold it against *us*, though." Bauer gives me a little nudge and an innocent-enough smile as a lock of brown hair falls over his forehead. The worst of the tension sheds away, leaving behind remnants of discomfort.

Monica clears her throat and asks, "Do you guys play sports?"

"Soccer and football," Bauer says, pointing back and forth between himself and Ranger. "Both of us."

"We cheer," I tell them.

"Ah, nice." Bauer smiles. "We'll have to look for you at the games next season and say hey."

Conversation comes easier now that Arik is gone, and thankfully he doesn't make his way back to us. Ranger gravitates to Monica, while Bauer takes an interest in me. He's not the kind of guy I could hang out with often—he's almost guarded, hard to read, like he's trying to say all the right things and come across too perfect. Still, he's kissable, and that's what matters.

I can tell he's starting to get a buzz when he cocks his head toward the trees and says, "Let's talk over there. It'll be quieter."

I give him a knowing look. "Quieter, huh?"

He cocks his head again and gives a nod, turning and walking confidently, like he knows I'll follow. And I do. But first I catch Monica's eye and she gives me a wink.

I get nervous when we're out of sight of the others. It's not like being alone with a guy from Peakton who I see every day. It feels different. I don't know this guy at all. Maybe I'm still feeling weird about Arik's rudeness. I try to shake it off so I can relax and have fun, but the uneasiness lingers.

When Bauer tries to walk farther, I grab his hand and say, "This is far enough."

My heart is beating too hard. *It's just a kiss*, I remind myself. *Get it, and get out.*

He turns back to me, giving me a confident, hooded look, and strides into my bubble. Without hesitation he cups the back of my head, kissing me harder than I've ever been kissed. My palms go to his chest as he backs me against a tree. He's holding me so tightly and pressing his mouth so hard against mine that I don't think he feels me trying to push back. *He's just a passionate guy*, I tell myself. *No need to freak*. I try to loosen up and kiss him back, but he's so intense. He wants to be in control, which I'd usually think was kind of sexy, but it feels . . . wrong.

Then, in a quick move, his hand is up my shirt, on my bare stomach and pushing downward, trying to get in my pants. Thank God they're too tight for easy access. I squirm as he goes for the button, and I'm finally able to wrench my head to the side, though he still clutches the back of my neck.

"Whoa," I say. "Just a kiss."

"What?" He gives a low chuckle. "Why?" As if "just a kiss" is the most absurd thing he's ever heard.

"Because that's all I want." *Duh.* I try to push him, but he wraps his arms around me, breathing down onto my neck.

"Just relax," he says.

"I think I'm done," I tell him. "Sorry." Ugh, why do I feel the need to apologize?

"Why?" he asks, not letting go. He chuckles into my neck again. "Come on, beautiful." His arms around me move until his hands are up my shirt, caressing my bare back as his mouth moves to cover mine again.

Nope. My hands push, and I'm met with a push back, my upper back digging into tree bark.

"Get off." I use all my might now to shove him away. In the flash of moonlight I see a look of surprise in his eyes. Disbelief.

"Dude, *chill.*" He reaches out and grasps my wrist. I yank back and holler when he holds tight, pinching my skin. A burning sensation sears up my arm and I whimper, still pulling against his hold.

"Hold on just a sec!" he says through gritted teeth, letting out a dry laugh as if I'm being unreasonable.

"*Hey.*" The calm male voice comes from within the darkness of the trees, and Bauer drops my wrist as Vincent and Kenzie show themselves. Oh my God, I want to run to them. Vin looks directly at me and speaks in his unwavering, gentle voice. "You okay, Zae?"

"Yeah." I put another step between Bauer and me, rubbing my wrist.

"Why wouldn't she be?" Bauer asks. "Just a kiss, right?"

He looks at me, and even in the moonlight I can see a mix of pleading and warning in his eyes. All I want to do is get far away from him.

"Let's go," I tell Vincent and Kenz.

I march out of the woods, trembling and suddenly freezing, to find Lin sitting on Parker's lap, sucking face. The sight sends a jolt of panic through me, and I have to tell myself it's okay. He's not hurting her. My eyes search for Monica, but I don't see her or that Ranger guy. Worry seizes me.

"Where's Monica?" I am practically panting as I look around.

"I'll find them." Vin rushes into the trees again.

"It's okay," Kenzie says, taking my hand.

Bauer speed walks past us, running a hand roughly through his hair as he makes his way to the larger group. It doesn't take long before I can hear whispers turning to louder voices and see people turning to look at us.

Bauer's voice rises. "Who invited the fucking psychos and that thug from Peakton?"

Lin is standing now, looking around with confusion. When she finds me, she whispers something to Parker and walks our way. Vincent comes out of the trees with Monica rushing behind him, a confused Ranger following.

I don't say a word. I start walking as fast as I can across the cold sand to the parking lot. By the time I pick up my sandals and get to the car, I'm shaking too hard to drive. Vincent takes the keys from me and I let him. I climb into the back with the girls, and Vin gets us out of there quickly.

"Oh my God, Zae, what happened?" Monica asks. She and

Kenzie are both holding me, and Lin is in the third row leaning over the seat, her hand rubbing my back.

"Nothing," I say automatically, because I feel stupid, but I have to tell them. "We were kissing, and then he tried to put his hands down my pants, and I stopped him, but he wouldn't let me go. He kept holding me tighter and his voice . . . I don't know. He was telling me to calm down and it was so creepy."

Monica and Lin gasp in indignation.

"I heard you say 'Get off,'" says Kenzie. "And it sounded like you were struggling, so we ran over. He was pushing you against the tree, and like, grabbing at you!" Her voice cracks and she wipes tears from her cheeks. "We should call the police!"

I shake my head. And tell them what? That I stupidly went into the woods with a boy I don't know? That he made a move I wasn't ready for, and got rough when I told him to stop? I know what they'll say. That I wasn't raped. That I wasn't quite assaulted. That he's a good kid from a good family in a good neighborhood. But what if Vincent and Kenzie hadn't been there? I don't know what that guy planned to do next. Could I have fought him off? I'd like to think so, but a shiver of apprehension zags down my back at the sense of powerlessness I felt.

"I can totally find out where he lives," Lin says. "We should egg him."

"No," I say. "He'll know it's me."

"Then we don't do it tonight," Vincent says quietly from the driver's seat. Kenzie sends him a look of complete adoration, and for once I don't begrudge her for it.

"Thank you, Vincent," I say. He doesn't respond, but he

doesn't need to. And then I remember . . . "He called you a thug."

We let that thought sink in, and then we're laughing. It's completely inappropriate laughter, brought on by our frenzy of adrenaline and horror, and when we're finished laughing, we wipe tears from our eyes and cling to one another.

We're quiet the rest of the way to Kenzie's house, where we drop off her and Vin. I'm feeling well enough to drive now, but a darkness still surrounds me, and my mind won't stop racing. I should have called him an asshole and been more vocal at the end when he tried to shush me. I'm haunted by the trepidation I felt when I walked into those woods—my gut instincts that I ignored. I think about the what ifs, and I silently send my love to all the souls in the world who weren't as lucky as I was tonight.

CHAPTER TWENTY

Friday

I'm having a hard time concentrating at work, partly because I hardly slept last night. I keep imagining that Bauer will come into the store and threaten me. I know it's ridiculous. I'm safe. All I have to do is pick up the phone and press one button to have security there. Each time I peer down at the button I feel a little better. Still, I stare at the store's opening into the mall.

My phone buzzes with a text from Kenzie: **My house tonight. Wear all black.**

All black, why? And then I remember and feel a jolt of excitement. I've never egged anyone's house before. The possibility of getting caught makes me nervous, but it will be worth it. Revenge is mine.

I'm so excited when I get off work, get home, and gather every black garment I own. I can't help but giggle in Kenzie's basement once we're all dressed like a pack of cute burglars. Even Vincent is decked out, though he's going to be the getaway driver. His only black pants were some fancy slacks from a suit and a black turtleneck that is too short at his waist and wrists. He lets us laugh at him for longer than necessary. And I have to admit, after last night, I welcome Vin's presence like a friend.

"I did some research," Lin says. "I stalked all of Bauer's social media pages. He has tons of pictures of his shiny red Jeep and calls it his baby."

I roll my eyes, and Monica gags.

"So," Lin continues, "I think we should focus on his car instead of his house. And we should use something that won't cause permanent damage."

Kenzie giggles and brings out a grocery bag. When she opens it, we all lean in, and I have to blink several times at the tubes inside.

"Biscuits?" Monica and I declare together.

"Yes!" Kenz and Lin are cackling like evil geniuses. "It's supposed to be the hottest, sunniest day of spring break tomorrow. We'll squash biscuit dough all over his car, and then it will rise in the morning sun."

Kenzie rolls onto her back, clutching her belly with glee, and Vincent smiles down at her like at a precious kitten.

Okay, biscuits are not exactly the big middle finger I wanted to give Bauer, but it's better than nothing. "Do we know where he lives?"

"Yes," Lin says. "Same street as my friend from gymnastics. And she can't stand him—says he's a cocky prick who gets away with murder all the time."

My heart skips a beat. "Wait, you didn't tell her we're doing this, did you?"

"No. She called me last night to ask what happened, and she believes you one hundred percent. Nobody outside this room will know. Got it?"

We all put our pinkies in the middle and twine them together. When Vincent just sits there, we stare at him.

"Well?" I say. "Get in here."

"Uh . . ." He wraps a long pinkie awkwardly around our conjoined ones, and we all laugh. Now it's time to get ready.

We go all out with our disguises. Full black. Cheap, stretchy black gloves and beanies from the dollar shop, courtesy of Lin. Kohl eyeliner thick around our eyes. To pass the time, we turn off all the lights and shine flashlights, dancing to Kenzie's cheer-dance mix.

At midnight, we go.

Vincent drives his own car, a black Honda coupe that will be less conspicuous than my big old minivan. I kind of love him for doing this. He takes control in a way that surprises us all and makes me feel like we're strangely safe.

We get to the neighborhood—old money—big, classic houses with sprawling lawns and lush trees separating properties. The kind of houses with pools and gazebos in the backyards.

"That's it up there," Lin whispers. "She said it's the one on the end, redbrick."

The street is quiet and empty as Vincent makes a slow pass of the house. Bauer's Jeep is parked in the driveway in front of the garage.

"They have floodlights at the corner of the garage," Vincent says quietly. "It's pointed toward the yard, so don't set foot off the driveway or you'll activate them. There's one over the front door, too, so stay close to the Jeep." He goes around the corner and parks, turning off the lights. "Don't bump the Jeep in case there's an alarm sensor. Be super gentle when you're touching it."

The four of us are nodding, and I know their hearts are beating just as hard as mine. Kenzie starts pulling the cans of biscuits out of the bag and peeling the paper, then smacking them against the dashboard to pop them. When she flinches and squeaks at the first pop, Vincent takes the others and opens them for us. We fill our hands. Since they're not as cold as they're supposed to be anymore, they've gotten sticky, and I can't help but giggle at the glop in my gloved hands.

Vincent comes around and opens our doors as quietly as possible. We slip out into the darkness, dashing quietly along the side of the road, and crouching as we rush up the driveway. I'm so nervous I could puke. Seeing my girls on the move keeps me going.

We work fast. I think about this guy, this jerk, who believes he has a right to take what he wants from a girl and then make her feel like trash when she doesn't want it back. I smear dough onto his back window and along the soft top wherever I can reach. I hear the gentle scuttle of my friends' feet on each side. When our hands are empty, we huddle together, take one look at his Jeep, which now appears pockmarked and gross, and take off back down the driveway, whispering "Oh my God!" and trying with all our might not to laugh.

We sprint up the street, push our way into Vincent's car,

pull the doors closed slowly, and Vincent guns it. He doesn't turn the lights back on until we're at the next street, and then we fall back into our seats, howling with laughter, exhilarated and wholly entertained. Vincent grins silently as he drives us back to Kenzie's, and we rehash every single detail of our mission.

"I just wish I could see his face tomorrow," I say. "Biscuited by four psychos and a thug."

Laughter. So much we can hardly breathe.

And in that moment I'm happy.

CHAPTER TWENTY-ONE

Saturday Afternoon

Thankfully Saturdays are super busy at work, which makes the day fly by, and the college girl I work with is nice. But I'm still on edge, staring out at people walking by, jumping at loud male voices that pass.

Lin messages us halfway through my shift, including a link. **OMG, look!! #success.**

The link takes me to one of Bauer's pages, which is public, and his message is clear: **Whoever fucked with my car, I will find you and you will pay.**

I cover my mouth to hold back a squeal of delight because Mrs. McOllie is in the back room. We've made Bauer seriously mad, and that's all I could have hoped for. I wonder if he cleaned the dough off himself or if Mommy and Daddy did it for him. Did it leave grease marks that had to be scrubbed?

Does he feel violated? I want to ask him how it feels to have someone touch something of his without permission. How it feels to be completely disrespected. I know two wrongs don't make a right and yada yada, but I have no regrets.

Still . . . I hope he never finds out it was us.

My good mood is ruined an hour before I'm supposed to get off, when I get a text from Dad: **Can you and Zeb come to the restaurant for dinner around 4:45 before the evening rush starts?**

I feel my lips curl into a scowl. Just the thought of seeing him makes me want to dive into my bed and cover my head with blankets. It takes me twenty minutes of deep breathing, pacing around the store, before I can text him back.

OK.

Great! See you then.

I'm tired when I get off, and I know it has everything to do with not wanting to see Dad. Then again, I feel tired a lot these days. When I pass the food court as I'm leaving, I hear my name being called and look over to see a huge group of Peakton kids. Basketball players and step teamers, and I see Joel and Kwami among them. I can't help but smile.

"Look at you, lookin' all cute," says Destinee, head of the step team. She motions to the skirt and blouse I'm wearing with flats.

"Thanks," I tell her. "I like the purple in your braids."

"Aw, you're too sweet." She waves off the compliment. "You coming to Quinton's tonight?"

Quinton is our basketball point guard. He's so good that college scouts came to nearly every game this season to watch

179

him. Quinton turns when he hears his name, and he looks me up and down with those watchful eyes. He's all wiry muscle. He gives me a wink and a nod, and I smile.

"Bring your girls," Destinee says. "We gonna light it up."

"All right," I tell her. "Thanks."

She turns back to the other girls and I glance at Joel, who's watching me. I go to him and get close enough to catch the scent of his cologne, which smells so yummy I rock back on my heels and have to clear my throat. I quickly check myself.

"Hey," I say to them.

"Hey," Joel and Kwami both say back.

"How many cigarettes have you smoked today?" I tease.

Joel rubs a thumb over his bottom lip. "'Bout a hundred."

Kwami laughs. "Man, you a damn liar. You ain't had one."

"Wow," I say, impressed.

He gives a cool shrug. "It's a recreational vice. I'll kill a pack at the party tonight."

"Will you?" I ask. "That's sad."

"Don't cry," Joel parries.

I roll my eyes and take out my phone to text Lin about the party.

"Your girl Meeka gonna be there?" Kwami asks me.

"I don't know. She's not really my girl."

"For real? Y'all cheer together."

"I know. We get along all right, but we don't talk much."

"Why you want that girl?" Joel asks him. "She thinks she's too good for you."

This prompts playful bickering between them. I ignore their conversation and respond to Lin, working out details about getting ready at her house. Then I tell the girls I'm having dinner at my dad's work.

"Why you frownin'? Fix your face." Joel nudges my arm and I look at him, my stomach turning with all the emotions. I shake my head.

"I gotta go. I'll see y'all tonight."

Naturally Zeb is super excited when I get home, and even Mom is smiling to see him so happy. She kisses my cheek as we're walking out the door.

"Try to enjoy it. Daddy loves you."

Yeah, so much that he abandoned us for some other woman.

Dad works at a barbecue sports bar known for its ribs. I *am* kind of looking forward to the food. He used to bring home ribs every Sunday, and I miss that.

He's waiting for us with two beaming waitresses at the hostess stand when we come in.

"There they are!" Dad's smile is so genuine that for a moment I forget I'm mad at him, and I just want to run into his arms. I swallow and hold back, letting Zeb be the one to run forward and hug him. I keep my arms at my sides when he gives me a squeeze and a kiss on the forehead.

Dad proudly introduces us to the two waitresses, who fuss about how adorable we are, and then he takes us to a booth. One of the waitresses comes over, a brunette probably in her midtwenties, still smiling.

"Zae, Zebby," says Dad. "This is Jacquie. She'll be taking care of you."

"Hi, guys," says Jacquie, overly chipper. "What can I get

you to drink? Wait, let me guess." She points to Zeb. "A choc-olate malt." Now me. "And a root beer float?"

Those are our all-time favorites. Zeb bounces in his seat and we look at Dad, who laughs. He must have told her before we came. It annoys me for some reason. Like everyone at his work thinks he's Father of the Year or something.

"Actually," I say, "I just want a Coke."

The waitress's smile falters, but she recovers quickly. "Sure. Be right back."

Dad gives me a funny look. "Too old for a float now?"

I shrug, even more annoyed because I really want that stu-pid float. Jacquie comes back to drop off two trivia remote boxes, still looking us over with that big, pretty smile, then leaves again.

Dad rumples Zeb's hair. "Get whatever you guys want. I've got a few phone calls to make—a waiter called in sick right before you got here—but I'll be back."

We busy ourselves with trivia, watching the big screens and answering with our remotes. One of the bar back guys passes us in a black apron, carrying a black bin, and he catches my eye, faltering. I blink in recognition. It's Elliott Fields from English class, the lanky, camo-wearing break-dancer. His hair, like pale-yellow straw, is sticking out from the sides of his restaurant-issued hat.

"Hey," I say.

He holds the empty bin against his waist. "How you doin', Zae?" He glances toward the doors where Dad went. "You know Xander Monroe?"

"He's our dad."

182

Elliott looks between Zeb and me, nodding, and his face seems to register something that he doesn't say out loud. I wonder what he's thinking. Does he want to tell me that Dad's a jerk? It seems like he's nice to his employees, but Elliott's expression makes me wonder.

Jacquie brings us an appetizer of fried onion straws with special sauce, and Elliott backs away, giving me a wave as he goes to clear a table.

I get ribs and Zebby gets a giant burger. Dad is able to steal ten minutes to sit down with us while we eat. I'm thankful because I know my brother needs this. And the food is amazing.

When Dad gets up to deal with a problem in the kitchen, I go to the restroom. More people are starting to show up now. Happy hour. We can't stay much longer. When I come out of the bathroom, there's a huge group at the hostess stand, so I go around the other way to get back to the bar. I'll have to cut through the waitress station, but Dad won't care.

As I'm passing the registers in the server alley I spot Dad through the window of the swinging door, in front of his office. He's standing close to our waitress, closer than is appropriate, gazing down at her. I stop and frown. Her head is tilted up to him, still with that smile, and she puts her hand on his arm. Everything about them screams intimacy and closeness. My heart rips. My throat dries and I can't swallow.

It's her. Jacquie. She's the other woman.

"Yo, you okay?" The soft voice is Elliott, right beside me. He glances through the door and blanches as he sees what I saw.

183

I try to say *I'm fine*, but it comes out a dry croak.

My face flushes with heat under his gaze, followed by a sickly cold feeling. I turn from his worried face, dizzy, and find my way back to the booth in a fog. I grab my purse. Zeb is staring up at the trivia screen, biting his lip, ready to answer.

"It's time to go," I tell him in a trembling voice. "Say bye to Dad."

"Huh?" He doesn't look away from the screen.

"Zeb!" My shout gets his attention. "It's time to go. It's getting busy. They need this booth."

"Aw, man."

My dinner is pressing its way back up into my esophagus, and I feel hot. It's too loud in here. I can't get her smile out of my mind. The smile of a woman without major worries. I haven't seen Mom smile like that in over a year. I nearly jump out of my skin when Dad and Jacquie are suddenly there.

"How was everything?" she asks brightly.

"Great!" Zeb tells her.

I fumble for my drink and suck down the last dregs as an excuse not to look at them. I can feel their presence, these two smiling people who now live together happily, while Zeb, Mom, and I are brokenhearted in our crappy apartment.

"Were your ribs okay, Zae?" Jacquie inquires.

I cannot look at her. My cloudy eyes go to Dad, but I can't focus.

"Can I get some money for gas?" I ask, even though I have a pocketful from my paycheck.

He pats his back pocket and frowns. "I'm not sure I have any cash. I can run to the ATM—"

"No," says Jacquie, reaching into her apron. "Is ten enough?" She holds it out to me, but I recoil from it, shaking my head.

"Zae, what's wrong with you?" Dad asks.

I slide out quickly, forcing them to move aside. "I don't feel good. I have to go."

I rush away, hoping Zeb will follow me through the crowd of loud talkers, holding drinks, completely unaware of the girl who is roiling with disgust and betrayal.

I sprint through the parking lot and lean against the minivan with both palms, my head hanging down, trying my hardest not to cry or barf. I can't get the image of them out of my mind or the injustice of it all. He should be looking at Mom like that, not her.

"Zae!" Dad's voice makes me stand and blink. He stops in front of me, his face pinched with worry. "Are you sick?"

"I'm fine," I say through clenched teeth. "Go back in with *Jacquie* and don't worry about me." His worry slowly morphs to realization, and he pales. His mouth opens. Nothing comes out.

I fling open the door and climb in. Dad slowly backs away, looking unsure. I see in the side mirror that Zeb comes out and hugs him one last time before getting in the minivan with me. I don't look at Dad again. I just drive away the second Zeb closes the door, hoping Dad enjoys his new life without me.

CHAPTER TWENTY-TWO

Saturday Night

While I was at dinner, Lin and Monica went bowling with Parker the gymnast and a few of his Garrison friends. Bauer was not there.

I try to be happy for her, but I've got a pit in my stomach that won't go away. I've been sitting at our tiny dining room table, zoning out since Zebby and I got home. I swear, I never used to be this negative and pissed off at the world. I hate feeling this way, but I don't know how to shake it. I can't make Jacquie go away. I can't get my parents back together. I can't make boys be faithful. I can't even make my own stupid heart not want Dean.

"I was thinking the three of us could go to church in the morning for Easter."

I snap my head up to where Mom is standing in the kitchen.

Zeb is staring with a similar look of surprise from the couch. We haven't gone to church in years.

She goes on. "I've been hearing things about that one by the mall. It's supposed to have really good music."

Zeb looks at me, as if I can fix this.

"We don't have to go to Sunday school, do we?" I ask. The thought of being in a small room with other kids I don't know, probably the only one who doesn't have Scriptures memorized, terrifies me.

"No, no," Mom says. "Just the regular service. It doesn't start until eleven, so you'll have plenty of time in the morning. I'll get home by ten twenty and we'll leave at ten forty."

If I wanted, I could refuse. I could get out of it. But then I think of Dad and Jacquie, all happy together, and I don't feel like I can deny Mom this one small request.

"Okay." And while we're playing nice, there's something I need to ask her that I've been putting off. "Hey, Mom? Um . . . tryouts are in May, and they're requiring a roundoff back handspring. Could I, maybe, take a few lessons?"

Her entire face sags, and my heart drops with it. I know she cannot afford it, especially now. "I'm working," I say. "So I can maybe pay half? And we can talk to Dad about pitching in."

"Honey, things are so tight right now. One month of lessons last year used up months of our savings."

"I know. Just . . . never mind. I need to get ready."

She exhales as I stand to go. I don't know what I'm going to do about cheer. The move isn't something I can practice on my own. I need someone strong to spot me. I know it's dumb, but I have an irrational fear of landing on my head. I have the best jumps on the squad. My motions are tight and I can dance my ass off. I'm one of the strongest bases, and I've never let a flyer fall, even if it means getting a black eye and minor concussion. But tumbling has always been my weakness. I can't believe it's come down to this. What am I going to do? Who am I if not a Peakton cheerleader? Every time I think about it, I feel like I'm going to have a panic attack.

In the bedroom, I stare up at my Eiffel Tower poster, then let my eyes wander over images of the Irish Cliffs of Moher and Egyptian pyramids. What would it be like to get away from all this? To go far away and experience an old-world culture? Even my far-off dreams cannot unroot me from my troubles right here, right now. I take out my phone and scroll, then stare at Dean's number for a long time. Then I take a deep breath and text him. **Party tonight at Quinton's.**

His response is almost immediate. **Sweet. Thnx.**

I hope that means he'll come. Nervousness courses through me. This is my chance with Dean—my chance to turn his eye away from Monica. I still don't know for sure if he was lying about the poems. Why wouldn't he be honest? Maybe because he's embarrassed or nervous. If he wrote them, I need to let him know I feel the same. I'll stake my claim, and if he finally lets the truth out, I know Monica will understand and back down.

A sense of foreboding fills me as I gather my clothes, flat iron, and makeup bag, but I try to shake it off. This storm cloud over my head cannot last forever. I'm going to take matters into my own hands. I *will* have fun tonight.

* * *

Monica gives me a quick, small smile when I get to Lin's, but she's quieter than normal. The past two nights at the Porpoise Beach party and then when we went biscuiting, things felt better between us, but now it's back to being tense. Maybe because I mentioned Dean might be there tonight? Whatever the reason, the atmosphere is noticeably less excited than our usual preparty vibe. As much as I'm not in the mood for butt kissing, I can't go on like this. I link my pinkie with Monica's and pull her aside.

"I'm sorry," I say. I need to say more, like *I won't let a guy come between us*, but *I'm sorry* is all I can manage at the moment.

She chews her glossy lip. "Me, too."

When she hugs me, I squeeze her tightly. More than anything, I need my friends right now. Kenzie went to an early movie with Vincent, but they're planning to meet us at Quinton's.

As we leave, Lin's parents are sitting on the couch, as close as can be, holding hands, watching a house-flipping show. They're older than my parents by at least ten years, and the sight of their obvious bond sort of crushes me in good and bad ways. They've made it together this long and still hold hands. I'm both happy and sad as I watch Lin kiss them before we go.

"Your parents are so cute," Monica says in the car.

"I know, right?" Lin smiles. "Relationship goals."

They both glance at me suddenly, like they're worried they've upset me by pointing out a happy marriage, but my fake-smile game is strong and puts them at ease.

I blare the music so Lin and Monica can sing at the top of their lungs, and all thoughts are chased out of my mind.

Quinton's house is down in Triangle, at the end of the street in an old neighborhood. We have to park far away and walk. Even though it's already dark, there are people sitting outside on creaky porches. Some of the men call out to us in slurring voices, laughing, and we ignore them.

Quinton's house is ahead, and it'll be filled with people I know. I don't have to be afraid, but after what happened with Bauer, I do have to be more cautious, which I hate to admit.

My mood lifts at the sound of music thumping as we approach the squat split-level surrounded by overgrown bushes. Voices carry from the backyard. We push our way inside, where the air is stifling with too many bodies, but it doesn't bother me. Just the opposite. I let myself get lost in the crowd, overshadowed by music and movement, my worries momentarily drowned into silence. I see Destinee and she smiles big, giving me a hug as we pass.

Lin, Monica, and I make our way right to the middle and dance until we're sweating. Guys from school surround us, dancing up to us. Hands on our hips and waists, everyone smiling and laughing, drinks held high. I spot a camouflage hat among the dancers and catch the eye of Elliott. Seconds later a circle is clearing and he's on the floor, spinning and swinging those legs and arms with precise control in a way that has everyone hollering with approval.

When he ends in a ball on his back, he puts his fingers on the floor by his head and throws his feet out, jumping up like he's made of springs. I clap, and he finds me, coming straight for me.

"Thought I saw you!" He dances up to me and I grin,

lifting my arms as his body comes flush to mine, one of his knees between mine, and we move together as one to the beat of the music. My girls cheer. Elliott moves around my body to the back, his hands out as he lowers himself to the floor, and I laugh. The boy is shameless, working his way back up my body in perfect sync to the music. When the song ends and another begins, he puts his hands on my shoulders and whispers, "Did you write that poem in class about your parents?"

I stiffen as the good cheer drains from me. Elliott moves around to face me, and the shifting bodies force us to get out of the way. We step against the wall and I look up into his tender, light-brown eyes.

"I'm sorry," he says over the music. I can smell beer on his breath. "I didn't mean to make you sad."

"It's okay," I tell him. I'm always sad lately. "What's it like working for him?"

"I haven't worked there very long. But he's cool." Elliott scratches his neck. "Did you know they were together? I mean, before today when you saw them?"

I shake my head and he cringes. "I didn't think so."

"It's okay," I say again, because I can tell he's feeling sorry for me, and I don't want to think about it. "Hey, Elliott? Did you write those poems in English class? About the girl and the Capri Sun?"

He laughs. "No, but that was some funny shit. Why?"

I shake my head. "Let's just dance, 'kay?"

His eyes brighten and he nods, pulling me back out there to where my girls are. I don't stop dancing until I feel my phone buzz and I look to see a message from Kenzie.

191

Me & V feel tired. Staying in 2nite. Sorry. Xoxo.

Well, that sucks. "Kenz's not coming," I shout to the girls. They crinkle their faces in disappointment.

Monica fans herself. "I need a drink!"

Lin and I nod in agreement and I say bye to Elliott, who gives me a wet kiss on the cheek, making me smile. My friends and I hold hands as we form a train through the party. In the hall, we see Joel and Kwami leaning against the wall. Seeing them fills me with a flicker of warm happiness. They hold out their fists, and we bump as we pass.

I call out to Joel as Lin pulls me along. "How many ciggies today?"

"Too many to count!" he calls back.

Kwami pulls his lips to the side and shakes his head, holding up his hand to form a circle. Zero? I open my mouth like *wow*, and Joel rolls his eyes. Lin yanks me forward as Monica yanks her. I keep my eyes on Joel's until we're out of sight.

Upstairs in the kitchen it's a disaster of bottles, cans, cups, and two-liters. Quinton is standing at a crystal punch bowl with a fancy pewter ladle that makes us laugh.

"Y'all like that, right?" he asks with a grin. "High class."

"What's in it?" Lin asks.

"Little o' this, little o' that," Quinton says.

He pours cups of red liquid and passes them out. I decline and grab an empty cup, filling it with ice from the freezer and water from the tap. I hold it up and we clink them together. Lin and Monica drink and then gasp simultaneously, coughing. Quinton brings a fist to his mouth and chortles. I'm guessing it's strong.

A huge new group of kids arrives, throwing their hands up and hollering lyrics as they come up the stairs, so we move out of the kitchen to let them in. We wind up in the dining room overlooking the backyard. The dining table is littered with trash, just like the kitchen. The whole place looks wild, like there's been a week-long party going on.

Wylie would love this party. The thought of him sends a pang of longing through me, and I brush it away. I miss that closeness. That feeling of being a partner in all ways. Having that one person who's *your* person. God, we used to laugh so much. Why did he throw that away? Am I doomed to always care for someone more than he cares for me, or vice versa? Is it possible that I'll ever find the person who loves me as much as I love him? Someone I'll still be holding hands with when we're old?

"What's wrong?" Lin asks, taking another gulp of her drink and giving her head a brisk shake.

"Nothing," I say. Then I decide to tell them. "I met my dad's girlfriend at the restaurant."

Both of their faces are mirrors of wide-eyed shock.

"What was she like?" Monica asks.

"Cute. Young. Nice."

"Well that's . . ." Lin glances at Monica. "Good?"

"I hate her," I say.

Monica nearly chokes on her drink and Lin says, "Okay, yeah, I hate her, too. Skank."

Now I snort a sad laugh. I stare down at the ice in my cup. "She's a waitress at his work."

They're both quiet, then Lin says, "I'm sorry, sweetie. I

know you're going through a lot. But in other news, your hair is on point. It's super smooth today."

I run a hand down my thick strands that took me two hours to straighten this morning, and still required a touch-up session before we came. "Thanks."

Monica peeks out the window. "Ooh, they're playing beer pong on a table out there. Let's go!"

This time we go out the sliding glass door and down a set of warped wooden steps to the back patio. Our feet trample weeds that have sprouted up through cracked concrete.

"I wanna play!" Monica says. She and Lin make their way into the teams of drunken players and I stand to watch, thoroughly content at that moment.

"Hey." Someone bumps me hard and I have to catch myself, spilling cold water over my hand. "Sorry!"

Dean's eyes are laughing when I look up at him, and my stomach spins. My smile is too big, but I cannot tame it.

"Hey," I say back.

He looks over at the game, grinning that dimpled smile of his. "This place is crazy, huh?" Beer pong players are fumbling and laughing.

"Yeah. And apparently the drinks are a little strong."

"I see that," he says. He takes his eyes from the game and looks me over, settling on my face with concern. "You doing okay?"

I nod. I'm about to answer him, when I feel compelled to look over, past the game, to where Joel and Kwami stand near the basement door. Joel is looking right at me, and something about his gaze is so strong, so focused, that all thought is knocked

194

from my brain. All I can do is stare back. Then his eyes slide to Dean. Before I can quite register it, Joel turns to Kwami and pulls out a cigarette. My stomach drops in disappointment.

"You sure?" Dean asks.

"Huh?" I look up at him and his expression turns funny.

"You sure you're okay?"

"Oh. Yeah." I look back at Joel, who is staring at me again as he moves the tip of the cigarette to the flame of his lighter. I give him a hard glare and shake my head. His returning grin is impish and challenging as he takes a drag.

"I'm gonna go get a drink," Dean says. "Need anything?"

Oh, crap. I was so distracted by Joel and his stupid oral fixation that I royally screwed up a chance for a conversation with Dean.

"No, I'm good, thanks. Are you coming back out?"

"Yup." He turns to go, and when I look back at the game, I catch Monica watching him walk up the stairs. Then she catches me eyeing her, and she quickly looks down at her drink. *Uuuuuugh*. Why, why, why?

I stomp over to Joel, wanting to rip the cancer stick from his mouth and crush it in my palm like She-Hulk.

"Something troubling you?" he asks coolly.

"I thought you quit."

He laughs outright, and God he's cute when his whole face smiles like that. "I don't recall ever saying that."

I put a sassy hand on my hip and exhale. "Whatever. Thanks for what you guys did that day at the mall."

Joel just looks at me, gives me a small incline of his head. "Rube's a stooge."

"Rube the boob," Kwami says with a laugh before walking off, leaving us. I step closer to Joel, crossing my arms.

He waves his cigarette at the crowd. "Who are you wanting to add to your list tonight, Zae?" Another drag. This time he makes smoke rings, which I reluctantly admire before his words hit me.

"There's *no list*."

He chuckles. "You're too easy to piss off. Relax."

"Why do you mess with me like that?" I ask. Then, wanting to mess with him right back, I ask, "You tryna get on my nonexistent list?" My stomach flips as he stills. Why did I ask that?

He looks straight at me and flicks his cigarette impressively far away.

"I'm tryna burn that list."

My body reacts before my mind does—flushing with warmth, my eyes glued to his, a weird pulsing in my belly. He steps toward me and I hold my breath as his face tips down, bypassing my lips and pressing softly against my neck. I involuntarily whimper at the feel of his mouth on my skin and the smell of cologne wafting off him.

He chuckles and walks away, leaving me staggering in a molten haze of lust.

Holy shit. I don't think I've ever been so turned on, and he barely did anything! I turn sluggishly to see Monica and Lin both gaping at me. They rush over.

"What was *that*?" Lin asks.

"I . . . have no idea," I say, reaching up to touch the hot spot on my neck.

"Oh my God, you should have seen the look on his face," Monica whispers in a loud hiss. "Girl, he wants you bad."

I shake my head. "He just likes to tease me. Did you know he used to hook up with Sierra?"

"Ew!" they both say in surprise.

"I know. Not my type." I'm going to keep telling myself that. Just thinking about the look in his eyes when he came toward me sends tingles dancing across my skin again. Things are going to be awkward between us now without a doubt, which makes me kind of sad.

"Isn't he a drug dealer?" Lin asks.

"I don't think so," I say. Though he definitely dabbles with that crowd.

"I need another drink." Monica holds up her empty cup and Lin agrees, so the three of us head back up the steps to the sliding glass door. The kitchen's even more crowed now and harder to get to the punch bowl, which Quinton is filling with generic-brand cartons of random juices, lemon-lime soda, and bottles of rail vodka and gin. He tosses the empty bottles to the counter. I find Dean just getting his cup. He walks over to me as the girls wait in line. My eyes slide over the room, wondering where Joel went. Then I remember how I ruined my last chance with Dean, and I force myself to focus.

"Wanna go downstairs and dance?" I ask.

He sips and nods. I smile. This is my chance.

Two of his giant football friends show, and we wait together while the girls get their drinks. Dean and his guys down their punch, and then Junior, by far the largest linebacker on the team, takes out the case of beer he's been carrying under his arm. The three of them guzzle beer after beer while I gawk. I glance around for Joel again, but he is nowhere. I wonder where he went. I wonder why I care. He's just a friend.

I'm tryna burn that list. I shiver. He didn't mean it.

By the time Lin and Monica are back, the guys are sufficiently buzzed and we squeeze our way down the crowded stairs to the basement. My heart bangs when we pass the place where Joel and Kwami were standing before, but they're not there.

The entire main basement room has turned into a dance floor, and the only light comes from a single dim lamp in the far corner. A thumping beat shakes the walls, and the football players lift their muscled arms into the air. We dance and dance. Junior lifts me high into the air by my waist and I squeal, locking my arms on his shoulders, and tucking my head so I don't hit the low ceiling. When he sets me down, I stumble into Dean, who smiles as he rights me.

I've been avoiding trying to dance with him, worried about upsetting Monica, but when he places a hand to my back and pulls me forward, I go with it. This is what I've been waiting for. I see Monica pull Lin from the dance floor, and Lin looks back to mouth *bathroom* to me. I nod and let myself focus on Dean.

Dancing with him is effortless. He smiles the whole time, and it's contagious. Everywhere I place my hands—his arms, shoulders, chest, waist—is hard with muscle. When he leans down, my heart pounds. But he's only trying to tell me something. *Ugh!*

"I'm gonna get another drink!" he shouts.

Impatience and frustration flare.

He holds up his cup to Junior, who yells, "Get me one, bro!"

Dean is proving to be a difficult target.

Across the basement I see Elliott still dancing, one hand up as he jumps to the beat. He's got a limitless supply of energy, sweat dripping down the sides of his face. I dance with Junior and the other guys for what feels like forever. My friends don't come back. Dean doesn't come back. An icky sensation slithers through me. Are they okay? Did they get caught up in a conversation somewhere and forget about me? Or is this like the Rex thing in middle school where he left me hanging at the dance with no intention of coming back? No. It couldn't be.

Without explaining to Dean's friends, I make my way off the dance floor. Down the small hall is a line for the bathroom, and an opening to a dark, doorless room that looks like a workroom. I catch sight of Lin's shoulder in that doorway, her back to the room. She's looking down at her phone.

My heart begins to gallop faster with each approaching step I take. I peer past her into the dark room, and sure enough, Monica and Dean are going at it. Kissing. Hands everywhere. I step back, stomach churning. Lin suddenly looks up and her eyes bulge.

"Zae . . ."

Oh my God.

I spin and press through the people on the stairs. I go straight up. Up through the packed kitchen, where Sierra and Meeka give me small waves, to where Quinton sits on the edge of the sink. I've been holding my water cup this whole time, long empty. I hold it out to him.

"I'm ready for a drink."

His grin is huge as he nods. "That's right." He scoops some into my cup and grabs a marker. "This one got your name all over it, girl."

Sure enough, it says *Zay, ZAY, zay* all over. I ignore the misspelling and thank him. Without moving from that spot, I chug the entire cup, not breathing through my nose. When I finish, my throat, esophagus, and stomach flame and I exhale in a hot rush. I hand him my cup and he gladly refills it. I chug again.

"Dang, Zae!"

I'm on the verge of either screaming or crying, so I hold up my cup again. "One more."

Now he slaps a leg and laughs before he fills it.

"Zae!" Lin's voice catches me halfway through my third cup. "What are you doing? You're supposed to be our DD!" Everyone in the kitchen turns to watch. The music thumps in my ears, making my head throb.

I think about how Lin kept guard for Monica.

"Get a new ride," I say.

Lin's expression wars between disapproval and guilt. I tilt back the rest of the cup and her jaw clenches.

"Who are we supposed to ask?" Lin demands. "Everyone's been drinking!"

Quinton steps down and slides an arm around both of us. "Y'all can stay here, you know."

"There you go." I point to Quinton and smile big at Lin. "Problem solved."

She slides away from him and crosses her arms. "That's fucked-up, Zae."

I move into her face, feeling the sudden whoosh of a buzz. "Don't talk to me about fucked-up."

Again, guilt flashes across her face. "I'm sorry!" she says through gritted teeth. She moves closer, whispering so only I can hear. "Dean didn't write those poems, Zae. He didn't even know they were about you." She sounds almost apologetic, but my whole body tenses with horror.

"You *asked* him? You told him I thought it was him?"

She pushes her hair behind her ears and turns her eyes down, as if she's realizing how much of an idiot that makes me look. The sting of betrayal swirls with the liquor in my belly, burning like acid, making me dizzy.

She shakes her head. "No. I mean—"

I move past her and the other people watching to pour myself another cup. I hear Lin let out a growl of frustration as she stomps away. Several people laugh, enjoying the drama. I cannot drink fast enough. I've only really been drunk once before, and I remember how numbing it was when it hit me. I need that again. I cannot believe they talked with Dean about the poems. It's beyond humiliating. The demoralizing feeling flooding my system is the same as I felt the night Wylie cheated.

Sierra and Meeka sidle up, their lips glossy and bright with smiles. Oh, no.

"So," says Sierra as I drink. "You and Joel?"

She takes a sip and eyes me over the rim, but I can see the calculation in her gaze.

"No," I tell her. "Just friends. Why? Do you still love him?"

Her nostrils flare and her eyes go wide. The laugh she emits is caustic. "I never loved him. *God*."

Meeka laughs at that notion and studies me. "Someone said y'all kissed outside."

"No, we didn't." What is wrong with people and their big, stupid mouths?

"But you're into him," Sierra teases. "This makes two parties that you've been spotted at together."

"*Talking.* As friends." The words are sour on my tongue. I blame the alcohol, not the fact that the feel of Joel's lips still lingers.

"All right," Sierra says. "If you're not into him, prove it. Kiss someone else."

I spin around to see who I can prove my innocence with, and the room spins with me. I reach for the counter, and Meeka and Sierra laugh.

"Whoa, girl," Meeka says. I nearly smile, despite how annoyed I am, because the alcohol is finally hitting me. And not a moment too soon.

My attention goes straight to the loudest voice and biggest smile in the room.

Quinton. Star point guard. Buzz supplier.

I go right up to him, pressing my body to his and putting a hand to his cheek. His smile falls as he peers down at me, frozen. To be honest, half the reason I'm all pressed against him is because I suddenly feel unbalanced, my equilibrium off. I try to blink away the memory of just how much alcohol he dumped in that punch.

"Can I help you?" he says in a low voice.

"Kiss me?"

His full, tender lips come straight down onto mine, and his

kiss is slow and sultry. The entire kitchen raises an "*OHHH!*"

Someone yanks me from behind by the belt loop. Meeka. She puts an arm around me, almost protectively, and says to Quinton, "I don't think so." The look she gives him is filled with warning, and he grins as he holds his palms up.

Meeka turns me away from him and the room goes splotchy. Voices mute and warp. Figures are fuzzy and shadowy. I rub my eyes.

"Now look what you've done," Sierra says. She runs her thumbs roughly under my eyes to get off the mascara.

In that moment I want to cry, because Sierra and Meeka are being nicer than my own friends.

"I love you guys," I say thickly.

"Oh my God, you're so drunk." Sierra laughs, rubbing my arm. "What the hell happened with you and Lin?"

"Nothing." My eyes well up, and I take another drink.

"No more." Meeka takes my cup and flings it into the sink where it spills out.

I stare at it, morbidly fascinated by the red splatter dripping.

"Are you about to puke?" Sierra asks.

It's hard to lift my head. "I need to sit."

"Take her outside," Sierra tells Meeka, and she complies.

We sit on the steps and I close my eyes as I lean my head on the splintery rail . . . so heavy. I flop over onto the cozy wood.

"You can't lie here," Meeka says. "People need to get by."

I feel her tugging at me, but I can't get up. It's the perfect place to lie.

. . .

. . .

203

"Damn, what happened?" Kwami? I try and fail to open my eyes.

"What does it look like, dumbass?" Meeka snaps.

. . .

. . .

. . .

"What are you doing?" Meeka.

Something touches my butt, but I can't move. I'm so heavy.

"I'm getting her phone to call her mom." Monica?

"*Noo*," I moan. "*Lee me lone . . .*"

Monica's voice sounds far away. Who is she talking to?

"We need to get her out front." Lin. "Sweetie, can you walk?"

I laugh, a slurred sound.

"I'll carry her." Dean!

"No, I got her." Joel . . . my neck kisser. I feel myself heaved and lifted, and I'm surrounded by his cologne.

"You *lefff* me," I murmur into his neck.

"You wanted to chase after Big Boy."

What? My body lightly bumps up and down as he walks around the house. I close my eyes, his words sliding around in my mind and then falling into the underbrush of my tangled consciousness.

. . .

. . .

. . .

Darkness.

. . .

I'm jostling, bouncing, and the world is spinning way too

fast. My stomach is turning inside out. My throat burns.

. . .

A single, comforting voice, murmuring.

"Ma . . . ?"

"Shh . . ."

. . .

. . .

. . .

Softness.

CHAPTER TWENTY-THREE

Sunday Morning

Utter confusion accompanies dizziness as I blink against the brightness. Nothing is where it should be. The window is on the wrong side. My vision begins to clear, and I hear breathing.

Mom is sleeping beside me. I'm in her room, in her full-size bed. With this clarity comes a wave of nausea and I roll the other way, so glad to see the trash can next to me. I grasp it and heave, my stomach muscles tired and sore. Nothing comes out. Mom rubs my back.

"You scared me last night," she says softly. "I almost took you to the hospital. No one could tell me how much you drank."

Tears of shame spring to my eyes. My voice rasps painfully. "I'm sorry."

She sighs and crawls past me, climbing out of bed. "You're

grounded for two weeks. You can take the van to school and work only. And you get to finish cleaning the inside of it today." She faces me, looking tired with her hands on her hips. "I know you're going through a lot, Xanderia, but this is not the way to deal with it." She leaves me and I look at the clock. 10:19. There is no way we're making it to church. And, oh, my gosh . . . did Mom have to take off work today because of me? They're always busy on holidays.

I'm shaking as I stand and take the trash can into my own room, where I cry tears of remorse and pity and humiliation. I'm terrified to look at my phone, which I'm so lucky she didn't take away from me. I never want to go to school again.

I cry for so long that I'm probably dehydrated.

At eleven Zeb comes in, approaching carefully with a grilled cheese sandwich on a plate. It actually smells really good, which I take as a positive sign.

"Mom said you're sick?"

I'm way past BS'ing my brother. "I drank too much last night, Zeb. It was stupid. Don't ever drink." I start crying again. "Please *don't ever drink!*" I blow my nose on a tissue.

Zeb backs slowly out of the room. "Okay," he says as he hits the door and rushes out, shutting it behind him.

I've just scarred him for life.

I nibble a quarter of the sandwich and manage to keep it down. Then I get so thirsty that I rush to the kitchen and drink three glasses from the tap in a row. My stomach immediately revolts and I pant as I bend over the sink, praying it will stay down. Mom gets up from the table and shuts herself in her room, and that's when I spot two Easter baskets on the table.

My heart squeezes with regret.

After a couple of minutes my stomach calms and everything stays down.

Zeb stares at me from the couch with dismay as I drag my wretched self back to my bedroom and collapse on the bed.

My phone dings and my heart explodes in fear. I don't want to deal with anyone.

When I see Kenz's number, I exhale in relief. She is about the only person in the world I can handle right now.

Are u OK? What happened?

I'm sure she's heard from Lin and Monica, and now she's looking for my side of the story.

Instead of trying to text it, I call her, lying back on the bed with my eyes closed. I tell her every detail I can remember. Bless her, she murmurs and gasps in all the right places.

"I feel like Dean kind of led you on," she says.

I pinch the skin between my eyes. "I don't know. Maybe. He's always been nice, though. I guess I just hoped, and I read him wrong . . . God, I'm so stupid. He never liked me." The thought is like a kick to the chest.

"It's okay, Zae. I probably would have felt the same, and I thought he was the one writing the poems, too. I don't think they should have told him, and I said as much when I talked to them. Now I think they're mad at me, too, but whatever."

"I don't want you guys to fight."

"I don't want them to fight with you either." She pauses. "You're not mad that they called your mom, are you?"

The thought of my mom is too much. "No. I mean, what other choice was there?" Worry prickles my neck. "Wait, how did they get home?" If Lin had to call her parents, she would be in so much trouble.

"You don't know?!"

"Oh, no, what?"

"It was a huge ordeal. Your mom drove you guys in the van. Then that Joel guy followed in your mom's car, and his friend Kwami followed them to take Joel home once they got to your apartment."

And I'm dead. I cover my face with a hand, as if I can hide from it all.

Dead.

"I should've been there," Kenzie says.

"It's not your fault." My hand still covers my face. A small knock sounds at my door, and Mom opens it. "I have to go."

"Okay, call me later."

I disconnect and sit up as Mom sits on the bed. I know it's completely pathetic, but I break down crying again. I have no idea how it's possible to cry any more.

"I'm sorry," I sob.

"Being the designated driver is a big responsibility."

"I know. I do. I never drink like that. I just . . . I got in a fight with Lin and Monica. And . . ." I sniffle.

"Let me guess," she says. "Over a boy?"

My face flushes with the shame of it, and I look down at my hands. "I can't go back to school."

"You can, and you will."

I moan. "Please, Mom. I made a fool of myself. I screwed everything up."

"And you'll have to face it. Life goes on."

209

"Please!" I beg.

"No." Her voice is firm, and my defenses spike.

"You don't understand!"

"I understand more than you know." She stands, giving me a pain-filled glare, then leaves me, closing the door hard behind herself.

I collapse face-first like a corpse on my bed until I hear a low sound coming from Mom's room. I get up and press my ear to the wall. When I recognize the muffled sounds of her crying, my insides feel like they're being pressed in a waffle iron. I snatch up my earbuds and shove them into my ears, blasting the music as loud as I can handle it.

It hits me then that I won the spring break kissing contest. I kissed five guys, Lin and Monica kissed four, and Kenzie kissed two. But I don't feel like I won anything. I most definitely feel like I lost. And now it's over. I'm done.

Back to School

End of Junior Year

CHAPTER TWENTY-FOUR

Before school the next morning I get a text from Lin: **My mom will take M & me 2 school on her way to work. Thnx**

K, I tell her. I knew that was coming, but it still hurts.

I pick up Kenzie and she makes small talk as I drive, trying to act like everything is fine, but my stomach is in a tight double knot when we pull into the student parking lot.

I linger at my locker as long as possible, spotting Lin and Monica as they pass on the other side of the hall, not looking my way. I feel heavy all over again as I trudge to math. I thought it was bad when I came to school without a boyfriend anymore. Coming to school without two of my friends at my side feels like I'm limping along without an arm and a leg. I don't know how to live this way.

And when Kenzie leaves my side after class, I feel more

alone than ever. I keep my head down as I walk to my locker to switch books.

"Hey, Zae." I turn toward Taro's voice. His locker is a few down from mine. He tilts his head, giving me a glimpse of both eyes through his hair. "You okay?"

"Yeah," I force myself to say. He wasn't at Quinton's party. Maybe he doesn't know about what a fool I made of myself. "You?"

"Good," he says.

We walk side by side to English, and I feel overly grateful not to be alone, even though we don't say a word.

We slink into English class, and I swear every single person is staring at me. I catch the intense gazes of Joel, Dean, Angelo, Flynn, Elliott . . . *everyone*, before I drop my eyes and slide into my desk, heart pounding.

When Mrs. Warfield calls on me to read a passage from the book halfway through class, I know she's disappointed that I don't use my usual clear, loud, animated voice. She gives me a funny look afterward, and I keep my head down the rest of class. When the bell rings, I bolt.

If I can just make it through this day, tomorrow will be better.

I meet Kenzie outside her AP English class and we walk to our lockers. When we turn the corner to the locker bay, Kenzie gasps, and I look up. Eight freshmen and sophomore JV baseball players are sitting on top of the lockers in a row. Every year the varsity team hazes them, making them do crazy things. What are they up to this year? When they catch sight of us, they each hold up a sign.

KENZIE WILL YOU GO TO PROM WITH
VINCENT?

She covers her mouth with a squeak, and a soft smile lifts my cheeks. Holy sweetness. Like, so sweet I'm about to get cavities. Vincent is standing in front of her locker holding a rose, looking bashful, and she runs, plowing into him with a hug. Then she looks up and nods, and everyone cheers.

"Get down from there!" a teacher yells, and the JV players hop down, running off.

I give my beaming friend a smile from my locker as I switch out my huge English book for French III. I don't want to go over and ruin their moment, so I shut my locker and head to my next class, keeping my eyes locked on the ground.

I can't believe it's almost prom time. Am I going? I have no desire. *Ugh.* Just another freaking thing to add to my plate of stress with a side of sadness.

As soon as I walk into French, Mrs. Hartt pulls me aside. She's also our cheer coach.

"I'm guessing you've heard about the roundoff back hand-spring?"

"Yeah." I glance away nervously.

"Listen, Zae, you know how competitive things are getting. I wouldn't have agreed to this requirement if I didn't think you could get it in time. We can't lose you. You're too good."

She has way more faith in me than I do.

"I don't have money for lessons."

She bites her lip in thought. "Can you practice with the other girls? Have them spot you?"

I want to laugh at the irony. My only friend I can ask now

is Kenzie, and she's so small. I shrug. "I'll work on it."

"Good." She smiles and gives my shoulder a squeeze as the bell rings.

I'm despondent and have a hard time focusing through class. I'm in a little bit of a daze when I walk into the hallway afterward. So much so, that I'm completely confused when Meeka grabs my arm and pulls me aside like there's a fire or something.

"Zae!" she whispers. "You need to watch your back. Camille Fletcher is after you."

Wait . . . "*What*?!" Camille is not a girl I'd ever mess with. "Why?"

"She heard about you and Quinton and now she wants to kick your ass."

Sheer panic overtakes me. "But she wasn't there! I didn't think they were together anymore!"

"They've been off and on since eighth grade," Meeka says. "But even when they're off, they're still on. You know what I'm sayin'?"

Yeah. He's hers. A tremble courses through me. This cannot be happening.

"I didn't know," I ramble. "There's nothing going on with us. It was just one stupid, little, meaningless kiss! Can't you tell her it was nothing?"

"Girl, we ain't friends!"

Oh, crap. Oh, crap. I am dead. I've never been in a fight.

"Just watch out for her," Meeka warns. "I gotta go."

My eyes dart around the hall. Camille, when she actually comes to school, is always surrounded by an entourage of scary-ass girls. She always seems larger than life with her voluptuous body, long nails, and platinum hair usually pulled up in a tight ponytail with extensions that hang halfway down her back. I cannot believe I forgot about her and Quinton. Stupid, stupid alcohol!

I speed walk to history and rush through the door, happy to see old Mr. Hawk. Camille won't mess with me in front of a teacher. I really wish I could tell Monica and Lin, but I feel cut off from them. Disconnected. Like I'm not allowed. I can't run to them for support when we haven't even made up.

"Today is guidance day," Mr. Hawk reminds us. I'd forgotten all about guidance day. It's when we talk to our counselors about our schedule for next year. We shuffle to our feet and I end up walking next to Angelo with his wide smile. I glance around the halls nervously, even though class is going on and hopefully Camille is in a room.

"I heard you took a siesta on Quinton's deck," Angelo whispers, nudging me with his elbow.

I give him a light shove, which makes him laugh.

"Quiet!" Mr. Hawk whispers over his shoulder.

I'm not in the mood to fake the funk when I sit down in front of Mrs. Crowley.

"How are things at home?"

"Awful. I don't want to talk about it."

Her penciled eyebrows rise. "I'm sorry to hear that. My door is open if you change your mind."

I tap the arms of my chair, my knee bouncing.

"And what are your plans postgraduation, Zae? Have you taken any time to think about it over break?"

"I don't know," I answer. "College, I guess."

She gives me a small smile. "And where do you plan to apply?"

I shake my head. I feel . . . inadequate whenever this subject comes up. Lin and her parents have already started college tours. All my friends know where they're applying.

"Where do you think I can get in?" I ask.

She presses her lips together and looks down at my paperwork. "Well, your grades are good. All As and Bs, but the problem is your course load. You've chosen all regular classes. I believe I urged you last year to sign up for an honors or advanced placement course. That's what colleges are really looking for."

I rub my sweating palms down my jeans.

"I only care about the foreign languages. I want to take Spanish four and French four next year."

"And you're doing very well in both. To be in the fourth level of two languages is impressive. Can you apply that same effort to English and history?"

I shake my head. I have no interest in taking those AP courses, reading all those boring old books, and writing millions of papers. My friends always have tons of homework.

"Mrs. Crowley, what kinds of jobs can I do with a language background besides teaching? What if . . ." I can't believe I'm saying this out loud. "What if I don't want to go to college?"

She examines me in silence for a long time, making me squirm. "I'm really not sure what language-related careers are out there that don't require a degree, but I can look into it if you'd like?"

"Yes. Please."

Mrs. Crowley nods and makes a note on my file.

My parents will be disappointed. They want me to be the first in the family to go to college. I wanted that, too—to make them proud—so the thought of abandoning it leaves me disheartened and anxious. But it's their dream for me, not mine. My dream is to travel and make use of my foreign languages, but there's not exactly a job for that, at least, not one I know of. I know I'm going to be stuck being a secretary or something, translating for immigrants who haven't learned English yet, and there's nothing wrong with that. Any job is respectable, in my opinion, but it doesn't make me excited. I guess not everyone can have a job they love.

Lunch is terrible, despite the number of people who approach me, laughing and giving me fist bumps. Apparently I was very entertaining in the kitchen at Quinton's. Kenzie and I can't stop staring around the room, waiting for Camille to show. Monica chooses to sit at a table across the cafeteria with a few other cheerleaders and dancers, and Kenzie looks sadder than I've ever seen her.

"Vincent's promposal was super cute," I say.

This makes her light up. "Yeah." She pokes at the chicken patty on her tray. I usually get on her case about eating, but I can't say anything today since I don't have an appetite either. "Maybe you can go with one of his friends. I'm sure Brent would love to take you."

I start shaking my head before she even finishes the sentence. I've been thinking about it since this morning. Prom is about romance and couples dancing and gazing and all that gag-worthy stuff.

"I don't want to go."

"Please, Zae?" She reaches across and grabs my hand. "What if you're on the prom court?"

"What? No." We both glance toward the busy table by the windows where student council reps are taking silent ballot nominations for junior-class prom prince and princess, and senior-class prom king and queen. There's no way I'll be nominated. I've pretty much ruined my reputation lately.

As I'm gazing around, alert, I see Joel and Kwami outside in the open-air courtyard. Joel looks over at that exact moment, and our eyes snag through the windows, making my heart grow hummingbird wings. We stare for two fat seconds before he turns back to Kwami and doesn't look my way again. My heart fluttering weakens. I should go thank him or apologize or something, but I'm so embarrassed.

"Come on." Kenzie stands with her tray. "Let's vote before the bell rings."

I have no interest, but I follow her anyway. I write Kenzie's and Vincent's names on ballots and put them in the boxes at the table.

Panic sets in when we part ways by our lockers and I head toward the foreign-language wing for Spanish class. I probably look psychotic the way I keep glancing behind me. And then, as I round the corner, everything in me seizes.

There, at the end of the hall, is Camille. With her sleek hair and nails that can shred a face. She and all her girls lift their chins when they catch sight of me across the expanse of students.

"Shit!" I breathe. I duck into the nearest set of doors, which happen to be to the guidance department, and come face-to-face with Joel. His eyes widen, and I'm so damn happy to see him.

I blurt, "Camille wants to kill me!"

He scrutinizes my face and says, "Ah. Quinton. Stay here."

I hiss, "What are you doing?" as he slips out the door. I sneak a peek through the glass pane of the door and watch him stop in front of Camille and her friends. He appears at ease. Unintimidated. The door is open a crack, and I strain to listen. As the bell time nears, the halls get quieter, leaving behind the rush of late feet on tile. I can hear their voices down the hall.

"Camille," he says politely.

"You tryna hide that girl?"

Joel sounds steady in comparison to Camille's sassy tone. She knows I'm in here. I'm glad all the counselors are in their rooms with their doors shut. The office area is quiet and calming, but my heart still thuds with the possibility of violence.

"I'm afraid I can't let you touch her," Joel says. "I was there that night. She was drunk, and her girls dared her to kiss someone. It was nothing. She's not after Q."

"I don't give a damn about some lil' peck in the kitchen. I care about her going in his room with him."

What?! My breathing halts. Is that what people are saying? Ugh, I freaking hate high school sometimes!

"She never went anywhere with him. After the kitchen incident I helped take her home."

I hear her smack her lips. "My friend saw him go up in his room with a cheerleading girl."

"You need to ask your friend to fact-check, because it wasn't Zae Monroe."

A long pause follows before she says, "All right. Imma check. But if they say it was her, you can't save your girl, you hear me?"

"I hear you, Cam. And I know the truth, so I ain't worried."

I flatten myself against the wall until the girls walk away. Two seconds later my heart jumps as Joel opens the door and slips in like smoke.

He eyes me. "You're good."

"Thank you." It comes out a pathetic blast of air. God, I'm a wimp.

"Don't worry about it."

I can't let it go. It's too good to be true. "You know her?"

"Kinda. Her best friend used to go with Kwami."

The bell rings and I let out a gust of breath, looking at the clock.

"I can write you a pass," he says. How awesome that the guidance aides can do that.

Joel might have a bad rep, and I have no idea what he did in the past, but he's now the nicest damn person I know.

"Thank you." Worst day ever.

I watch Joel scratching words on the green notepad with his left hand bent over it. He tears off the sheet and hands it to me, but I'm not ready to leave him yet.

"Hey." I fidget with the pass in my fingers. "About Saturday . . ."

"Nothin' to say." His eyes are bright blue under the

fluorescent lights. He seems taller than usual. Maybe because I've raised him to hero status.

I spit it out. "Thank you for helping me, and I'm sorry."

He cocks his head, regarding me thoughtfully, and I can't help but look at those lips that kissed my neck so softly. The memory makes me jittery and nervous.

"Your mom's cool," he says.

Weird. Such a clash of my worlds. I survey him, and he stands there and lets me.

"Joel, were you high when you . . ." I touch my neck.

His lips tighten. "I haven't been high in seven months, not since my brother was thrown in prison for dealing. And you think I'd drive your mom's car while I was high? Come on now."

"Oh. No, I'm sorry." I just can't figure out why he said and did what he did at the party when he doesn't seem interested any other time. And, wait, his brother was a dealer? So that's where the rumors come from.

"Did you meet with Mrs. Crowley today?" he asks.

His complete change of subject makes me blink. "Uh, yeah."

"Okay." And that's all he says.

I glance down at my pass. "I guess I should go."

We stare a few seconds longer before I turn, feeling way warmer than the moment warrants. Before I walk out, I go on my tiptoes to peek out the glass pane of the door. Joel comes up behind me to look, too. I'm suddenly very, very aware of him against my back, his breath warm on my neck as he peers out beside me. My whole body stiffens and my breath hitches as I turn my head to catch his eye, so close. He freezes, too. Then, I swear, he moves forward an inch more, and I feel the front of him brush against my backside. It takes every bit of willpower not to press against him.

And just like that, I'm on fire. Practically panting from a boy's breath on my skin and the whisper of a touch through our clothes. Oh, my damn, I really want him to touch me and kiss me and—

He abruptly pulls back from me and juts his chin at the door, shoving his hands in his pockets.

"All clear. See you 'round."

I can't even talk. All I can do is force a stiff nod as I pull the door open. I rush down the hall to Spanish, using the pass to fan my heated face. Joel is a hard guy to read, but I find myself wanting to read him more and more each time we meet.

CHAPTER TWENTY-FIVE

I show up at Zeb's bus stop after school with a giant Slurpee in hand. Bribery. It's impossible not to notice that he's now as tall as me, but skinny like a string bean. I hope he's up for the challenge I'm about to propose.

"I need your help today," I say, pulling into a parking spot at our apartment building. "I need you to keep me from breaking my neck as I try to learn a roundoff back handspring."

"A what-a-what?" He takes a long pull on his red straw as he climbs out of the van and follows me to a grassy area between our building and the next.

"Gymnastics," I explain. "I need it for tryouts."

He sits crisscross on the grass while I warm up and do backbends to stretch. When he finishes his drink, I pull him to his feet and show him exactly what he'll have to do.

225

"Bend your knees. Keep your palm flat to my lower back. Just follow my movement. If I go too low, keep the pressure there. You gotta be strong and firm."

"Are you gonna kick me in the face?"

"Hopefully not."

He laughs, and I can't help myself. I grab him and pull him into a tight squeeze. His arms flail and he swivels to get away from me, so I shove him away with a smile.

"Let's do this."

We start with standing back handsprings. I'm a little rusty, and I forgot how much I hate doing this. I don't know how the other girls dive backward so gracefully without a worry in the world. It's unnatural to me. I do several, nervous each time, and Zeb starts to get the hang of it.

"Okay," I tell him. "It's going to get tricky now. I have to go straight from a running roundoff into the back handspring. So you have to follow me as I go and get your hand in there." I do several roundoffs so he can get a feel for how far I'll move.

He wets his lips and nods. "Got it."

The first two times I chicken out, jumping straight up in the air to see how much height I can get. On try number three, I twist to the side, coming down on my wrist. Zeb dives forward to try and help. We both end up in a pile.

Laughter tinkles down to us, and we look up to see Mom on the balcony, motherly pride and adoration on her face. I rub my wrist and get back up.

"Again," I say.

The failed attempts go on longer than I care to admit. Half the time I freak out and stop. When I do it again, Zeb growls.

"Zae, just do it already! I'm getting hungry."

"You just had a huge Slurpee!"

"That was, like, an hour and a half ago."

I look up at Mom, who nods that he's right. I flop down on the grass, frustrated and tired. And then, to my amazement, Zeb runs, does a sloppy roundoff with his feet too far apart, throws himself backward, and does a back handspring, stumbling but staying upright. My mouth falls open.

"How did you do that?!"

His eyes are as huge as his smile. "That was awesome!"

"It's because he's not scared, sweetie, and you are," Mom says from above us.

My hands clench. I *am* scared. I don't know how to stop being scared. I yank out a handful of grass and throw it. "I'm done."

When we get upstairs, Mom pulls a piece of grass from my hair. "How was school?"

"Bad."

She sighs. "I brought broccoli soup and sourdough bread from the shop. Let's eat."

The rest of the week is more of the same. I avoid everyone but Kenz, and everyone avoids me. It's really freaking depressing. How long are we going to do this? I feel sick about it every day.

Friday morning comes, and there is a crowd around the grassy knoll at the side of the school. Kenzie and I press in on our way up from the parking lot to see what everyone is murmuring and smiling about.

On the side of the green hill, written in colorful, real flowers, is a message:

Monica, prom? Dean.

It hits me way harder than it should, in a jumble of harsh emotions.

Kenz gasps at my side and *aw*s. It's beautiful. It really is. I have to swallow several times. Looking around, I don't see Dean and Monica, so I assume she's already seen it, said yes, and gone happily inside the building.

I trudge with the crowd up the stairs and into the school. When I get to English, I slump into a seat. Am I jealous? Yes, but not in the traditional way. I had a mad crush on Dean, but I have to face the fact he doesn't like me like that. The knowledge is humbling, but mostly because I was mistaken. He only ever liked Monica. He was my friend, and he wanted to get to her. That's fine. It's not Dean that I want, it's love in general, which makes me mad at myself. I don't *want* to want love, but it's part of who I am.

And then there's Monica. I never dreamed we'd not be friends. It's hard to accept the fact that she just got the most gorgeous promposal I've ever seen, and I wasn't at her side to jump up and down and hug her. It's all wrong. The loss is gutting me.

A figure stops beside me and I suck in a breath as I look up at Dean. My face heats with embarrassment.

"Hey," I say, clearing my dry throat.

"You okay?" he asks.

I nod. "Mm-hm. I liked your, um, the flowers. It was pretty." I force myself to look up at him, despite the knowledge that my face is embarrassingly red.

"She said no," he tells me.

My abs squeeze, and I frown. "What?"

"Well, she said 'maybe,' which is a no." He shrugs, like it's no biggie, but it's a show. He is hurt. I stare up at him in shock, at a complete loss for words. He's telling me this for a reason.

The bell rings, and he moves to the back to sit. I turn to watch him go, but what I end up seeing is Joel watching me, unsmiling. He pulls his hood up to hide his eyes, leans back, and crosses his arms. What is his problem?

I face forward, trying to digest Dean's revelation. Why on Earth would Monica not say yes? The only conclusion I can come to is . . . me.

"Good morning, Panthers," says the senior president over the announcement speakers. "Please stand for the Pledge of Allegiance."

I push to my feet with the others, covering my heart and reciting the pledge. Then we sit again.

"Here are your top three nominations for junior-class prom princess and prince. Quinton Green. Kyle Fairchild. Dean Prescott." The class cheers. I glance back at Dean, who doesn't even crack a smile. "Monica Sanchez." My insides squeeze with pride for her. "Meeka Washington. And Zae Monroe. Now for your top three senior nominees . . ." *What?!* The announcements are lost in an array of excited voices congratulating me and my own blood pounding in my ears. People pat my shoulders. I cannot believe they just said my name. I do *not* want to go to prom. And now Monica and Dean need to go more than ever.

I glance back at Dean again, but he's not wearing his

trademark smile. He's staring off into space. Then my eyes shift to Joel, whose eyes are cracked open at me. When he sees me looking, he closes his eyes and keeps them shut. Fine.

I catch Taro looking at me with his one revealed eye, reflecting kindness and concern. It makes me emotional and I have to turn away.

I'm a wreck until the bell rings. Monica is all the way upstairs in science. It'll be difficult to get to her without being late, but I have to. I run. I nearly bowl her over outside the smelly science hall that reeks of sulfur. I grab her arm and she looks at me with surprise, a hint of red around her eyes.

"Monica!" I'm panting.

"What?" She gently pulls away, looking down.

"Why didn't you say yes? You should say yes!"

Her jaw clenches with surprise. "I didn't tell anyone that yet."

"*He* told me." Her eyes widen, and I go on. "He's really sad, Monica."

Guilt shrouds her face and makes her shoulders hunch. "He'll be fine. It's not worth it." I was right. She said no because of me.

"Look, Monica, I'm sorry." I'm still trying to catch my breath. "I never should have—"

"No, *I'm* sorry." She chokes up. "I've been feeling like crap since Saturday. It's not worth it if you're not going to talk to me anymore."

Me not talk to her? "Monica, I'm over it, okay? You should

go with him. He's . . . a good guy."

"I don't want you to be mad at me. Or sad."

"The only thing I was mad or sad about today was that I wasn't by your side to support you when you saw that message." I swallow hard. "It was so perfect, and you deserve it." My voice cracks.

Monica wipes under her eyes. "But if I go with him, who would you go with?"

"I don't want to go."

"You have to! You're up for prom princess!"

"I don't care."

"Miss Sanchez," calls her science teacher from the doorway.

Monica gives me one last look before dashing into her class. I run down the hall as the bell rings. I will happily take the tardy.

The three of us are together at lunch again. The atmosphere at our table is strained, and we're all quiet, but we're together. Nobody mentions prom. Nobody mentions Dean. Nobody mentions anything that could be a trigger.

"Lin is visiting Virginia Tech this weekend," Monica says. Lin hasn't apologized to me, but I haven't said sorry to her either. I think we both know we equally screwed up.

"I can see her as a Hokie." Kenzie smiles and takes a nibble of her yogurt. "My mom is taking me dress shopping today." Her cheeks darken, probably realizing she just brought up prom in a roundabout way, but nobody reacts.

"Send us pics," I say. That seems to make her happy.

"Wait, aren't you grounded from your phone?" she asks.

"I'm grounded from going out the next two weeks, but I get to keep my phone, thank God."

We eat quietly together.

During Spanish, my stomach does a flip when Joel shows at the door with a pass for me to go to guidance. He doesn't talk or acknowledge me as we walk. After about two seconds I can't take it anymore.

"Are you mad at me?" I ask.

"For what?" He keeps his eyes straight ahead.

"I don't know. Anything?"

"Nope."

"Because I thought we were cool, but you're acting weird."

"Weird?" He doesn't pause in his walk. "You hardly know me."

Ouch.

I'm still confused and kind of hurt when he drops me at Mrs. Crowley's office. He leaves her door open a few inches, and I'm betting he's totally eavesdropping from the office area. For some reason, I don't mind.

"Miss Monroe," she says with a smile. "I've done a bit of research, and I hope you're doing the same." Whoops. "Being bilingual or multilingual will be an amazing addition to your résumé for any job. Do you feel that you are bilingual?"

I shake my hand in the air to say so-so. She nods.

"Well, I came across this and thought of you." She hands me a pamphlet. *Study Abroad!*

"Is this a college program?" I ask, confused.

She twines her fingers on the desk in front of her. "No. This would be for your senior year. Like a foreign exchange program, but different. You would have a choice of going to one country for the entire year, or splitting it up and doing one country for the first semester and another country for the second. For you, I would recommend Argentina and France."

My heart jumps. "Wait, you mean I'd be gone the whole year? How would I graduate?"

"I've looked at your credits. The study abroad program would give you credits, and you would need one more math and one more English class, both of which you could take online or at the community college this summer."

I stare at her, still so confused. This kind of thing cannot possibly be an option for me. It's huge.

"Who . . . how much . . . ?"

"It is pricey, but the price drops if you agree to stay with a host family." She opens the pamphlet to the price page and all I see are thousands. Every tiny hope that had just danced to life is crushed under an ugly bulldozer.

"I can't. My family can't afford it."

She presses her lips together. "I understand. I still think you should take it home and show them. You'd be surprised how parents are able to make things work when they put their minds to it."

I want to yell at her that my parents have zero savings and cannot afford a loan payment. Maybe in her perfect world people can "make things work," but not in mine.

"Thanks." I start to stand when she pushes a list toward me.

"Here are some respectable jobs you can think about in the meantime." I look it over: banking, social services, secretarial work, yada yada yada, and then the last one catches my attention. Flight attendant.

I stare at those two words as I exit her room and stop in the office area.

Flight attendant. Huh.

I look at Joel, who's sitting with his head leaned back against the wall, his arms crossed, looking back at me. He says nothing, so I don't either. But it feels wrong. When I get to the door, I stop and turn.

"Whatever I did to upset you, I'm sorry."

Joel raises his chin to examine me for a second before responding. "And I'm sorry I've given you the impression I'm upset with you." He stands and walks toward me. Without permission, he takes the pamphlet, looks it over with a nod, then hands it back.

"I can't do it," I say, feeling irrationally peeved that she gave it to me as an option.

He says nothing, just shoves his hands in his pockets.

"What are *you* doing after graduation?" I ask him.

"Working for my dad at the shop. Maybe taking community college classes to pass the extra time." He sounds totally unworried and unhurried. I envy him.

"I don't know what I'm doing," I admit. The words make me feel so anxious. Like I'm on pause and everyone else is still going forward full speed. I'll never catch up.

"You'll figure it out," he says softly. "You're a smart girl."

Pfft. Right. My chin drops, and he lifts it back up with a finger. My heart trembles.

"You're too hard on yourself." I try to look away, but he touches my chin again. "Look, with or without something like this"—he flicks the pamphlet—"you'll do great. Stop letting society tell you that you have to do a certain thing. You don't gotta do what everyone else is doing."

I know he's talking about the college path. His words hit me, and I take a shuddering breath. All I can do is nod and turn away, because I'm feeling overly emotional.

"Thanks" is all I can say. I can't look at him as I go.

I take my pamphlet and list of jobs back to Spanish, where everyone's doing silent work. Mrs. Hernandez peers up at me inquisitively through her glasses, so I show her the pamphlet and whisper, "She wants me to study abroad next year."

Her eyes twinkle, and she whispers back, "*¡Maravilloso!* How perfect for you!"

"*Sí.*" I feel stupid saying the next part. "We don't have the money, though." I try to smile so she won't feel bad for me. It doesn't work. She tilts her head and her face scrunches with pity. I shouldn't have shown her.

"That's really too bad, Zae. You are the textbook candidate for it."

"It's okay." I smile again to show my gratitude for her compliment.

"By the way, congratulations on making prom court."

"Thank you," I say before I take my seat.

While I'm flattered that my fellow juniors like me enough to elect me for the court, I really wish I could give it to someone who wants to go—someone who will appreciate the honor.

It's hard to concentrate on my classwork. I really wish Mrs. Crowley had never shown me that pamphlet. Everyone always tells you to "dream big," but when you're stuck, you're stuck. Not everyone has the means to reach higher. It's unfair and that's just how it is.

CHAPTER TWENTY-SIX

I fly under the radar for the next few weeks, even after my grounding is over. No parties. No kissing. No hanging out with my girls. I learn about their lives via text.

Monica makes it official with Dean.

Lin continues to get kisses from Parker the gymnast and for days I get texts like: **Parkerrrrr!**

I think she likes him.

Then we get a group message from Kenzie. She and Vin had their first fight. It was over food, of all things.

He's mad cuz I don't want to eat around him.

Why don't you want to eat around him? Monica asks.

IDK . . . I just feel like a pig or something.

Oh, Kenzie. **He just wants to know ur comfortable with him.**

Y'all know I don't eat a lot.

Lin writes: **B— eat the damn food! U don't have to stuff urself but it sounds like ur not eating anything around him. He's probably worried, too.**

It takes Kenzie a long time to answer, and I know she's upset, probably crying. It breaks my heart for her. I hate that she deals with this.

She finally writes: **I don't need a guy policing what I eat or don't eat. I deal with enough comments from everyone else in my life.**

Sigh.

Vincent has grown on me, and I don't want this issue to be the thing that does them in.

I tell her: **How about a compromise? Just let him see you eating a little.**

She fires back: **Then he'll be like, "That's all ur gonna eat??" It won't be enough!**

Baby steps. Lin's text is the last one for a while.

I make the decision to do something dangerous. I pull Vincent aside at school when Kenz leaves for a dentist appointment. I make him swear not to tell Kenzie about our conversation. I know he cares about her, and he needs to know about her struggle and to be patient with her. I love him even more after we talk, because he seems to get it, and he's thankful that it's not just him who worries. I give him some pointers on dealing with her gently. That was days ago, and nothing more has been said. I can only hope that means the baby steps are working.

On a Sunday afternoon in late April, when prom is on the horizon, Kenz texts us and it's apparent that things with her and Vincent are good again. Better than good: **V's brother is getting us a hotel room for prom. His parents think he's staying at Kyle's. Zae, can I tell mine I'm staying with u?**

Ummm . . . first things first. **Yes, OK, but r u going to have sex?????**

Lin: **OMG.**

Monica: **?? Are u??**

Kenzie: **Maybe? IDK, guys.**

Me: **Aaaaahhhhh!!!!**

Lin: **Tell him he has to buy condoms.**

Me: **Love gloves!**

Lin: **Willie hats!**

Me: **Don't be a ding-dong, cover your shling-shlong.**

Kenzie: **Ew, lol!**

Monica: **Bawhaha! We want details.**

Kenzie: **Rae says it's going 2 b awkward.**

Her big sister. She's probably right. Nothing's like it is in the movies.

Me: **I can't believe our lil' K-bae won't see unicorns anymore!**

Kenzie: **Stop it! Don't make me cry.**

Lin: **Have u n him talked about it?**

Me: **Wait, does V talk?**

Kenzie: **I do most of the talking and he smiles at me.**

Monica: **ROFL!!**

The conversation makes me laugh, but for some reason it also leaves me feeling sad. Things are changing. We're growing up, and there's no going back. And in a weird way I constantly feel like I'm being left behind. Maybe because they all have guys. And futures. I don't know. I'm just thankful for my job, which keeps me busy and makes me feel mature. Mrs. McOllie has started trusting me with closing duties on Wednesday nights, which means I get to count the drawer, put the earnings in the money bag, and lock up the store. A security guy comes to walk me to my car since I'm underage. I feel very official.

After a week of rain, and not being able to practice my tumbling outside, I'm excited for a sunny afternoon. Plus, Kenzie's news about prom has left me needing to run and jump and possibly land on my head.

I'm determined to get this dang thing, and I hope it happens soon because I'm getting tired of buying Zeb Slurpees. The man at the register definitely thinks I'm a Slurpee junkie.

As luck would have it, I cannot land it. I cannot get past the barrier of fear. Every single time I come out here, I'm filled with hope that this is the day, only to remember very quickly that I can't do it. It's useless.

"You're not even trying," Zeb gripes.

"Shut up."

"I'm not going to help you if you just yell at me!"

It's hard to take him seriously with blue Slurpee lips. Or to be mad at him.

"Sorry," I say, letting out a giant, frustrated sigh. I'm never going to get this. What will I do if I don't cheer next year? The thought seizes me with panic, and the feeling of being left behind is stronger than ever.

"Kids, time to come up," Mom calls.

I trudge up the steps behind Zeb's bouncy strides, my legs heavy.

In the living room, Mom looks nervous. "I just talked to Daddy, and he'd like you to both come over to see his place today.

"Yes!" Zeb jumps and punches the air. "Finally!"

My stomach has flattened and flipped like a rotten pancake. "I don't feel good."

Zeb glares at me. "Seriously, Zae? I want to go!"

"Then go. I'm not stopping you."

Mom's lips purse tightly. She points to my room. Great. I go and she follows, closing us in. I sit heavily on the bed with my arms crossed.

"You've avoided him long enough. You will take a shower and get dressed. Your dad will be here in an hour, and—"

"No way!" I leap from the bed. "I don't want to see them!"

Mom closes her eyes as if gathering patience. "She won't be there. Lower your voice."

"I don't want to see him either! I hate him!" It's the first time I've said it out loud and I nearly choke on the filthy words. I have to cover my mouth.

"Please don't hate him, Zae." It comes out a desperate whisper.

Her face . . . why does she look so hurt on his behalf?

"Please," I beg. "Send Zeb, but don't make me go. And stop sticking up for him!"

Mom faces me straight on. "He is not a bad man. He loves you."

"He abandoned us for a waitress!" I remind her.

Mom sits on the edge of the bed and puts her face in her hands. She sits there long enough for me to catch my breath and lose steam. I almost don't hear her when she speaks.

"Sit down."

"Mom—"

"Sit *down*."

My jaw rocks and I sit, crossing my arms, my knee bouncing.

"I have something I need to tell you. Something I'd rather Zeb not know at this point in time."

"What?" I ask, though by the sound of her voice I really don't want to hear.

"As you know, your father was pretty young when we met. I was a twenty-six-year-old bartender, and he was a twenty-year-old fry cook." I know the story, and I love it.

"Yeah. He was persistent and won you over after a year."

She nods, staring off in nostalgia. "I was twenty-seven when we married. At that point I'd been living on my own almost eight years. I was independent, not used to answering to anyone but me. Our first year of marriage was . . . hard." That pained look tightens her face again. "I wasn't used to having to explain what money I was spending and if I wanted to go out with my friends. Your father was always more financially conscious than me, and I felt like he was trying to control me. I know now that wasn't the case, but back then . . ."

Foreboding fills me. I rub my arms as she goes on.

"I . . ." She clenches her jaw as if gathering strength. "That year I had an affair. I almost left Daddy." Now she is choking up, and my guts are in a grinder. I stare at her, and she suddenly morphs into a stranger, someone I thought I knew but really didn't.

"I didn't tell him. I'm not sure what kept us together—a

242

miracle, probably. But I broke things off with the other man, a marine, and he was restationed. Everything made itself very clear to me during that time. I knew I didn't want to lose your dad. I knew the problem was me and not him. I knew I made a horrible mistake and I was lucky to have a second chance. I worked hard to be a good wife after that, to be worthy of his love. Well . . ." She wipes her eyes. "Fast forward to last year. Seventeen years later, that man found me again. He contacted me. I told him I was in a happy place and wanted nothing to do with him. But he started stalking me. I was scared." She wipes her face again. "It got so bad that I had to get a restraining order, and I had to tell Daddy."

Oh, my gosh. I am so floored. This cannot be my mother telling this story. All I can do is stare at her, my emotions coiling like writhing snakes. I knew something was off last year, but I had no idea . . . I was so focused on my friends and cheer and Wylie.

"The man ended up confronting Daddy in the parking lot of his job, and they got into a fight. They both spent the night in jail. That's when Daddy got fired."

My heart is buzzing with quick speed as I remember back to last year. My parents were both on edge. Daddy without a job. Mom looked like she'd aged ten years overnight.

"We tried to make it work. We tried to get past it. He got a new job. We tried . . . but it's like there was this unfixable crack in our marriage after that. He met . . . *her*, at work, and she was there for him. She was what he needed. I couldn't even be mad."

Tears are streaming down her face now. For the first time

in ages, I don't cry. It's like it's too much. I can't process it. Images from my family's story in my mind are changing and morphing, pages are flipping and rewriting themselves.

My mom cheated first.

"Zae." She places her hand over mine, and I let her, though I feel like a cold, undead thing. "Please don't be mad at him. He tried. He really did. We both did. And we love you and Zebby so much. You are the light of our lives. He misses you." She sucks in a huge, ragged breath. "I don't blame you for being mad at us. We both made mistakes, choices that we regret and wish we could change. I'm sorry."

I say nothing. It's still too big. Mom pulls her hand back and stands. I stare at the spot where she sat until she leaves me.

For five minutes my brain throbs, overloaded, and I can't think. Then thoughts come rushing at me, bombarding my senses, and I fight to catch my breath.

My parents are a mess, just like me. Just like Zeb. Just like Lin who kept watch for Monica, and Monica who couldn't help but like the guy I liked. We're all . . . human. We're messy. We've all made mistakes. Sometimes we're lucky and it ends up being a "learn from it" mistake, and sometimes it's a mistake that reaches out with its claws and snags other people you love, dragging them into it, shredding the bonds of a relationship, and turning your life completely upside down.

I stand, as stiff as a lifeless zombie, and gather a change of clothes. Then I head to the bathroom to shower.

When I'm ready, I sit silently on the couch with Zeb until Dad comes to the door. Mom opens it, and they share a long glance in which she gives him a telling nod. His whole demeanor seems to soften with relief. I don't say hi to him or bye to Mom. I walk past them into the late April evening and let myself into the back seat of Dad's car. Zeb happily takes shotgun.

I stare from the window as we drive across town to a cute condominium neighborhood. Inside has a noticeable feminine touch. Cream couches with pastel-flower throw pillows. And best of all . . . Dad goes to a huge dog crate in the corner and lets out a yellow Lab who dances around excitedly, wagging a heavy tail and nearly knocking us over as she greets us. Zeb and I both laugh and get down to pet her.

"You have a dog!" Zeb cries, letting her lick all over his face. We've always wanted one, but Mom is allergic.

"Yep. This is Sadie."

Dad clicks a leash onto her collar and we walk outside together. He gives Zeb the leash and Sadie takes off down the sidewalk. He runs after her, lanky limbs flying. Dad chuckles and crosses his arms. As he stares at Zeb I stare at him, this man who everyone says I look like. Those round, chocolaty eyes—my own eyes—those dark curls that we both work so hard to maintain. And my heart squeezes at the thought of all he's been through—all that I put him through with my attitude and my anger.

I slip an arm around his waist and snuggle into his side. He hesitates, as if surprised, and then his arm goes around me tightly, protectively, lovingly. I don't want to let go, and neither does he, so we don't.

We hold on.

CHAPTER TWENTY-SEVEN

I feel different at school on Monday. Changed. For the first time in a long time I sense the warmth of the sun shining through the proverbial cloud that has plagued me.

Lunch is kind of weird because Dean comes over to sit with us. I don't look at him much because I'm still embarrassed about everything. And having a boy at the table means we can't talk about certain things, but I refuse to let myself feel grumbly about it.

I look up at the clock a few minutes before the bell and decide it's time to drop a bomb on my friends. Something I've been dreading.

"I'm not trying out for cheer next year."

Both of them stare at me, aghast. Even Dean looks shocked.

"Is it the tumbling?" Monica asks. "Because mine is rough,

too. We can work on it together."

"It's really no use," I say. "I've been practicing hard and I can't get it." Saying all this out loud, seeing their faces, it dredges up every horrible feeling of failure I've managed to tamp down. The thought of not cheering, it's like I'm abandoning my people. For the first time ever, I won't be a part of the hustle, the craziness, the uniforms and games and . . . my friends. But they'll go on without me, just like when they'll be off at college next year without me. A sensation of alarm and loss splits me from the inside, but there is nothing I can do to change the situation. It's hopeless.

"You *have* to be on the team," Kenzie says. "You have perfect jumps, and you're an amazing base. I can't stunt without you!"

"Yes, you can," I say, but I hate the thought of not being the one to catch her.

"This is crazy, Zae," Monica says. "You were all-star at camp last year. You have to talk to Mrs. Hartt. She has to make an exception."

"She won't," I say. "I already talked to her, and it wouldn't be fair anyway. You guys need tumblers. Maybe this will help the squad actually win."

Monica glares. "The reason we don't win isn't because of tumbling. We're just as good as every other squad in the county, but we're *Peakton*. Nobody cares about Peakton. Mrs. Hartt can change the requirements all she wants, but we'll still be seen as the thug school full of losers who don't matter."

We're all quiet as that truth sinks in. With other sports our teams can win because of the point systems. Our guys have won states twice in the past five years for basketball, and qualified for states in football and baseball. Cheerleading is different, though. So much about the scoring is subjective, based on individual judges' opinions. Every year we work so hard, and every year we feel cheated out of a first- or second-place win. It really is exhausting.

"We do it for us, remember?" Kenzie says. "Not for them. It doesn't matter what they think."

It kind of does, but I don't want to burst her bubble. I know she means well.

A scream and crash come from the other end of the cafeteria, followed by a frenzy of scuffling feet. From what I can see through the hordes of people jumping to their feet, two girls are going at it, grabbing hair and scrambling to overpower each other. I recognize the puff pigtails and long, slender legs of Meeka.

Sierra screams for someone to help. Next to her, Raul takes off running toward the doors where the officer usually stands. It takes less than a second for students to leap from their seats and converge on the fight, yelling, standing on tables and chairs to see. We jump up and grab our bags.

"That was Meeka," I say, feeling ill at the sounds of violence and the ensuing mob of bystanders.

"Yeah," Dean says, lifting his chin to see. "And Quinton's chick."

"Camille?" Kenzie asks. She and I share a *holy crap* look. I remember the way Meeka pulled me away from Quinton at the party. And how someone told Camille he went into his room with a cheerleader. Oh, Meeka . . .

Teachers and staff come running, pushing through, and the bell rings. Sierra runs from the cafeteria, looking shaken.

I'm despondent as I walk to my locker, realizing fights and things are what people think about when they think of Peakton. We're defined by the negative, no matter how much good stuff goes on here. No matter how much passion we have. I wish I could change it. I wish I could fix it all.

When I open my locker a piece of folded paper falls to my feet. I bend and pick it up. Was it in my locker? Because I don't recognize it. I open it and see typed writing. Air fills my lungs as I gasp. It's a poem.

I see your smile.
It looks good on you.
A welcome change from the heavy hue.
Is it here to stay?
Or will it go away?
Hold tight to every new day.

"What's that?" Kenzie asks. I breathlessly hand it over, my hand trembling. She reads through and sags into me. *"Ohmagarsh!!"* Then she stares up at me with doe eyes. "Holy crap, Zae! Who wrote this?"

We both look around, but only random guys are passing, none of them paying a bit of attention to us. I shake my head, still dazed, then I fold the paper carefully and slide it into my back pocket. We're smiling like idiots as we jog to class through the locker bay and main hall.

In a strange sort of slow-motion vibe, I catch the eye of

249

guys as we pass their groups, and a weird sensation of realization flits through me. These guys are not out to hurt anyone. With the exception of possibly Rex Morino, they're nice. In fact, I'd been no better than Rex during my conquests. These guys could be little brothers like Zebby. And I'd treated a bunch of them with disdain as I went on my tirade against males, not caring if I hurt any of them. Now, as I pass them, I feel bad. Male, female, and all the other ways we categorize each other—we're all just people—individual personalities, making mistakes and trying to get by. I want to do better. I never want to return to that dark place, even though part of my soul still aches, and might always.

Brent watches me with a grin from beneath his Peakton varsity baseball hat. Taro gives me a shy smile from his group of skinny-jeans friends. Rex wears his bad-boy glare from his group of guys in black, like he hates me but he can't look away. Flynn pulls a book from his locker and swishes his loose, dark-red curls to the side when he sees me, tucking them back and giving me a wave. Elliott walks past with his buddy in Carhartt hunting pants. He holds up a palm and I smack it, followed by Kenz.

Then there's the double whammy of Quinton and Joel standing with Kwami and our star basketball forward, whispering. But all four glance over as we pass. Joel's gaze and nod heats my neck as it sweeps over me, like I was somehow branded when he kissed me there.

I don't hate the feeling, and I'm not sure what that means. My anger at the male sex may have dissipated, but I still don't want to fall hard for Joel when there is a super romantic mystery guy out there. And what if mystery guy is someone I don't like? Are the poems enough to change that? I have to ask myself, what burns hotter: The poet's words on my heart, or Joel's lips on my neck? They're pretty darn close. This is killing me!

We run to our next class, where I'm distracted by all that's happened today. I check my locker thoroughly between each class, hoping for another poem, but there's nothing.

After school, I rush out to meet the girls in the parking lot.

Lin has her hands on her hips. "Excuse me, missy, but what's this about a poem?"

I pull it out of my back pocket and experience a squishy, ooey-gooey pride as they read it and freak out on my behalf. When they finish, Monica peers over her shoulder and looks back at me, fiddling nervously with the strap on her book bag.

"Hey, Zae? Do you mind if, um, if Dean drives me home today?"

My heart falls at the fact that she feels nervous even asking me. "Dean can take you home anytime you want, Monica. I'm not upset about him, I promise." I realize as I say it that I mean every word, and the relief is a balm to my soul.

Monica gives me a hug and jogs away to Dean's coupe.

Kenzie spots Vincent across the lot, walking to baseball practice with the other guys. "Ooh!" She jumps as high as she can, several times, waving. Vincent lifts a long arm in the air, and she giggles.

Lin's phone dings. Her face lights up when she reads it. "Parker wants to see me this week! I have a feeling he's going to ask me to be his girlfriend."

"Yay!" Kenzie exclaims. "What are you going to say?"

"Yes, of course! The boy has abs and thighs of steel and he can kiss. Good lawd, can he kiss!"

And just like that, all three of my friends are pretty much taken. And though I'm happy for them, I am now an outsider in every way.

CHAPTER TWENTY-EIGHT

This week I'm pulled out of math class and sent to guidance again. I'm happy to get out of math but nervous about what Mrs. Crowley wants now.

I come to a dead stop in her doorway at the sight of both my parents sitting there, looking up at me with puzzled expressions. What is this?

"Zae!" Mrs. Crowley says. "Here's a seat for you. Join us."

I sit, peering around at the three of them in worried confusion.

"I've called you all here today because I have good news. I'm sure Zae shared the pamphlet about studying abroad."

Holy crap! Is she for real? I wince and squirm. "No," I say. "I told you we couldn't afford that."

"Were you supposed to bring something home to me?"

Mom asks in her parental voice. Dad leans forward, his eyes searching me for answers.

"No." I look pointedly at Mrs. Crowley. This is wrong of her, but she looks zero percent regretful. I can't believe she called both my parents in for this.

She stares right back at me and asks, "Did you speak to them about your hopes and plans for after high school?"

I bite my lip hard as anger sparks and flares.

"I haven't heard about any change of plans," Mom says.

"Me either." Dad folds his hands and all of them watch me, waiting.

What kind of crappy guidance is this? Forcing me into this awkward conversation when I'm not ready? Wasting everyone's time? I barely open my lips to grumble the words.

"I don't want to go to college."

The looks on Mom's and Dad's faces crush me, making my heart gallop.

"I don't think it's for me," I say. "I feel like it'd be a waste of money, just to say I did it, for a job I won't even love."

Mom looks down at her hands, and Dad's eyebrows droop.

"I'm sorry," I whisper, silently cursing Mrs. Crowley.

She clears her throat and reaches for another pamphlet, sliding it across, where my parents open it and look together. Guilt surges inside me like a churn of acid.

"This really isn't necessary," I say, my voice raised. "I didn't show them because it's not possible. This is a waste of time."

She ignores me and focuses on my parents. "I'm sure you're aware that plenty of respected people don't have college degrees. Steve Jobs, Bill Gates, Mark Zuckerberg." My parents look unimpressed by this fact, but she soldiers on. "While it's a necessary option for many, there are wonderful work opportunities out there for young people today. In Zae's case, I think it's important that we focus on her prolific language skills and seize this particular prospect. I'll let you read through it."

I want to snatch the pamphlet away and run out. Dad exhales in a huff before turning his eyes down to the paper in obvious disapproval. Mom makes a sound in the back of her throat when she gets to the prices at the bottom.

"Mr. and Mrs. Monroe," says Mrs. Crowley. Her eyes sort of sparkle when she glances at me. "Zae. What if I told you there's been an anonymous donor who would like to sponsor you?"

The room gets so quiet. So still. I'm afraid to breathe. I can't . . . What did she just say? Oh my God, my heart feels like a racehorse just shot out of the gate.

Dad clears his throat. "Someone wants to pay for her?"

"Yes." Mrs. Crowley looks ready to burst with the news. "They wish to stay anonymous, with no strings attached. Every expense for the entire year."

"Wait." Mom closes her eyes. "A year . . . away?"

"The first semester would be in Buenos Aires, Argentina. She would come home at Christmas. Then the second semester would be in Paris, France. She would be home in time for graduation. The donor has also agreed to pay the community-college tuition fees for her to get the final credits she needs this summer before she leaves."

Argentina! France!

The room is spinning. I'm in a dream. Mom covers her mouth and tears spring to her eyes.

Dad is staring at me like he doesn't know me. "Xanderia? This is something you want?"

"I . . ." OH MY GOD OH MY GOD OH MY GOD. "I don't know?"

"It's an amazing opportunity," he says firmly. "But I'm not going to sit here and act like I'm not surprised. I wish you'd confided in us sooner so we could wrap our minds around this. And keep in mind, we're talking about your senior year. You're a very sociable, active girl in school. Are you willing to miss all that? Because this is not something where you can get over there, get homesick, and easily come home."

I can't believe this is happening. I'm going to hyperventilate. I put my elbows on the desk and breathe, letting my head hang down. Mrs. Crowley chuckles.

"It's a lot to take in. Listen, Zae. You have two weeks to decide. Think about it. Talk it over as a family. Weigh the positives and negatives."

"Thank you," Mom whispers.

We stand together, and my legs are numb and trembling. Mrs. Crowley stays in her office while my parents and I converge in thick silence in the guidance room. Thankfully there's no aide in there right now to stare at us. When I look up at Mom and Dad, I feel lost, scared, excited, hopeful, worried. I don't know what to think. I can't imagine leaving my friends, my family, my school. Senior year was going to be the best year of my life. Traveling has always been my dream, but an unattainable dream. Not something right at my fingertips for the taking. Stuff like this doesn't happen to girls like me.

"Zae." Dad finally breaks the silence. "I don't know what to say. This is huge."

"I didn't know," I tell him. "When she first showed me the pamphlet and told me to share it with you, I knew we didn't have the money, so I threw it away."

"Who could the donor be?" Mom asks. "Do you think they'll expect something from us?"

"If they're anonymous, then no," Dad says. He looks at me. "Do you have any idea who it is?"

"No!" I'm just as shocked and baffled as them. "I don't know. I don't know what to do."

"Ultimately, I think it needs to be your choice," Dad says. Mom nods her agreement through teary eyes. "But we will be happy to work on the pros-and-cons list to make sure you consider every angle."

We. My parents aren't together, but we're still a family. They're still my team, both there for me. I swallow hard and nod. "Okay."

I hug each of them, and my brain seems to shut down on the way back to class. Emotions are gone, too. Nothing is computing. This cannot be real. It can't be my life.

I want to tell my friends, but at the same time I'm terrified. I don't want anyone to try to talk me into or out of it. I've never been so torn about something. But this is monumental for me.

"Are you okay?" my friends ask me after school.

"Fine." Not fine. In disbelief. Utter freak-out mode. Forced smile activated.

Brent jumps in front of me on the sidewalk down to the parking lot. He grasps the back of his neck.

"Uh, hey! Are you going to prom with anyone?"

My stomach sinks, sending a wave of yuck over me at the thought of prom. "No," I say soberly. "I'm not going at all. I'm sorry."

"Oh. With anyone?"

I shake my head. "No."

"Why not?"

I shrug. "I just really don't feel like it."

His lips pull to the side, and he nods. "Okay, then. See you around." And he runs off toward the baseball field.

"Zae," Kenzie starts.

"I'm serious," I tell her for the millionth time. And then it hits me. If I don't go this year, and I'm in France next year at this time, that means I won't have gone to any proms. I start shaking.

"Why do you look like you're about to cry?" Lin asks.

"I feel like there's stuff you're not telling us." Monica cocks her head at me.

Ugh, why can they read me so well?

"Guys . . ."

"You're scaring me." Kenzie twines her fingers through mine.

"Do you have a minute," I ask. "Before I have to drive?"

They exchange glances and nod.

"But you have to promise me you won't try to give me advice or pressure me about what I'm gonna tell you. I know that sounds weird, but I need you to just . . . listen."

Another round of glances is exchanged, this time alarmed, and I can't blame them. We move to the side and sit on the grass, away from students and teachers, and I tell them everything. It's the first time ever that all four of us cry together. Lin's tears are usually stored in a steel vault. In fact, I don't think I've ever seen her cry.

Nobody says anything, they just cry, and I know we're all thinking the same thing. We knew things would change when we graduated. But to take one of us out of the equation a year early would mean that soon, very soon, nothing would ever be the same for the four of us. It would be the end of our carefree days together. But if I stay, we'll have one more year together. Then again, if they get serious with Dean, Vincent, and Parker, and they all cheer without me, things will be changing anyway . . . I don't know what to think. I don't know what to do.

They stick to their promise and don't try to sway me one way or the other, even though part of me wants to scream *Tell me what to do!*

We're quiet and thoughtful the whole drive home.

Mom wraps me in a long hug when I walk in the door, and I let her hold me. Zebby, usually clueless, says, "What's going on? You're both acting weird."

Instead of answering, I go over and hug him, too, rocking him back and forth as his arms swing and flop until he wiggles away and says, "Never mind, I don't even want to know." I'm glad to hear it, because I can't handle another single tear today.

CHAPTER TWENTY-NINE

In the course of five days, I've successfully decided on giving Mrs. Crowley an absolute yes, and then a firm no, no less than fifty times, back and forth.

Oh, and no more poems, though I scour my locker and the floor around it every day. Mystery poet has probably had a change of heart. I don't want a fickle guy anyway.

Prom is this weekend, and the entire junior and senior classes are stressing. Between dresses, tuxedo rentals, corsages, limos, nail and hair appointments, and finding last-minute dates, school has taken on a humming atmosphere of anticipation. Everyone wants everything to be perfect, and I'm extra glad not to have those worries. My friends have helped deflect boys who want to ask me—and thankfully most of them ask my friends first, like, "Hey, does Zae have a date yet?" And they tell them I'm not going. So far, the only one who showed interest that I felt bad about was Taro.

But by the end of the week, all those stray guys find girls to ask, and hardly anyone is left without a date. Some groups of friends choose to go together. It's funny how everything works out.

I do feel sad . . . and left out, though I know it's of my own device. I'm regretting now that I'm not going to at least be with my friends. On Friday I go to Mrs. Hartt, who's running the prom court. Kenzie comes with me for moral support.

"There you are!" Mrs. Hartt smiles. "I've got your prom ticket and sash." She digs around on her desk and pulls out a big yellow envelope with my name on it. "I'm so proud of my girls. Do you know this is the first time in nine years that all three nominees are cheerleaders?" She holds out the envelope, but I don't take it.

"I didn't buy a ticket."

"You get one free since you're on the court." She shoves the stuff into my arms.

"I'm sorry," I say. "But I'm not going."

Mrs. Hartt puts both hands on her hips. "Zae, I think you will regret that."

"I know," I whisper. "But it's too late now."

"It's never too late. You drive, right?" She looks at Kenzie. "Surely you or one of the girls, or even your sisters have an extra dress Zae can wear."

My cheeks burn. "No! It's too much."

"Zae," Kenzie says softly, "it's really not too much. You can come to my house today and we'll find you a dress. We can call the restaurant and add one more to the reservation."

I shake my head, feeling humiliated that I'm waffling the day before prom. It's just that all the reasons I didn't want to go feel so flimsy now. I'm regretting not taking advantage of this experience with my friends.

"I've already told guys no," I say.

Mrs. Hartt laughs at that. "Who cares? Believe me, they'll get over it and move on."

I look at Kenzie and her adorable smile slides into place. "Pretty please?"

I sigh and look down at the prom sash. Mrs. Hartt grins. "See you there, hun. No regrets."

All right, fine. No regrets.

I opt out of the dinner, and decide to show up to prom an hour late. I'm wearing a maroon, strapless, long satin dress that Kenzie's big sister wore as a bridesmaid. It's tight in the chest, but at least I know it won't fall down. Mom put my hair into fat curls and piled them on my head in a regal upsweep. I did my makeup in black, gray, and silver.

I don't know why I'm so nervous when I show. I keep smoothing down the white prom-court sash that lies over my shoulder. I've rehearsed what I'll tell anyone who asks why I changed my mind, "Mrs. Hartt said I had to make an appearance because of prom court." It's a half-truth, but oh well. It'll save my butt from looking too stupid or hurting some nice guy's feelings.

I wobble just slightly in the gravelly parking lot on my heels, borrowed from Monica, as I walk around the side of the hotel. Two guys in tuxedos are smoking, and I move to the edge to give them a wide berth. A sweetness like cotton candy wafts over.

"Thought you weren't coming," says a familiar, smooth voice that makes my insides jump. I wobble a little as I stop and face Joel in a black-and-white tux. Next to Kwami. Both their bow ties have been undone and hang loose around their necks. I can't help but smile at how slim and dapper they look.

"Dang, y'all clean up nice," I say. "But I think it's against the rules to smoke at a school event." I put a hand on my hip and eye the tiny vape in his hand. "New toy?"

Joel's cool half grin makes me shiver. "Oral fixation, remember?"

"Maybe you should find something better to do with your mouth."

I'm so glad it's dark out because I feel the blood rush to my face as Kwami bends over, laughing in spurts.

Joel's easy demeanor never wavers. "Perhaps I should."

I look around. "Are your dates inside?"

"We came stag," Joel says. "Kwami's my date."

"Yeah, J thinks he's gettin' lucky tonight, so I'm gonna have to fight him off."

Joel's laugh is slow and smooth. "Right, right. Can we escort you inside?"

"Sure," I say. "Thanks." They each hold out their elbows, and I slide my hands in.

It dawns on me as we're walking in that people might think I came with a date after all, but I'm so happy not to be alone that I don't care. Inside the ballroom, lights twinkle, and everyone looks like young movie stars. People are excited to see me, stopping to hug me.

"You look beautiful!"

"Look at your hair!"

"Girl, I love that dress."

Every single girl is busy complimenting another, and it warms my heart to see us building each other up.

Kenzie is the first at a table to spot me and jump to her feet. I meet the girls halfway, and we converge in a group hug, squealing and laughing. Parker, Dean, and Vincent jump up and hug each other, bouncing in a circle with their heads thrown back as they fake yell. It's pretty funny, especially to see Vincent letting loose, and Parker, who just met these guys tonight. I turn around and Joel and Kwami are nowhere to be seen. I strain my neck to peer around the room. Where did they go?

"Selfie time!" Lin says.

We spend the next ten minutes posing together and with any other friend who comes along. When a dance song we all love comes on, "Girl Anthem," we scream and run to the dance floor, leaving the dates in the dust. In fact, almost every girl at prom rushes onto the floor with their hands in the air, and we dance like crazy, laughing, beautiful, and free. I feel so lucky, so *grateful*, in that moment, realizing I almost wasn't part of this.

No regrets.

Our song is followed by a slow song, so I take my exit as the guys come up to find their dates and hold them in their arms. This was the moment I thought I would hate—the moment I wanted to avoid—but it turns out I don't care after all. They look happy. They're being treated nicely. Come what may in the future, on this night they are smiling, and that's all I can ask for.

The chair next to me whispers across the carpet as Joel pulls it out and sits in it backward, straddling the seat. He's sipping from a clear plastic cup as he regards the crowd.

"Why did you decide to come?" I ask.

"Surprised?"

"Kind of." Totally.

He shrugs. "Something to do. Parties. Prom. All these things are entertaining."

"So, you just like to people watch."

"Precisely."

"You don't ever join in? You don't dance?"

"Not usually." He keeps staring out at the dance floor, and my hope dissipates. He turns to regard me with serious eyes. "Why did *you* decide to come?" It's really a loaded question, and to answer it would mean I have to reveal all the sadness and insecurity I'm facing. So, instead of responding, I stand and hold out my hand.

"Dance with me?" I ask.

He looks at my hand and hesitates. My heart pounds in preparation for rejection, but after half a beat he stands and puts his warm hand in mine. I let out a breath and lead him to the dance floor, my fingers falling into place between his. I pull him into the crowd of bodies until we're submersed in the sea, then he lifts my hand to his shoulder and takes my other palm in his own. I feel his free hand circle my waist, warm against my lower back as he pulls me until our bodies are flush. He smells like cologne and spun sugar from the vape. The latter I can do without. The former makes my knees weak.

We don't speak a word. I take nervous glances at his serious blue eyes before deciding to rest my head against his shoulder. He feels . . . nice. Steady. I let myself relax and the song is over too soon. It's not until I pull away from him that I realize just how much of us was touching.

Monica catches my eye as Dean leads her off the dance floor, and she's looking back and forth between me and Joel in question. I can't exactly respond, so I just give her a smile.

To my surprise, Joel hangs out with me. We go up to the cake table for a slice when it's cut, and then we both make gross faces when we realize it's lemon, not vanilla.

"So wrong," Joel says, and I laugh a little too hard.

Flynn Rogers, the bassist, passes us, holding hands with Emi. I guess they're together now.

"Hi, Flynn," I say. "Hi, Emi."

"Hey!" Flynn smiles, but Emi just stares me up and down as they go by. Ouch.

Joel's eyes widen, and I can tell he's trying not to laugh.

"I guess she doesn't like me," I mumble under my breath. I don't recall doing anything to her other than talking to Flynn.

"Girls are harsh like that to each other," he tells me in all his wisdom. I wish he wasn't right.

The microphone system screeches, making everyone flinch and some cover their ears.

"May I have your attention," Mrs. Hartt says. "It's now time for our junior- and senior-class prom court to come to the dance floor so that we may announce the prince, princess, king, and queen!"

People lightly cheer, and my stomach flops.

"Get up there, Miss Popular." Joel nudges me, and I groan. "But you might wanna wipe the frosting from your face first." I gasp and wipe at my face, making him laugh. "Nah, just messing with you." I slap him, and Monica joins us, taking my hand and leading me onto the dance floor. We move next to Meeka, gorgeous in sleek, thin braids. She got suspended for a day and Camille got three for attacking her. But Meeka has healed from her scratches and bruises, and holds her head high.

I take her hand, too, and the three of us stand together with the three junior guys to our left. The spotlights make me squint.

"First, I'd like to announce our junior-class prince," Mrs. Hartt says. "Congratulations, Dean Prescott!"

I clap, and Monica whistles through her fingers, nearly blowing out my eardrums and making everyone laugh. Mrs. Hartt puts a manly, thick, gold circlet on his head. The obnoxious one with red velvet is reserved for the king, along with a velvet cape.

"And now, for your junior-class princess!" I grasp hands with the girls again. *Please say Monica, please, please, please . . .* And then . . .

"Zae Monroe!"

I stand there frozen. The sound of applause warbles in my eardrums. Both Monica and Meeka shove me. I turn to Monica, and she gives me the kind of smile that only a friend can give you when she is surely feeling wrecked with disappointment.

"Go," she mouths.

Mrs. Hartt is trying to adhere a tiara to my curls, and I trust her not to mess it all up. "There," she whispers, giving my shoulders a squeeze and beaming at me before she urges me to stand next to Dean.

I'm in a complete daze as the king and queen are announced. I smile for pictures and marvel at how this is my life. I didn't believe my name would be called. I really didn't.

"And now it's time for the royal court dance!" says Mrs. Hartt.

The what? A slow song comes on and Dean turns to me, not meeting my eye. Ugh. Freaking ugh. We pause long enough to make things uncomfortable. Then I suck it up and put both hands on his tall, wide shoulders. He puts his fingertips to my waist. We proceed to hold each other at arm's length as we rock stiffly back and forth, looking everywhere but at each other, fully aware that everyone is staring at us and taking pictures.

Most awkward moment of my life. And I'm pretty sure it's the longest song in history. I glance toward the cake area where I left Joel, wondering if he's laughing at me, but he's not there. I look all around and find him in a corner talking to Sierra. My mouth and throat suddenly go dry.

As the song ends, I mutter, "Congratulations," and he says back quietly, "You, too."

Dean and I walk back to where we were all sitting and proceed to get dogged by our entire group of friends. Kenzie is giggling too hard to talk.

"What the hell was that?" Lin asks us.

"You looked like prom zombies," Parker says.

Dean's face is red, but he gives that dimpled smile. "I was just trying to be respectful."

Monica squeezes herself under his arm and gives me a wink. I wink back.

"Look at this picture," Kenzie says, showing how ridiculous we looked, like middle schoolers afraid to touch.

I push her phone away with a laugh. "No, thank you." I lived the moment, that's enough for me. I look toward the corner where Joel and Sierra had been talking, but they're not there anymore. I don't see either of them anywhere.

"Who did Sierra come with?" I ask.

"Bodhi," Dean answers. "But he's wrecked from drinking in the limo."

"Where did Joel go?" The question slips out, but I don't care.

"I think he left with Sierra," Vincent says.

Left with her? I turn away from them and pretend to be looking for my drink so they won't see the disappointment on my face. Why did they leave together? Are they . . . ? I shake the thought away. I have no claim to him. But that fact doesn't stop my stomach from hurting.

"We need a group picture with the crown and tiara now," Kenz says.

We pose for more pictures, and though plenty of time passes, Joel does not return, and neither does the feeling of happiness I had while he was here.

I have no right to be upset. I sort of adopted him as mine tonight, but he's not mine. I give myself a pep talk. We're not together. He doesn't answer to me. I'm here for my friends. I don't need a guy.

Speaking of guys, Taro Hattori strides over at that very moment, looking fine with his black hair shining under the lights, hiding part of his face. He's with a guy and girl I've seen at the skate park. I notice he has a new eyebrow ring that is beyond sexy.

"You came," he says. Guilt makes my skin flush. Before I can give him an excuse, he says, "I guess Mrs. Hartt made you." He raises his chin to the tiara.

"Yeah . . ." I clear my throat. "Who's your date?"

"Just here with my friends."

"Me, too." I smile at both his friends and they smile back.

"Want to dance?" Taro asks.

"Sure!" We all head to the floor, lifting our long gowns, and squeeze our way onto the dance floor.

Taro doesn't have the moves of Elliott, who has apparently abandoned his date somewhere on the dance floor as he dances his way around the entire place, making everyone laugh. But then again, nobody's as good as Elliott. Taro and I laugh, and there's a comfort between us that I appreciate right now.

"Hey, Taro?" We're dancing close.

"Yes?" He tilts his head.

"Are you a poet?"

He looks at me funny. "No. Just a skater. And an artist, sort of. Why?"

Disappointment flares and wanes. "No reason."

He puts his hands on my waist as the song changes to something slower.

Monica leans her head toward me from where she and Dean are dancing and whispers, "Aren't you glad you came?"

Love rushes through me as I have my sights on her, Lin, and Kenzie. I could have missed this.

I answer honestly. "Yes."

CHAPTER THIRTY

An unexpected, unwelcome surprise is waiting outside my apartment complex when I get home. Wylie. He's sitting on the hood of his parents' BMW, and he jumps down, his face coming to life when he sees me pull up in the minivan. I now regret not taking Taro up on his offer to hang out after prom, but I was tired, mentally and emotionally.

"Zae!" Wy runs over. "Damn, girl, look at you." He puts both hands on his head and stares unabashedly. I'm not wearing the tiara anymore, but being looked at like that makes me feel like a princess, especially from the only boy who's ever seen me naked. The boy who broke my heart so thoroughly I still feel the residual hurt.

All I can think to say is, "How do you know where I live now?"

"I asked around and found out the apartment complex name. Then I drove around until I found your mom's car with the cupcake sticker on the back. Remember when you put that there?"

I cross my arms, refusing to reminisce. He moves closer, opening his hands and pulling them back to his sides. He wants to touch me. I can tell he still thinks he has the right, and he has to put himself in check.

"Why are you here?"

Wylie could never hide his emotions. His face is more expressive than anyone I've ever known, which I always loved. What I'm seeing is sadness and regret. Genuine pain.

"I'm sorry," he whispers. "What I did, it was the worst mistake of my life. I'm going to be fifty and still saying it was the worst mistake of my life." My heart squeezes. "I'll never forgive myself for losing you. I think about you every day, Zae. *Every day.*"

When was the last time I really thought of Wylie? It's been a while.

"I've been punished," he says. "You have no idea. That girl, Vonia?" It takes me a second to remember that's the name of the freshman girl. "She told me she was pregnant. For a month I was completely freaking out. I told my parents and they . . . God, it killed them! And then one of Vonia's girls told me she was lying." I watch in surprise as Wylie actually chokes up. "She was trying to get me to be with her and then she was gonna act like she had a miscarriage or something. See, you would *never* do something like that to someone."

"Most girls wouldn't," I say, and all I can feel is pity. Pity for Wylie. Pity for Vonia, who thinks so little of herself she has to take desperate measures to try to get the guy she wants. I rub my face.

"Wylie, I'm sorry that happened—"

"I miss you!" He grabs my hand with both of his. He's standing close, and he smells so familiar, like happy memories. "Give me a second chance. Please."

"Wy—"

"*Please!* I can't live without you anymore. I don't want to. I'm no good without you. I'll die—"

"Don't say that." Anger flares inside me, and I push his hands away. "Don't try to manipulate me. It's not fair, and it's bullshit. You were screwed up when we were together. I can't make you good, Wylie. Only you can do that."

"I need you," he whispers, like he's begging for a life raft. But Wylie's going to have to learn to swim on his own.

I look at his lost eyes, and realize that was me for months. Lost. And I don't want that to be me anymore. A solid sense of clarity breaks me out of a too-long stupor, shoving me into reality and the life choice that I'm facing.

Suddenly I declare in a rush, "I'm spending my senior year overseas."

Shock hits his eyes like a blast of wind, and I feel as if my own breath has been sucked from my lungs. In that moment, I feel kind of faint. I've been indecisive, but as the words come out, as terrifying as they are, they are . . . perfect.

"What?" he whispers.

My voice quavers. "I'll be busy this summer taking classes to get all the credits I need. Then I'm going to Argentina

274

and France for language studies."

I'm going to Argentina and France.

I see the moment he loses hope, and it's like it transfers to me instead, blooming with fragrant life. But not just hope. It's a lightness I've never felt. Like all my worries are suddenly gone and in their place is new possibility, new chances that brighten the shadows inside me and fill me with blinding purpose.

I'm going to travel! I'm going to see the world and experience languages with native speakers! I cover my mouth as an ecstatic, disbelieving smile comes to me.

"That's . . . amazing," Wylie says, shaking his head. "It is. Wow. I mean, I guess I'm not surprised. *You're* amazing."

I swallow hard and whisper, "Thank you."

And then we're quiet as he shoves his hands in his pockets and we look at the ground. What's left to say? He is my past, and we're headed in different directions. But I'll still always care about him.

"I'm sorry," he says. "For what it's worth." He grasps the back of his neck.

"Me, too," I whisper.

When he moves forward to hug me, I let him, breathing in his familiar scent. We hold each other for a minute and then I give him a goodbye smile.

"Good luck, Wy. I really think you can do whatever you put your mind to. You are your parents' son."

I turn, clutching my tiny purse in both hands and feeling more steady on my heels than I have all night. I can't stop smiling as I ascend the stairs and let myself in. Zeb is asleep on the couch—it's past midnight—and he barely stirs. I stare at his peaceful form. I know my brother is going to grow up a lot while I'm gone. I won't be here to stick up for him or just hang out with him. That thought is like a rock in my gut, but at the same time, I know he'll be okay. I'll make him keep in touch with me. I won't forget my baby brother.

I kick off my heels against the wall and pad quietly to Mom's room. Her door is open a crack, but I can see the light of her phone where she's playing a game on it. She sits up and flicks on the lamp when I open the door.

"How was it?" She pats the bed and I sit beside her.

"It was good. You should be aware that your daughter is officially a princess."

Mom squeezes me in a hug and laughs. "I already knew that. Congratulations on making it official, though."

"Hey, Mom?"

"Yeah?" She pushes a stray curl from my forehead.

"I want to do the international program."

Her hand falls heavily to her lap, and she gets a faraway look in her eye.

"Of course you do," she whispers and takes my hand. "And it's only the start for you, baby."

CHAPTER THIRTY-ONE

I'm here. Kenzie's text comes to me at eight thirty the next morning, and I quietly go to the door to let her in. Mom left for work before dawn, but Zeb is still asleep on the couch, so we tiptoe back to my room. She's wearing shorts and a Peakton sweatshirt. Her updo from last night is now in a messy bun on top of her head after a night at a hotel with Vin. She tosses her overnight bag to the ground and climbs onto my bed. I sit on the edge.

"*Well*?" I pester. My heart is pounding.

She picks at my blanket, curling into herself bashfully.

"You did it!" I hiss.

She bites her lip and nods, still staring at the blanket.

"Are you okay?" I ask. "Did you use protection? Did it . . . hurt?"

"Yes, yes, and not really."

I'm overly fascinated and can't stop staring at her, half expecting her to look different, but she doesn't.

"Did it, like, feel *good*?"

"Not the first time. It was weird. But it got better."

I can't stop staring. "How many times did you do it?"

"Three?" She giggles, and I cover my mouth so I don't let out a loud, immature cackle.

I can tell she doesn't want to go into detail; Kenzie isn't a big sharer, so I don't ask anything else and she seems relieved.

Once we hear Zeb moving around, I get up and make us all egg sandwiches. I steal glances at Kenzie until it's time to take her home.

"What?" she asks when she catches me staring at her in the car while we're at a light.

I need to stop, but it's so weird. Kenzie's got this new knowledge, this new experience, that the rest of us don't.

"Do you feel different?" I ask.

"I thought I would, but I feel the same. I love him."

"I know," I say. "You guys are lucky."

This makes her smile and ponder. "Do you know he wants to apply to James Madison, too? He could maybe get a baseball scholarship and we could be together. Wouldn't that be cool?"

"Yeah." I like the thought of her not being alone when she goes off to college. But that's over a year away. I hope they stay together. I hope she stays this happy.

I decide not to tell her just yet about my decision for next year.

The first place I go Monday morning is Mrs. Hernandez's room. She's just putting down her purse and sipping coffee from her *¡Buenos Días!* travel mug. Her eyes practically sparkle when she sees me.

"*¡Buenos días!*"

"*Buenos días, señora.* Can I talk to you?"

"Sure, if you don't mind me arranging some papers."

I nod as she gets to work. "I've decided to do the program abroad."

Mrs. Hernandez drops the papers to throw up her hands. "*¡Bueno!* You decided to take the offer!"

The offer? Wait, does she know about the anonymous benefactor?

Her face pales. "I spoke with Mrs. Crowley," she explains in a rush. "She gave me an update. I hope you don't mind." She won't quite meet my eyes, and it's so bizarre that my heart beats hard against my ribs.

Oh, my goodness.

Is Mrs. Hernandez my benefactor? I consider what I know about her. She has no children. Her husband died several years ago of cancer. It's totally possible. But it's so much. It's huge. For her to be my silent angel . . . she has no idea how much it means to me.

"Yeah," I say, my voice thick with emotion. "When I first heard about the program, I felt kind of mad, you know? Like it was unfair that I couldn't do it. But it turns out someone else was willing to dream big for me. *With* me."

Her eyes water.

The rest of my words come out as a whisper. "I'm really thankful."

She takes my hand and uses her other to wipe under her eyes. "I'm thankful there are bright, open-minded students like you out there, making the world a better place."

I hug her and don't let go until first bell rings, signaling the five-minute warning.

***

I see you switched from Capri Sun to Hi-C today.
How can you mess with my emotions that way?

That's all it says, typed up neatly, and I stand there, giggling like a fool at my locker after school. My girls come sprinting when they see me holding the paper. Kenzie snatches it, and the three of them fight over reading it.

"He was watching you at lunch!" Lin says. "He's the sweetest stalker ever!"

"Who is this?" Monica demands. "Every time I walk by your locker I look to see if anyone is there. Agh!"

Kenzie can't stop smiling.

"Hey, can you guys give me five minutes?" I ask. "I need to talk to Mrs. Hartt real quick. I'll meet you at the van." I hand Monica my keys and jog toward the foreign-language wing.

Mrs. Hartt is wiping her whiteboard clean when I get there. Her smile is weary when she sees me.

"I'm glad you're here," she says. "I made a decision today." She brushes off her hands and comes over. "Several other girls from JV who are trying out for varsity came to me saying they couldn't get the tumbling in time either. I'm changing it back to just a standing back handspring."

Oh, crap. I can still cheer. I can . . . no. *No.* I've made my decision. I stand taller, trying to give myself strength to resist this temptation.

280

"I'd rather have a big squad," Mrs. Hartt explains. "I can't turn you and the others away. And even if every single one of you did have a roundoff back handspring . . ." She waves the thought away. "Never mind."

"I know," I say. "It wouldn't matter. We're still Peakton."

She crosses her arms and gives me a sad smile. "Screw 'em, right?"

"Right," I agree. "Because Peakton's the real deal."

"That's right," she says. "I wouldn't trade you guys for anything."

A lump lodges in my throat, considering what I'm about to say. I suck it up and tell her, and her mouth drops open. She envelops me in a hug.

"That's incredible, Zae! I'm so proud of you! What do the girls think? Are they being supportive?"

I chew my lip. "I haven't told them yet."

"Ahh." She presses her lips together. "Be strong, 'kay? I can't imagine the squad without you—I can't imagine your group of girls without you—but some things are too important to pass up." She holds my shoulders at arm's length to make sure I listen.

"Thank you," I say. "I'll miss you."

I have to leave before I can think too much about cheer going on without me. I can't have everything. I know if I decide to stay here and experience my senior year with my friends, I can still be on the squad, but I'll always wonder what would have happened if I had gone. Maybe I'd be happy here, and other opportunities would come up, or maybe I'd always regret it.

I jog down to the parking lot, holding the straps of my book bag so it doesn't bounce too much. The parking lot is quiet now that most of the cars have gone.

The girls are leaning against the van, watching me as I come to a stop.

"You've been in la-la land today," Monica says.

"What did you need to talk to Mrs. Hartt about?" Lin asks.

Kenzie hunches a little.

They know I've come to a decision. For a moment I balk, ready to lie so I can avoid this, but I have to tell them eventually. They deserve my honesty. But I'm worried. I'm scared they'll try to make me change my mind. I'm even more terrified they'll succeed, and I'll chicken out of going. I still haven't confirmed with Mrs. Crowley.

I take a deep breath and say quietly, "I'm going."

The three of them stare at me. I feel everything inside. I'm excited for this chance but already mourning the times I won't have with these girls. I'm filled with hope and loss all at once, and it's making me fragile. I don't know if I can handle their sadness. I can't handle any guilt or negativity. I'm too weak and damaged.

What I'm not expecting is all three of them to come at me and tackle me in a group hug, holding me so tight I can barely breathe, their love and acceptance acting as glue to every brittle crack I've come to carry. They mend my heart and strengthen my soul. And as they hug me I realize this is not the end for us. High school is not the end. It is just the beginning. Come what may, near or far, we are a team. This is my squad.

CHAPTER THIRTY-TWO

Things feel different since I've made my decision and solidified it with Mrs. Crowley. All the drama that used to feel like such a big deal suddenly carries no weight. People gossiping about me? Doesn't matter. Bad hair day? Who cares! My entire outlook on life has changed. With my new attitude, plus the end-of-year buzz, I feel on top of the world.

The girls are frantic about tryouts. Not that they're in danger of not making it, but learning and perfecting the new cheers and dance in four days is always stressful. We meet in Kenzie's basement after tryout practice every night. I control the music as they work on the dance, and I critique them. Except for Wednesdays when I have to work.

Mrs. McOllie is sad to be losing me in three months, but says, "I'll take what I can get from you!" which makes me feel good. I'm saving as much as I can to have spending money while I'm away, and Mrs. McOllie says I'm welcome to work during the month that I'm home at Christmas. We'll see. I might have to take her up on it so I can go shopping in Paris.

Paris! I have to pinch myself daily.

The girls make the squad, of course, and our next stressor is final exams, and for me, signing up for those two online classes. But this stress feels different. It feels like a necessary evil, a burden of responsibility that will let me move forward. So I try to embrace it.

I'm glad to be on cloud nine, otherwise I'd be harping on and on about why my mystery poem guy has stopped writing, and why Joel has sort of avoided me since prom. I haven't seen him and Sierra talking anymore, but that doesn't mean they're not hanging out behind the scenes. I'm not sure what I did to him, but maybe it's better this way. A guy right now would complicate things. Still, I kind of miss him.

Since school is almost out, I write a note and stick it through the slats of my locker, poking out just enough for mystery poet to hopefully see it.

I don't know who you are. I wish you would tell me, but I guess you have your reasons. I need to thank you. You don't know it, but you helped me through a really hard time in my life. There were some days when your words were the only good thing. So thank you. I'll never forget you. Zae

When I go back later, the note is gone but nothing is left in its place.

On the last day of school there's a huge crowd in the main hall after the final bell.

"Is there a fight?" Kenzie asks.

And then I hear someone say, "Rap battle!"

What? Yes! I smile at Kenzie, and we wiggle our way to the front. When we get close enough to see, my feet come to a skidding halt and Kenzie slaps my arm.

"It's your friend Joel!"

Holy crap! Joel's standing in the middle, arms crossed, hat on backward, feet spread, staring at a straight-faced Kwami like they're about to fight. All around us people are cramming in. Some girls are hoisted up on shoulders to watch. Some climb on top of lockers. I hear the gym coach shout, "What's going on here?" And a student says, "Hurry up, y'all!" People are holding up their phones to record.

Kwami's voice rises, hushing the crowd. I feel nervous and excited.

"Y'all, break out your phones, get those vid buttons hit,

'Cause I'm takin' on white boy, it's about to get lit!" He steps to Joel and goes on.

"Imma take you to task, wipe the floor with these rags.

Dirty up that yellow head, walk out wit money in bags."

Joel claps back without hesitation and the hairs on my arms stand straight up.

"You can go ahead and try, you know I love a good laugh.

You'll be cryin' by the end, enough tears for a bath.

God showed his humor when he made me, pale skin droppin' def beats,

285

The day you came along, he was yawnin' in his shredded wheats."

Kwami rubs a thumb against his nose and grabs at his crotch.

"Bro, please. You think you all that and more.

I got the rhymes and the time, Imma settle the score.

Back down, on your knees, go hug on some trees,

You about to feel the sting of my words, killer bees!"

Joel never loses his blasé expression despite the hollers from students.

"On my knees? Think again. You get no action today.

In fact, you get no action anytime, the rumors say.

Kwami's tame. It's a shame. The dude needs some sin.

He can't even grow hair on his chinny-chin-chin."

He tweaks Kwami's smooth chin while the crowd reacts in laughter and cheers. Even teachers are watching with smiles.

"Oh, now it's on, Slim Shady, with a side of gravy.

I got the balls to tell a girl when she can have my baby.

Unlike you, Romeo, who slips a poem in her locker.

Wherefore is her love? Not with you! Big shocker!"

Pow. My head spins. The crowd's cheers are lost on me as Kenzie grabs my arm and screams. I'm staring at Joel's serious face as he smirks at Kwami, and things click into place. Every inch of me is on fire.

"It's called romance, my man, you should give it a try,

Instead of chasing every tail till the day that you die.

Call me puss all you want—we both know I ain't soft,

Keep being wack. I got your back. I hold my standards aloft."

Everyone is cheering like crazy, punching the air; and

teachers start hollering for students to clear the hall, fire code violations, busses being made late, blah, blah, blah. I get jostled side to side as I stare at Joel.

"It's him!" Kenzie is shouting.

I know. I think maybe I've known for a while, and I *so* did not want to fall for him.

But now. Oh, now. It is on.

I push through the throng of smiling, laughing, shouting faces, people clapping both guys on the back and smacking their hats. When I'm finally in front of Joel, he is as collected and unreactive as ever. Only the slightest lift of his eyebrows responds to my face in his.

I say nothing because he's said enough for both of us.

I just kiss him.

Cheers erupt as my hands go around his neck and his go around my waist. He smells just as heavenly as ever, even better because there is no tinge of cigarettes, and his mouth is hot on mine. His lips are just right. His tongue is soft but firm, not overpowering or underwhelming. His kiss is just like him— understated, poetic, sensual. I kinda sorta wish we weren't surrounded by hundreds of people.

"Enough!" a teacher shouts, too closely, breaking Joel and me apart. "Clear out, everyone! Be safe! Have a good summer!" The coach makes his way closer to disperse the crowd and holds out a fist to Joel and Kwami, saying, "Nice lyrics."

They both bump his knuckles and the teacher moves on.

Kwami looks at me and says, "Where's my love?"

I go to hug him, and Joel pulls me to him, putting an arm around me. "Uh-uh, bro."

Kwami laughs. "Man, you selfish."

"I'll hug you!" Kenzie says out of nowhere. She does, and Kwami picks her up like the pixie she is, making her laugh. She smiles at Joel, then me, and says, "See you at the car?"

"Yeah," I say.

Kwami leaves us, too, and Joel takes his hand from around my shoulder, leaning against a locker.

"You could have told me," I say quietly.

"You're going away." He looks down and puts his hands in his baggy jeans pockets.

"Yeah, but you haven't talked to me since prom. You didn't know I was going away then."

He lifts his chin just enough to peer up at me guiltily.

"Wait . . ." I put a hand on my hip and pretend to be mad. "Did you look in my file?"

He lets out a dry chuckle. "Let's just say Mrs. Crowley's filing system is piling everything on her desk for the world to see. It wasn't hard."

I cross my arms as things suddenly feel more serious.

"You're on the rise, girl. I'm not gonna hold you down. You've gotta build up that list of yours with Latino and Parisian names."

I roll my eyes and shake my head. He'll never let me live down the stupid non-list.

"Zae," he says gently. "You're going. And I'm staying. Those are the facts."

I take a deep breath, my blood pumping hard with nervousness. "I don't have to be single when I go. People have long-distance relationships all the time."

He gives his head a slow shake. "You should be single on this journey. It needs to be about you."

I feel torn. He's being selfless, willing to let me go, but am I willing to let him go? Leaving him behind feels like an opportunity lost. He makes me feel tingly and special and I want a future where I can kiss him every day.

I swallow hard. "How do you know what I need? I'll be the judge of that."

"You'll be a changed woman when you get back, Zae. Your aspirations will probably be higher than me, and that's a good thing."

My lips purse with displeasure. "This trip's not going to change who I am or turn me into a snob."

"I didn't say that—"

"Does this mean you won't even write to me?" I'm shaking now, realizing I'm losing this great guy before I ever had him.

"If you want me to write you, Zae, I will write you every day." He means it. His sincerity makes me inhale and let it out slowly, calming me down.

"How about this," he says. "We'll write. No pressure. Life happens. When you get back, if you still want to give it a go, I'll be here. I ain't going nowhere."

"You might fall for another girl between now and then." My stomach sours at the thought of him being there for some other girl, slipping her poems.

"And you might fall for another guy. We can't get mad about that."

But I already feel mad about it.

He reaches for both my hands and pulls me to him,

holding me to his chest and nuzzling my hair with his face. I let him hold me until my heart stops hammering and my stomach stops churning with jealousy of girls I don't even know.

"Can we at least hang out this summer before I go?" I ask.

I close my eyes as I wait for his answer, which is a long time coming.

"I think that'll be dangerous," he says.

"Why?" I whisper.

His laugh is airy. "Because I don't want to fall for you any harder. I've been trying to talk myself out of liking you all year."

I pull back. All year? His serious gaze assures me.

"And I knew you were after Big Boy. I could tell the second you were single."

I shake my head, feeling defensive and embarrassed. "And what about you and Sierra? I know you went home with her after prom."

He's steady in his response. "I drove her home 'cause her date was trashed and she was upset. The end. I know better than to fall back with someone who burned me, but I'm not gonna leave her hangin' either." A slow grin grows on his sexy lips. "Were you jealous?"

"You didn't say goodbye."

His humor dissipates. "That was rude of me. I saw you dancing with Dean, and then . . ." He shakes his head and I realize he was jealous, too.

"I had no more feelings for him by the time he got with Monica. I promise."

"Well." He scuffs the floor. "I knew I needed to distance myself, regardless."

I go up on my toes and give him a soft peck until he lets out a quiet moan. When I pull back, he runs a thumb over my cheek. "Make me a promise."

I nod.

"Don't get mad at me if I need to keep that distance." He's still going to hold back? I lock my jaw, hating the thought. After all this, I'm pissed.

"There's that fire," he says. "Let me explain." He picks up a loose ball of paper from the floor and holds it in his open palm. "That's you." He points to the trash and I glower. "Only you're prettier, of course. Imagine it a little less dirty with sexy lips."

I smack my lips and cross my arms. "Keep going."

"And my hand is me. This is my instinct when I think about you leaving." He curls his hand closed tight around the paper, crumpling the life out of it and eyeing me. When he opens his hand again, the paper looks sad. Smaller. "But I gotta fight that instinct and keep my hand just like this." He keeps it open. "So you can go where the wind takes you."

"You don't want to be together," I say quietly, understanding.

"Yet," he reiterates.

I tend to be an all-in kind of person. Holding back will be hard, but at the same time, it feels wrong to force him, *us*, into something serious when we know it's going to be difficult to be far apart.

"Okay," I whisper.

We walk side by side out to the parking lot, bumping each

other with our hips and shoulders as we go. I spot my squad waiting by the van, huddled, smiling when they see us coming. My heart expands and snaps back, stinging. I have so much to stay for.

As if reading my mind, Joel says under his breath, "Up you go, Zae Monroe. No looking back."

Senior Year Abroad

PeaktonTravelPrincess@Umail.com: Hey Lin, 你好吗？
我想你。

gymbunnyforlife@Umail.com: WTH, Zae? You know I
can't read that. What does it say?

PeaktonTravelPrincess@Umail.com: Figure it out. And
don't use an online translator. Use the alphabet booklet I
got you.

gymbunnyforlife@Umail.com: Ugh! You suck! Fine!

gymbunnyforlife@Umail.com: Aww. I did it! I'm doing
great and I miss you, too! This is actually kind of fun . . .

KenzieCheers@Umail.com: OMG, Zae! You'll never
believe this! Vincent and I are homecoming king and
queen!!

PeaktonTravelPrincess@Umail.com: Gahhhh!!! Of course I believe it! Send all the pics!

KenzieCheers@Umail.com: Also, I ate a whole hot dog in front of him before the game. I know that sounds stupid to anyone else, but it was a big deal for me and I know you'll understand.

PeaktonTravelPrincess@Umail.com: I am so proud of you! Stop making me cry!

Zae,
I see you in my mind's eye, feasting on carne and cerveza,
Smiling and laughing, still loca en la cabeza.
I see your friends in the hall, like a three-legged cat,
Missing their Zae, it ain't the same, that's a fact.
How's your list? Never mind. I don't want to know.
Things at Peakton are fine, but every day is a show.
To answer your question I'm still single,
This kid's too busy to mingle,
Learning days, working nights.
Enjoying Friday night lights.
I saw a juice the other day, said he's missing your lips.
I told him, Have some pride, my man, but he ain't open to tips.
For real, I hope you are well, and learning all the big words.
From your friend in America, flying high with the birds. J
PS—not really high, just needed a rhyme . . . and I'm done with cigs, too. For real this time. Though I partake in vaping on occasion. Oral fixation and all that.

EPILOGUE

Joel was right. My kiss list did grow while I was in Argentina and France. Fun kisses. Spontaneous kisses. Moments with gorgeous foreign boys that made me laugh and smile but did not reach my heart, which I kept heavily guarded with someone else's name on it.

Joel kept his promise to write me, and I've saved every word.

We learned each other's favorite songs and books. I told him every weird new thing I ate, and he dared me to try more. I confided in him about my family, and he told me about his brother and how close they were, and how his letters from prison depress the hell out of him. We told each other so much in those letters, and yet I felt the distance between us with each word. His careful avoidance of intimacy. He was always kind, always uplifting, never closing his hand on me.

Monica and Lin weren't great about emailing, but I could always count on them to video chat. Kenzie was the best about keeping me up-to-date on every sordid, dramatic detail of Peakton life.

Monica and Dean broke up the first month of senior year. Apparently they were both so busy with sports that they grew apart. Lin and Parker lasted until after homecoming in the fall when they got early acceptance to schools in different states. Meeka and Kwami were spotted kissing after a basketball game—guess he finally won her over. Quinton and Camille had a baby in March. Señora Hernandez asked Kenzie about me all the time, and the cheer squad took third place at regionals.

Through senior year, Vincent and Kenzie were still going strong, both accepted to James Madison University. Monica's headed to University of Virginia, and Lin to UVA's rival school, Virginia Tech. That gives me three colleges to visit this fall. I can't complain.

Mom started dating a guy named Dennison, and according to Zebby she keeps laughing like a teenager and humming show tunes around the house. Dad and Jacquie are still together. I officially met her, as his girlfriend, at their condo before I left on my trip. It was weird, but I was nice and so was she.

Everything in the United States feels surreal when I return for graduation. I'm now fluent in three languages. I've been looking into jobs, but I keep going back to the flight attendant thing. I've heard it's not as glamorous as it seems, but is any job? I'm just not ready to be behind a desk. Plus, flight attendants get a certain amount of free airline tickets each year, and let's just say there are a lot of places I want to go.

But first things first. I have a graduation to attend and a score to settle with a certain Mr. Joel Ruddick, who cannot avoid me any longer. According to Kenzie, he wasn't spotted romancing any other girls while I was away, which gives me hope. She kept a special eye on him and Sierra, but Sierra was almost always dating other guys. I have no idea if Joel's feelings are still the same as mine. A year is a long time to wait. But I intend to find out today.

The school stadium is a madhouse of families all dressed up and roasting under the sun, and graduates. The guys wear navy-blue robes while the girls wear white. I made a glittery Eiffel Tower on my mortarboard graduation cap. Parts of my heart are still in Buenos Aires and Paris. I envision their streets when I close my eyes. I know I missed a lot, but I will never regret a single moment.

It's good to be with my loved ones again, though. I link hands with Monica, Lin, and Kenzie in the gymnasium where graduates are called to line up. They keep saying I look different, but when I ask them to elaborate, they can't. They just look at me like I'm glowing or something, and I know what they mean. I see it in them, too.

I search where the *R* students are lining up until I spot Joel, his hat doing the hip-hop lean to the side. It's undecorated. Of course Joel couldn't be bothered with that. As I stare, I see that he's changed, too. He's taller. Slightly broader, his face . . . squarer or something. But even from a distance his eyes are just as light blue. His lips just as shapely and kissable. Looking at him makes my insides dance like the music is on speed.

I head to the rows of *M* names as the band begins playing. We march outside onto the field to the tune of "Pomp and Circumstance." Everyone is smiling, all our worries and grudges from the past four years suddenly gone.

We cross the stage.

We throw our caps.

We find our families in a rush of excited chaos. People are all over the stadium, lawn, and parking lot. I agreed to meet my parents by the car. Zeb is two inches taller than me now, a fact he loves to point out at every opportunity. He also has braces and armpit hair. So weird.

Jacquie is at Dad's side, sporting a tiny diamond on her left hand. Yeah, that happened while I was away, only weeks after my parents' divorce was finalized. It's a little awkward between the two of them and Mom, but they're cordial enough, mostly focusing on me and not looking at one another.

I opted for no graduation party since none of our relatives from afar could afford to come. Tonight I'll go to Kenzie's graduation party at her house with the girls. I can't wait.

"Pictures!" Mom says. I pose with every member of the family, and Zeb finds my three girls and ushers them over so the four of us can get a group photo—both serious and silly. As we're saying goodbye I spot Señora Hernandez getting in her car.

"I'll be right back," I tell my family.

For the past year Señora Hernandez has followed my journey on social media, always commenting on my pictures and supporting me with occasional notes. I will always feel indebted to her. All my life.

I catch her before she climbs in, and her whole face illuminates.

"Ah, Zae! So good to see you!"

She takes me by the face and kisses both my cheeks, and then I hug her.

"I have enjoyed every moment of your journey," she says. "Thank you for sharing it for me to see."

"It was the best year of my life," I tell her honestly. "I feel so lucky."

She pats my cheek. "I can't wait to see what you do next. Keep posting."

"I will. And someday, I want to pay it forward."

Her eyes fill with tears. We hug again, and I run back to my family.

Dad gives me one last hug before he and Jacquie get in his car to wait in the long line out of the school's parking lot. I'm going out to eat with Mom and Zebby, but first there's one more person I need to see.

I look all around until I spot Joel by an oversize pickup truck with his family. His gown is unzipped, showing a fitted T-shirt and long shorts. His grad cap is long gone. His blond hair a mess. The man he's standing near has a potbelly and scruffy face. The woman is short with her blond-and-gray hair in a braid. I jog over.

His eyes flash with something like surprise, or maybe worry, and he raises his chin in greeting.

"Hey, Joel." I clasp my hands in front of me, feeling strangely shy.

"Hey." He looks at his parents. "Mom, Dad, this is Zae Monroe."

His mom's face widens in a smile and she looks ten years younger. "The girl who was overseas?"

"Yes, ma'am," I say. She puts out her hand, and I shake it.

Joel's dad just gives me a grumbly once-over, nods at me, and heads toward the driver's side of the truck. Joel sort of tenses up at his dad's rudeness. His mom gives me one last smile before heading to the passenger seat.

"I guess we're going," he says, but doesn't move, just stares at my eyes. "Your hair is longer. Look at these little spirals." He touches the ends of my hair, and it makes my heart flutter. He opens his mouth like he wants to say more, but his dad hollers.

"Let's go, boy!"

Joel grits his teeth, his mouth clamped shut.

"I'll call you," I say quietly.

He gives me a nod, but I can't read him as he walks and gets in the truck. He seems . . . sad. I need to find out what's going on with him. I stare as they drive away.

"It's not you," says Sierra from beside me, making me jump. She pushes her hair over her shoulder. "It's his dad."

I look at her, surprised. "What about his dad?"

"He's an asshole." I watch his father maneuver the truck into the line, using its girth to scare the little cars into submission out of his way. "I probably shouldn't tell you this, but fuck it. Our dads used to be partners, and when Mr. Ruddick broke away, he went bankrupt. Like, totally broke. They lost everything. So Joel and his brother, Marcus, started selling pot, then meth and other shit, and giving the money to their dad. Joel was only a freshman." My stomach plummets and I feel chilled despite the sunshine. He really had been a dealer.

"He used their drug money to get them a place and start a new business. But the whole time he treated his sons like they were trash. Like he was ashamed of them. Marcus went to jail and Joel got clean and started working for him, but he still treats him like shit."

I might be sick. I flash from cold to hot. I can't believe I didn't know any of this about him.

Sierra peers over and eyes me up and down. "You look great."

"Thanks." I stare at where the Ruddicks' truck accelerates around the corner, out of sight. "You, too. But you always do."

She smiles. "Okay, so which country has the hottest guys?"

I can't bring myself to smile, but I can answer this one honestly. "It's literally a tie. So much hotness."

"Lucky." She bites her lip. "See you around."

I nod and go back to my family, but I have unfinished business. That was *not* how things were supposed to go today. I need a do-over ASAP.

At home after lunch, I do some stalking. I call Meeka for Kwami's number. I call Kwami to find out which house is Joel's. I only know the neighborhood.

"Your best bet is to find him at work," he says. "He's there more than home these days."

Kwami tells me what time he'll be there tomorrow, and I mentally prepare. While I'm at it, I research airlines and make a few calls. Then I play video games with Zeb for old time's sake and can't help but tease him about his changes.

"Oh my God, and look at your feet!" I point to them. "They're man-size!"

"Quit being weird," he says, still laughing.

"He's also got a girlfriend," Mom calls from the kitchen, where she's prepping green-chili chicken enchiladas for tonight.

"Aw, Zebby, stop growing up!" I grab his arm and shake him.

Zeb curls inward and covers his head to ward off the embarrassment.

It's good to be home.

I pull up in front of Ruddick's Auto at nine the next morning, armed with a piece of paper in my pocket that I've had since Paris. Today, if Joel's receptive, I'll give it to him.

I'm light-headed with nerves as I approach the doorway. I clasp my fingers and let them go, smoothing my shirt. With a heavy inhale and exhale, I pull open the door and cringe when it dings. My eyes go straight to the counter, where Joel stands in his navy-blue button-down shirt. He's wearing his matching hat the proper way, instead of backward, and it makes me almost laugh.

Joel looks up from where he's having a man sign something, and his eyes go comically wide. He checks himself super quick and focuses on the customer. I look around at the small room that smells like rubber and oil. There's a seating area with two old love seats and a dingy coffee maker. In the middle of the room is a display of tires. Along the walls are car accessories.

"Have a good day, sir," he says. The guy walks out, and it's just us. I approach with caution, and he looks toward the door that leads to the mechanic area. Joel pales when that door bursts open and Mr. Ruddick comes in, wiping his hands on a rag. He stops and looks back and forth between Joel and me. My heart drops.

He frowns at Joel. "You socializing on the clock?"

"No, sir. She . . ."

I swallow to wet my throat. "I need, uh, windshield wipers."

Mr. Ruddick looks at Joel. "Well, get the girl some wipers!" he shouts, making me jump. He glowers at Joel and turns to go back into the mechanic area. Another guy comes in, a young mechanic, and he shuffles through some papers on the counter.

Joel sighs, looking ashamed or embarrassed or maybe both. "Can I call you when I get off?"

"Okay," I whisper, shaken to see how his dad treats him. "Do you get a lunch break?"

"Not really," he says tightly.

"Hey," says the guy next to him, "my next car's not for another half hour. Go outside and talk. I'll cover you."

Joel hesitates, glancing toward where his dad went.

"Yeah, okay."

Joel turns his hat around backward and comes out. We walk around the side of the building, and my heart starts jumping like I did a bunch of burpees. He shoves his hands in his pockets as I cross my arms. I almost laugh. Are we strangers now? How do I bridge the gap that this year apart has caused?

"You gave me freedom," I say. "Thank you. It was an amazing year."

His jaw tightens as he nods. He won't look straight at me. He's nervous.

"But you know what the best part was?" I ask.

"No drinking age?"

"No." I poke his taut tummy and he reluctantly grins. "Your poems."

Again, he looks away, and it makes my stomach tighten. I'm starting to get nervous.

"Are you done with me, Joel?"

His hands go deeper in his pockets and his elbows lock. He looks guarded, vulnerable even. "I wasn't sure how you'd feel when you got back. About us."

I tone down my frustration and move even closer, inches away, talking softly, taking his uniform shirt gently between my fingers.

"If you could go anywhere in the world, Joel Ruddick, where would you go?"

His lip quirks up like I'm crazy. I tilt my head, waiting.

"Zae. Come on. I gotta get back in there."

"Just answer, and then I'll leave you alone."

He huffs out a breath and stares off at the building next to us. "I don't know. A big city, I guess. Somewhere I can get lost in the shuffle. Somewhere musicians camp out on corners playing and you can just stop to listen. Like New Orleans or New York. London, Dublin, Amsterdam, shit, anywhere but here."

I can't help but smile. It's such a Joel answer.

"Let me take you."

"Stop." He shakes his head. I reach for his hands and he stiffens a little, but lets me hold them.

"I did a phone interview yesterday," I tell him, "to be a flight attendant. They're flying me to Houston tomorrow for a second interview. The airline's second hub is in DC, so I'll most likely be stationed here." I start talking faster as I see his lips press together. "I would do international flights, like four days away, then two or three days off at a time. Latin America and Canada to start. Then Europe. We can hang out on my days off, and a few times a year we can go where we want! We'll have to stay in hostels and stuff until we save some money, but we can get away from here together."

His grip on my hand tightens as his gaze drops to the side, downward.

"Dream with me, Joel, *please*. Dream big." I move in, my legs pressing against his, clutching his shirt tighter. His hands go automatically to my waist, but he still won't look at me. I pull back and slide the folded paper from my back pocket. My heartbeat gains momentum, because this is the last trick up my sleeve.

"Remember my so-called kiss list?" I ask. "The one up here?" I touch my head.

His eyes darken, and he looks down at the paper in my hand, frowning.

"I burned it," I say. Now he looks at me, his eyes searching. "Metaphorically speaking. And then I made a new one—a wish list."

I hand him the paper, and he eyes it nervously.

"Go ahead," I say.

He opens it slowly, and I swear his hands are trembling. I can't see the writing, but his entire body freezes as his eyes scour it. I imagine what he's seeing. His name. Written a thousand times in different ways. Curly letters, blocky letters. Tiny lowercases, huge caps.

"I'm here to collect," I whisper.

I've never been as nervous as I am when his eyes roam from the paper to me. Slowly, so slowly, he folds the paper and tucks it into his back pocket. Then, without a word, he reaches for my neck, sliding his hand around it as his other splays out on my lower back. Instead of kissing me though, his forehead presses to mine and he shuts his eyes. My heart explodes into a glittery mess.

"Is it stupid that I'm scared to dream? That I feel stuck here forever?"

"No," I whisper. "I was scared, too, until someone helped me. I can dream for both of us until you get your feet wet. It's easier than you think. You just have to say yes and jump."

He grins and opens his eyes. "You'll hold my hand?"

"The whole time."

His face moves down, and I gasp as his mouth lands on my neck again, just like at Quinton's party. I grasp the back of his neck as that same shooting sense of need rages through me.

"Joel," I breathe, pressing closer.

He answers by pulling the strap of my tank top down so he can run his hot lips over my shoulder. I'm grabbing on to him like I might fall if I let go. Then a moan slips from my throat that surprises me and makes him laugh low and sultry.

"You're mean," I say.

He lifts his head from my shoulder and gives me a stare hot enough to make steam form around us. Then he kisses me in a way that really makes me wish we were alone, somewhere

306

private. When he pulls away, I fight to catch my breath, and he runs his tongue over his bottom lip.

"I gotta get back in there and make some money. My girlfriend wants us to be globe-trotters."

Girlfriend. Holy gushy feelings. I'm a pile of gelatin with a goofy smile.

"That's right," I say, flicking a pretend pile of bills into the air, one by one. "Make it rain, baby." He laughs and takes my hand, walking me back to the front of the building. We let go and grin at each other as he walks backward to the door and I step to the minivan. I laugh when he bumps the door with his back, then straightens up, turning his hat forward before going in.

I can't wait to see where the future takes us.

ACKNOWLEDGMENTS

Thank you, Alyson Day, my editor, and Jill Corcoran, my agent, for believing in me and supporting me through the telling of my first contemporary novel. You know my struggles with roadblocks along the way, and most important you know my heart. I appreciate you both.

Thank you to all my friends from Potomac for the throwback memories that inspired so much of Zae's story—especially to my Panther squad: Hilary, Kristy, Holly, Meghan, Carol, Christine, Danielle, and Stacey.

And to my early readers for your feedback and excitement: Nyrae Dawn, Jen Fisher, Valerie Rinta, Hilary Mahalchick, and Katie McGarry. Kisses!

So much of this story parallels the drama my friends and I experienced in high school. The highs and lows many American teens understand. Zae's story, much like my story, was filled with love, even in the hard times. Not every young adult is so lucky. But you, and your story, are important. Whoever you are and whatever you're going through, you're not alone. Ultimately, high school is just one phase in your life, and though it often seems as if it will never end, in retrospect, it's over in a hazy flash. And then the real fun begins. I wish you the very best.

2 Timothy 1:7